FRACTURED DAWN

HARMONICS
BOOK 3

COLLIN EARL

CHRIS SNELGROVE

SILVERSTONE BOOKS

Fractured Dawn

Harmonics: Book Three

By Collin Earl & Chris Snelgrove

ISBN-13: 978-1-967473-17-5

CHAPTER 1
TODAY IS THAT DAY

Time: Mid-morning
Scene: Jade Empire

The Jadian sunrise stretched over the landscape of the Seven Cities, pouring out light and color in an unabashed and bold wake-up call. Sasha was already up and working, as were all the personal assistants. The heads of each household arrived shortly after the dawning sun, and with their arrival came the single-minded fulfillment of the director's needs. Since Sasha was the personal assistant to the Madam, she had to work especially hard.

Today, Sasha's job was poised to become a bit easier as her new assistant would arrive at any time. An assistant to the assistant—it was a bit on the poetic side, really.

Sasha did not have to wait long and smiled as her new attendant walked demurely through the door. This one was a keeper, a beautiful girl with jet-black hair and the darkest of eyes, a rare gem from the shores of the Black Sea. Sasha was looking forward to the additional help. Since her last attendant left, she'd been running around to the point of absolute exhaustion. Sasha searched through her data feeds. Now, what was the girl's name? Sasha's smile grew as she found the information stream she was searching for.

"Hello, Alena. Welcome to the Seven Cities."

The girl dipped her head respectfully. "Your Premier Eminence Alexandra, personal assistant to the Madam, the Emperor's favorite wife and holy mystic. 'Tis an honor to stand before you, Mistress."

Sasha sighed. Alena was going to be another one of those girls.

"Alena, please, stop being so formal. My blood is no more 'premier' than yours. Please call me Sasha. All my friends do, and I hope we'll be friends, as we're going to be spending a lot of time together."

Alena's eyes grew wide from shock. "Your Premier Eminence, I simply—no, there isn't any way that I could refer to you in such an informal manner. The Ladies Finishing School—"

Sasha cut her off. She would get the measure of her new assistant with a simple command. "Alena, I *order* you to call me Sasha."

Alena's voice went dry. She did not speak. She turned her eyes downward.

Sasha held back a smile. Alena was a groomed assistant. Orders from above were absolute, even if they conflicted with propriety or a rule of etiquette.

"Well, Alena? What do you say?"

The girl's chin rose. "May I call you Lady Sasha?"

Sasha smiled. Alena passed her first test. "Of course you can, Alena, and like I said, welcome to the Seven Cities."

Sasha curtsied to Alena. The girl smiled.

"Now let me show you around the offices where you'll be working. I've only got a few weeks to get you trained."

———

One Year Later

"Oh, good morning, Alena! I'm so glad you are here. I trust your vacation was good. How is your family?"

"Wonderful, Lady Sasha. And how was your time with the Madam?"

"Splendid, good, good. But enough chitchat. It's so good to have you back. I've been running around ragged all week. Would you be a doll and bring the Madam her morning tea?"

"Yes, Lady Sasha," answered the girl. She sounded a bit on the scared side and averted her eyes.

"Is there something wrong, Alena? You're not having flight sickness, are you?"

The girl started to fidget. "No—it's not—well, I just...."

It clicked for Sasha. "You're scared of the Madam."

Alena nodded her head. "She's a mystic of the highest order, Lady Sasha. What if she senses evil in my heart and decides to punish me?"

Sasha laughed. "I apologize, Alena, I forgot that you've spent precious little time with the Madam. I've been hogging you all to myself."

She touched the young Slavic girl on the face. "Go and fetch the Madam's tea set and then meet me in front of the Inner Sanctuary."

Alena's eyes grew to the size of dinner plates. She obeyed wordlessly.

Ten minutes later, Alena, tray and expensive china in hand, walked into the Sanctuary behind Sasha. It was such a sharp contrast to the rest of the building making up the Divine Offices that Alena nearly dropped her tray. The Sanctuary was the shrine, a holy place for the development of mystics and their mysterious abilities. Protected by a special squad called the Red Guard, entering without the blessing of the Emperor himself was unheard of. Lady Sasha steadied the young girl.

"Careful, Alena—you wouldn't want to drop those cups. They are a thousand years old."

Alena and Sasha made their way towards three ancient but perfectly maintained buildings.

"OK, Alena, pop quiz. Tell me about these three buildings."

Alena rattled off in a low, hypnotic voice: "The Sanctuary is made up mostly of the remnants of the Chinese Purple Forbidden City. The parts that weren't destroyed in the Battle of Ming were moved here to the Seventh City and retrofitted with some of the modern amenities to make them more functional. The Inner Sanctuary, where we are now, holds three buildings: The Palace of Heavenly Purity, The Hall of Union, and the Palace of Earthly Tranquility. These were once the residences of the Emperor and Empress of China. The Emperor of Jade uses them as a reminder of the Jadians' past. The palaces and halls are home to some of the Emperor's most sensitive projects. This area is basically impenetrable because of the seven displacement shields from each of the rings of the seven cities. The Jadian Restpit and the Emerald House are modeled after the Palace of Heavenly Purity and Palace of Earthly Tranquility."

Sasha touched Alena affectionately. "Perfect. You're smart, Alena. Just be yourself, and you'll be fine."

Alena and Sasha slowly made their way through security, gaining access to the Palace of Earthly Tranquility. Alena had a particularly tense moment when one of the Jadian special security forces was unable to find her ID in his system and pulled a light shiv on her. Sasha stepped in before the soldier took his zealotry too far. She calmly threatened him with a visit from the Madam herself if he touched Alena. It was probably the only thing that could have kept the soldier from attacking.

The interior of the Palace of Earthly Tranquility—the Jadian Restpit—was almost exactly what Alena expected. Technology of the highest caliber melded seamlessly with woodwork, art, and structural materials from fourteenth-century China. The blend of old and new was perfect, taking the Zen concept and refining it. Alena was so impressed, she actually stopped to admire the surroundings.

Lady Sasha gave her a nudge. "The Madam is waiting, Alena. Come."

Several minutes later, Lady Sasha and Alena stood outside an opulently decorated door depicting a massive dragon head. Huge griffins, carved out of single blocks of quarried jade, stood as sentinels on either side of the door. Lady Sasha ran her hands through her hair and smoothed down the front of her dress. She took a few calming breaths. Alena did so as well. Seeing Lady Sasha flustered was foreign, like some kind of out-of-body experience. It made Alena nervous.

Lady Sasha knocked on the massive door before Alena had the chance to ask what was bothering her. Instantly, the doors slowly drew back, letting a puff of sweet-smelling incense waft through. Opulence in all its astounding glory greeted Alena as she walked through the doors. The chamber was draped in crimson and green so vibrant, so alive that it was difficult to focus on or comprehend anything else.

Golden pillars a meter across and many meters high lined a plush velvet carpet that led directly into the room. The incense grew stronger the farther Lady Sasha and Alena moved along the rug, but with slight changes in the scent. Lavender turned into jasmine, into sandalwood, into frankincense, and then into something that Alena did not recognize, but that nearly knocked her off her feet with its binding and encompassing fragrance. They reached the other side of the room without Alena noticing. Her pull-back into reality came as a terrible shock as Alena and Lady Sasha neared the focal point of the room, a carved granite desk. At the desk, the lady herself, the Madam, sat poring over a tablet.

Lady Sasha bowed deeply. Alena did the same, trying not to dump her charge.

"Please be at ease, Sasha." The Madam's voice was bright and musical, like she was casting a spell.

"Good morning, my Madam. It is an honor, as always."

Alena looked up just as the Madam smiled. A mind-numbingly beautiful woman, the Madam sat in robes of liquid jade, blonde hair falling past her shoulders in rolling waves of curls. Piercing blue peered out from long arching eyelashes as a sense of warmth radiated from her eyes. Alena started openly, then remembered her manners. No wonder she was the favorite wife.

"My dear friend. Please do not address me so formally. We are familiar enough that you may call me by my name. How many times must I tell you this?"

"At least one more, Madam."

Sasha's head remained down. Alena chanced another look. The Madam caught her ruse. The Madam gave her a warm, endearing smile.

"Alena—my dear girl. It's wonderful to see you again."

Alena returned the smile. She had no choice; it was too infectious not to. "You honor me, Madam, by allowing one such as I in your holy presence."

The Madam laughed. "Holy? My dear child, I am anything but holy. If I am cut, I bleed just as you do. Please come and sit, both of you, and let us talk of affairs."

Sasha and Alena seated themselves on large cushioned chairs. Alena placed the tea tray she brought with her on the small table and started to prepare the tea. Sasha pulled out a tablet and launched a calendar.

"You have a meeting with the Counsel of Elders at ten o'clock, followed by lunch at the Hall of Unions at noon. The Emperor's new bride is being inducted, then you have a testing with some new mystics. This evening...."

Alena passed cups of tea to the Madam and Sasha; both gave her a smile in return. Alena settled herself into the cushions and let Lady Sasha's voice roll over her, choosing instead to watch the Madam. Alena considered the Madam's age. She was famous, a longstanding and integral part of the Jadian leadership. Before she met her, Alena had pictured the Madam as someone older, severe, and task-oriented. But what sat before her was the furthest thing from that. The Madam was a beauty beyond compare and exuded a soft ambiance, one that made a person feel safe and comfortable. Alena found herself drifting.

"Alena."

Alena heard her name ring out from what seemed like a far-off distance.

A hand clamped down on her shoulder, and Alena returned to full awareness. Sasha gave her a forceful shake. "Alena, are you OK?"

Alena came back to reality, the faces of Sasha and the Madam returning fully to view. She stared back at the two women, horrified.

She fell to her knees. "Lady Sasha, Madam, I do apologize. I did not—I am—I could not—I am sorry. I will humbly take any punishment."

The Madam laughed. It was a magical sound.

"Stand, child."

Alena did just that.

"You need not fear. You are new to my presence. You need some time to adjust. It's to be expected. Now come. I have much to show you."

The Madam stood and whisked herself off, gliding to a door on the far right of the room. She exited with Alena and Lady Sasha right behind her.

———

"Madam, is it really alright for me to be here?"

Alena, the Madam, and Sasha stood at the balcony entrance of a massive complex. The building was huge and stretched for kilometers in either direction. Far from completely open, the room in front of them was divided into cubby-like spaces separated by large steel curtains with no roof, which spread into an intricate labyrinth of individual rooms. It felt like a giant rat maze. While various subject-testing was visible from their overlooking vantage point, no sound penetrated the space. It was quite unusual.

"Displacement shield technology is quite remarkable, isn't it?" the Madam commented softly. "It's amazing what can be done these days."

"It is truly amazing, Madam."

"Oh dear," said the Madam, looking back towards Alena, "where are my manners? Alena, welcome to the Valley of the Mystics; this is where we do some of our most sensitive work. Come—you must have a tour."

"But Madam," answered Alena, "I've no clearance into—"

"Nonsense, you are with me. That is clearance enough," said the Madam, veiling her face as they descended a long winding staircase. Alena shot Sasha an inquisitive look. Sasha simply smiled.

The Madam, Sasha, and Alena boarded a small six-person shuttle at the bottom. This shuttle area contained lines of people, all of whom moved slowly to one side or the other as the Madam walked through them. Each person bowed respectfully as the Madam passed. The shuttle ride took them past all sorts of strange and amazing things, most of which were difficult for Alena to describe. There were experiments with animals, weapons, people and planets, new technologies, and a variety of amazing and wondrous things. Alena's head whipped back and forth like a child at a twentieth-century amusement park, filled with wonderment, bewilderment, and awe as they passed each subsequent corner and turn. The trip might have taken hours, and Alena would not have noticed. It was truly incredible.

The journey eventually came to an end. At long last, they rounded a final turn and stopped in front of a steel platform where more than ten Jadian security guards stood watching. Alena felt ice shoot through her veins as they neared the men.

"The Red Guard," said Lady Sasha in Alena's ear. "No sudden movements."

A handsome guard, young and energetic, probably of Russian descent, ran to the side of the shuttle and bowed deeply to the Madam. He offered her a hand while still bowed, not looking directly into the Madam's veiled face.

The Madam took his hand and allowed him to help her out of the shuttle. The guards stood shoulder-to-shoulder at full attention on either side of the carbonized steel door, presumably the entrance to their destination. They bowed as the Madam neared. She paid them no heed but moved past them through the door that opened as she approached. Alena and Sasha, who had jumped from the shuttle unassisted, followed closely behind her.

The room behind the carbonized steel was far less spectacular than Alena was expecting. The room was plain but brightly lit and brimming with life. Many individuals in lab coats inspected monitors, reviewed charts, or gathered around other people—men, women, and children—discussing various topics that Alena did not understand.

"Welcome to the Mystics' Abode, ladies, my life's work and home to some of the most powerful mystics on the planet. Allow me to show you—"

"Madam! Thank goodness you're here." A sleep-deprived boy, approximately eighteen or nineteen at the most, came running to the Madam. It was obvious he had been up for hours; large bags under his eyes, slurred speech, and ill-coordinated movements said as much. He stopped in front of Sasha first, shooting her a boyish smile.

"Your Premier Eminence Alexandra, I didn't know you'd be accompanying the Madam today. If I had—"

The boy blanched as if realizing he had committed a huge mistake. He turned to the Madam. "I apologize for my rude behavior, Madam. I should have greeted you first."

"Nonsense, Shioon, I am well aware of your infatuation with Sasha, and be of good cheer—she likes the attention you give her."

Sasha put her head down and burned a flagrant color of crimson. Alena gawked as a wicked grin crept onto the

Madam's face. She addressed Shioon. "Now, my young friend, can you tell us why you look like the walking dead?"

"The Delphic Candidate, Madam. The Mogui and the Sun have found the Delphic Candidate."

There was a cheer that let out all around the room. It was as if the people were waiting for this exact moment to express their excitement.

The Madam smiled a strange smile, one that Alena didn't quite know how to take. She thought the Madam looked sad.

"Excellent," said the Madam, intending to move forward. She stumbled, nearly falling to the ground.

"Madam," said several people all at once. Fortunately, Alena was there. To her surprise, the Madam was muttering. "Today. Today was that day...that day...oh, Beloved, I wished. I did. I wished that I was wrong...."

CHAPTER 2
DREAMS ARE NEVER THE REALITY

Time: Unknown

Scene: Escape craft

He held me, my arms wrapped around his neck. My arms clung to him for safety, those arms that were small and weak. I couldn't move them, only clasp my fingers together in the hopes that he wouldn't let go. We moved quickly but quietly in the dark. I whimpered at the jostling of my body. I was tired, so very tired.

"Hush now," he said as we came to a corner of two hallways. "I need you to be quiet."

The light, the little there was, hurt my eyes. There was another who neared. I could feel his presence ravage the air. His stench and darkness filled my all, my...everything. He dominated me from touch to taste; all my senses fell under his darkness, his evil. I laid my eyes upon him.

I saw only a monster.

The monster spotted us and stalked forward. He held me close, shielding my body and fighting the monster. The monster was strong. I wanted to help. I wanted to fight. My hands wouldn't move. I attempted to cry; I attempted to call, but my voice could not be heard. He pulled out something, I didn't know what, and struck the monster, struck the monster with bright holy light. I looked up to see his face, and he smiled.

"You're...you're...just...like...a magician."

———

Sam opened her eyes and rubbed at her head. She blinked. Why couldn't she see anything? The memories came like a tidal wave, and Sam remembered. She remembered S&D, the fortress made of boulders, and Richard—fighting—alone. She remembered the rocket ship that leveled out into a hovercraft. She remembered MESA decimating the whole of Richard's secret base. She could still feel the effect of those tears and the lingering puffiness of her eyes.

After the revelation, the realization that Richard was gone, things became a great deal fuzzier. She recalled laying her head back to rest her eyes, hoping, praying for some type of reprieve. She needed rest and got it. She must have fallen asleep, and somehow the plane recognized that. Now it was time to get up and figure out her next move. The space in the craft was too dark to see, and that could be a problem. There wasn't much that was going to be accomplished in the dark.

Sam sat up and felt around a bit. Not surprisingly, her recollection of the layout of the cabin of the rocket ship-turned-hovercraft was hazy at best. The problem was further complicated by the fact that she had no idea where the light switch was.

Sam stood tentatively, trying to locate something, anything that might engage a control panel. She only succeeded in tripping and using her face to break her fall. She felt blood drip from her nose.

"You've got to be kidding. Where the flipper-flak are the lights?"

It was as if she only had to ask.

The lights popped on immediately, blinding Sam, whose eyes had already adjusted to the darkness. She waited for a short while, then, with a certain amount of hesitation, opened her eyes again and waited for them to accommodate the brightness. Once she was able to look around without it hurting, she did just that, searching for anything that might be helpful. She didn't find much.

The craft wasn't terribly large by hovercraft standards. Everyone knew that the Floating Fortresses of the UWC and Jade Empire could house thousands and stay in the air for months at a time, assuming that all the power generators were up and running. Sam didn't know how Ariel Navy Officers and the enlisted did it. The whole idea of being thousands of *feet up in the air on a piece of metal weighing thousands of tons was not something that appealed to her. Sam's Uncle Roger used to tell her horror stories about the Ariel Navy vs. UWC Ground Forces football game and how the Ariel teams would always practice on the uppermost flight deck of the UWC's flag carrier, the UWC Clinton. Uncle Roger used to tell her that every year, every single year, there would be one enlisted who would get blown off the deck. He laughed every time he told that story, like people falling hundreds of meters through the air was funny. Uncle Roger had a strange sense of humor.*

Actually, Uncle Roger reminded Sam a great deal of Richard—well, fat Richard, not super Richard. They had similar personalities, though Uncle Roger was quite a bit more jovial. They cared in the same way, were there for her in the same way; heck, they scolded her in the same way. Perhaps Uncle Roger was the real reason that Sam gravitated to fat Richard so quickly. Fat Richard just reminded her of Uncle Roger.

She pushed Uncle Roger out of her mind. She didn't want to think about another sad thing. It was painful enough thinking about Richard.

Sam sighed. Stupid Richard, why the heck would he go out of his way to protect her, to die for her? It didn't make any sense. He was a soldier, right? He had a purpose, some sort of goal. How did protecting her and dying further that goal?

Well, I'm sure he didn't mean to die, thought Sam. *Not even Richard can anticipate everything.*

She yawned and stretched as she considered that line of thought. No one can anticipate everything, but Richard caught that unaware? No, it wasn't possible unless there was something so unexpected, so unlikely that he simply did not account for it affecting them. That thought brought another to mind.

The tin box.

She closed her eyes, thinking back to the conversation that started it all. That box, Richard recognized it. Back when she thought that the box was the reason for this whole mess, that she was just a bystander who happened to get roped in because she was there and found the silly tin jinx, Richard recognizing the box would not have surprised her. She knew better now, and Richard's reaction to the box was nothing short of unnerving.

What was it about that box that had him so upset? Sam adjusted, trying to find a comfortable position. She ran through their escape, going back to the beginning. An exchange with Richard jumped out at her...

"A war is defined as an armed conflict between nation-states, Samantha, and I'm pretty sure you, I, and MESA don't qualify as nation-states. Granted, MESA has the GDP to pull it off."

"I could do without the sarcasm."

"I could do with you not giving away our position."

"What's that supposed to mean?"

"Never mind. Just get in the car."

She was having trouble remembering everything. It all happened so fast—Richard coming into her room, the arguing, and together running to Richard's little lair. What did he say...what did he say after that?

"Why didn't you take the box?"

"Because leaving it might give us a chance to escape, and I can't stop the transfer now that MESA knows where we are."

"Richard, that doesn't make any sense. Don't we want to keep the box out of MESA's hands? Isn't that the whole reason for this whole freaking circumstance?"

"Sam, what are you talking about? What would have given you the idea that MESA was after that box? MESA made that box. They've made thousands of them. Why would they go through so much trouble just to retrieve it?"

"But isn't—isn't that why they came to Academy City 676? Weren't they after the box? I thought you said—"

"Sam, MESA was never after the box. MESA came to Academy City 676 for one reason and one reason alone. MESA came to our school to find and capture *you*."

. . .

The conversation echoed over and over again and brought Sam to the only logical and obvious conclusion: MESA wasn't looking for the box but using the box to look for her. She had brought the box. She was responsible for leading MESA to them.

Sam felt the tears again. Not only was Richard dead, but she was responsible. It was all her fault. She was responsible for the death of probably her best friend in the world. He might have been a fake. He might have lied to her for years, but she didn't care, or her heart didn't care. Richard, fat or super, was important to her, and now he was gone, and she would never get the chance to tell him. She wasn't sure how she was going to deal with all this. Sam felt the warmth from her eyes. She wiped at them before the path of her tears became too ingrained in her skin.

Sam rose; she had to do something, or she was going to lose it. She searched the craft for anything that might take her mind off Richard. This one was probably something that Richard had constructed with bubble gum and duct tape, so she wasn't sure how much faith she should have in its structural integrity. Not that she had control of what the craft was doing anyway. That was probably the first thing she should figure out.

The primary control board appeared to be located at the very front of the craft. Sam walked unsteadily towards it and found conductor's gloves located in a glass half-pillar just under the board. The holo-screen was black with only a smiley face on it. The smiley face made Sam smile. She wanted to think that Richard left that, though that probably wasn't the case. Richard, especially new super Richard, didn't have a sense of humor.

Sam moved the conductor's gloves. Never having used them before, she hoped there wasn't some sort of boot-up or recognition program. Fortunately, the gloves lit up as soon as she finished strapping them in place. The cockpit came alive. The holo-screen increased in length, stretching out to envelop Sam completely and reaching from floor to ceiling. Directly in front of Sam, the blackness changed to a white background with a superimposed word: "Engage."

Sam reached up and touched the screen. The holo-screen phased out the pitch black of the standby screen and loaded blue skies and mountains as far as the eye could see. Sam felt like she was floating, standing freely on a gust of wind like a bird. It was a sensational feeling. Stretching out her own wingspan, Sam barely noticed the conductor's gloves starting to glow. Curious as to what the gloves were doing, she moved her hands and felt the craft jerk. She almost bit it.

Sam caught herself before she fell flat on the ground and looked again at the gloves, trying not to move them.

"No way...," she said aloud. "He couldn't have possibly...."

She tested the gloves, moving her right hand upward and twisting it. Instantly, the craft turned to the side sharply, and Sam fell down hard.

Sliding from the angle of the ship's tilt, she hit the wall; the lights on the gloves went black but were replaced by lights from the bump she received from the wall. She sat for a moment, letting the impact-related dizziness pass. While she waited for the lights and vertigo to subside, the ship leveled out, apparently having had enough of hanging on its side. Sam got to her feet and walked cautiously back to the center of the room. The conductor's gloves began to glow the closer she came to her original position. Not wanting to repeat the experience, Sam kept her hands stationary. It worked. She made it to the middle of the holo-screen area, which was once again filled with blue skies and mountain scenery.

"Well, now what?" she grumbled. "How am I supposed to fly this plane just by standing here? Every time I move the silly thing, I'm going to swan dive into the wall."

Complaining wasn't going to get her anywhere. She needed to try a voice command. It worked for Richard; why not her?

Sam was suddenly thrown aloft as something collided with the craft. She did an encore performance of her earlier tumble and face-planted into the side of the wall. Again the gloves went black, the blue sky/mountain scenery faded away, and everything went dark. The shaking lasted only temporarily, stopping before she could wrap her head around the current situation. A weird sound, one that Sam didn't recognize, whined from somewhere in a disembodied way. The source was simply indistinguishable.

Bright light replaced the question of *where* the sound was coming from to *what* it was. It started out small, no bigger than a thumb, on the far side of the cockpit. It grew slightly to the size of the palm of her hand but did not remain still. The light thrust downward, moving from its point of origin to the floor. It made three more passes and melted three more light paths. All four paths connected, enabling Samantha to comprehend: It was a door. Someone on the outside was cutting a door straight into the side of her craft.

Sam realized this too late—not that she was in any position to do anything to the intruders or stop them. She didn't have any weapons, and if the ship did, she had no idea where they were. No, she was at the mercy of whoever came through the door. She hoped it was a friend, not a foe.

The makeshift door fell inward, clanging against the ground and kicking up debris that she didn't know was there. She saw the outline of a single individual that disappeared from view as soon as the newly cut door fell away. Sam's stomach dropped into her feet while her heart jumped to her throat.

Sam caught the view of a long hallway, one that shouldn't have been there, before soldiers, one after another, filed into her craft—soldiers she recognized as Jadian. They wore the uniforms of the Jadian death squad, the Mogui, the same unit that attacked Academy City 676. It was them, she was sure of it. She tried to ignore the recollection of a Jadian soldier splitting her shirt as he and his cronies moved in around her. Sam cringed; she was not going down like that. She would die first.

The soldiers panned out, moving swiftly and silently around the craft and lining the walls. Sam watched them; what else could she do? Once the craft was lined with soldiers, they bowed and stood silently at attention, shoulder-to-shoulder. The silence was broken only by the pounding of approaching footsteps, which caused them to bow their heads and say something in Mandarin that she couldn't understand.

From the darkness of the hall, a large and rugged man with thick black hair and a matching black beard streaked with gray stepped through the opening into Sam's ship. Though Sam really had no idea, the man looked important. She guessed he was some sort of commanding officer. In reality, he could have been a busboy, and he would still have Sam's respect and awe. He was intimidating, period. Sam stood straight and tried not to cower.

The man approached her with no visible expression. He walked right up to Sam and then, to her total and utter surprise, he kneeled down on one knee and said, "Gōng Zhǔ."

Each soldier mimicked the words and the movement of the first, kneeling and bowing their heads towards Samantha. They remained like that for what felt like forever. Finally, the captain stood, saying, "Gōng Zhǔ, it is so good to see you again. We would have you command us. Please."

Sam was speechless, totally speechless. She expected a lot

of things to happen, pictured a great many scenarios once she saw those soldiers come through the side of her craft. None of them involved her being called some strange Chinese word and asked to command a Jadian death squad.

"Captain, please, you're scaring the poor girl. Give her a little room to process this."

Sam literally froze. She recognized the voice.

Sam looked out and around the captain, who shifted from in front of her. A boy, tall and handsome with striking features, stepped from behind him. Sam's jaw dropped.

"Hello, Samantha, it's been a long time."

"Yes, yes it has, Adam."

CHAPTER 3
PRIMUM NON NOCERE

Time: Early Saturday morning
Scene: Local cafe

Professor Thurman sat at the small cafe, sipping his tea. The sky was clear, and the day was just starting to warm up. The tea felt warm in his mouth and soothing to his troubled mind. It seemed that all of his emotions were coming to a head. The frustrations he had been tolerating were growing each day, and his resolve to ignore those heavy emotions appeared to be cracking. He set the tea down and looked at his leather-bound book of notes. With MESA limiting the scope of his research, he found himself postulating more and more in his notes about Harmonicum, its beneficial uses, and the possibilities that could become a reality in the not-too-distant future.

Over the last few weeks, his pondering had gravitated towards two main topics. Thurman knew in his gut that

Harmonicum was the physical incarnation of the theory of everything that had eluded physicists for well over a hundred years. And while the theory had morphed and changed since Einstein's days, the ability to succinctly define everything occurring in the universe still proved to be elusive. Harmonicum could change all of that—Thurman just knew it. Yet the question remained: How? How did Harmonicum do what it did? How did it act as it did and not violate the laws Thurman knew to be fact? Were those facts actually fiction?

He had strung the idea back and forth in so many mathematical paths that his notes looked more like spider webs than equations. No matter which avenue he took, he seemed to always run into the same problems. Namely, the ability to decode universal DNA and use the same knowledge to code it into something else. While Thurman knew Harmonicum did that with ease, the *how* was maddeningly difficult to find. There had to be a way to *see* how that process worked. Thurman hypothesized that it was a three-step process of identification, deconstruction, and reconstruction, but how did an inanimate material understand something else? The conundrum was akin to a lump of gold sitting up and reciting the Pythagorean theorem.

Additionally, Harmonicum could not just have a database of sorts that listed the composition of all things. It was not some hyper-computer that made a query and retrieved a result. Therefore, the process had to be somehow built in. There was some way that Harmonicum could identify elements and then copy them. As Thurman sat pondering, he felt he was attributing more and more anthropomorphic qualities to this mysterious rock. If he kept it up, maybe he should just *ask* the rock how it did what it did.

The topic that came in a close second was more now-focused. Who cared how Harmonicum worked; the fact was, it did. What could he do with it? His usual first-day-of-the-semester lecture came to mind again. Sight to the blind, legs to the paralyzed...was there anything that Harmonicum could not do? And yet this topic came with its own questions, equally slippery as those belonging to the first. While Computer Human Interfaces had been a part of medicine for decades now, the complexity they would require to integrate Harmonicum would certainly be a daunting task.

Thurman recalled speaking with his father as a boy and how he had instilled in him the value of "first do no harm." His father abided by that principle in his practice and taught it to Thurman. While he didn't follow his father into medicine, he had always remained adamant about that core principle. And it was that moral injunction which caused his mind to think outside the CHI box. Thurman knew that CHIs had come a long way since their inception. Most today were minimally invasive and required little maintenance. However, a CHI designed to integrate someone with Harmonicum would be brutal. Hours of surgery implanting receptors and artificial nerves, months if not years of therapy to adapt to the new nervous system—not to mention the side effects of the energy transfers. You would need to identify genetic markers that would indicate the subject's ability to handle the amount of free radicals that the interface would produce. Almost constant monitoring of the subject would be required. You would need an entire...

Thurman sat up as a thought struck him. *First do no harm,* he thought. The most complicated aspects of the CHI were those elements designed to connect the user with the Harmonicum. You would basically need to rewire the entire nervous system. Thurman grabbed his pencil and began scribbling:

"Given that the procedure for fully interfacing Harmonicum into a human subject would result in too great of harm to said subject, the problem then becomes how to connect the subject to the interface using a minimally invasive process. With this in mind, why couldn't the Harmonicum itself become the medium in which the subject was connected? Harmonicum abides by the laws of conservation; therefore, it must produce measurable inputs and outputs. If a CHI could be designed to process these signals, then only a small system would be required. These signals would, of course, need to be identified and databased as the changes to Harmonicum occurred. But once they were, as long as the CHI could detect and communicate in the same signal language, the Harmonicum would act

as both carrier system and facilitate the desired physiological changes."

Thurman sat back as he finished his thought. The surgery required for such a procedure would be minimal at most, perhaps a small connection to the brain stem. The implantation of Harmonicum lines could be accomplished via ingested micro-robotics or natural orifice endoscopy. Scarring and recovery time would be nominal. Better still, if the lack of Harmonicum was exaggerated, and from the copious amounts MESA had access to, that was a real possibility, even the cost-prohibitive nature of using a rare element would not preclude the masses from benefiting.

Thurman refilled his cup from the warming pot. As he sipped, he rolled this new idea around in his head, looking at it from different angles. Minimally invasive procedures to cure all manner of disease. Genetically onset diabetes eradicated by Harmonicum controlling insulin production, macular degeneration reversed via Harmonicum transmitting the sights of the world to the brain, even amputees having near-perfect control of their prosthetics through a Harmonicum interface. There would be very few medical maladies that could not be alleviated.

First do no harm. That phrase kept lingering in his mind. *No harm.* No invasive measures, no unnecessary pain.

Thurman could feel his mind start to really run with the idea. Setting down his tea, he grabbed his pencil again:

"I fear that the centuries of medical thought and procedure are leading me to confine my theorizing to a past-based outlook. What I really need, and desperately desire, is to share these ideas with a futurist. Someone that is always seemingly looking beyond what the current day's box has provided us. Even as I sit here and think, I see more of the flaws in my thinking. If Harmonicum is truly the Universal Rosetta Stone, why would we stop at a minimally invasive CHI? Couldn't Harmonicum be used as a bio-mechanical interface? Surely the element has the properties needed to become "one" with the user so that the medical procedure required to interface would be completely seamless. If Harmonicum can act as both the carrier system and the second set of neurological connections, why stop there? Why not design a Harmonicum-based CHI? This would be the world's first true bio-mechanical computer system. Not some foreign object piggybacking on the human infrastructure, but rather one fully integrated with it, because it becomes a part of the user."

Thurman sat back again, somewhat overcome by the emotion of it all. His initial understanding of Harmonicum had been so infantile when he first arrived at MESA. Yet, with ideas like this one, he still was a mere toddler in what could be accomplished by such an incredible gift. Thurman believed in a god. Many of his colleagues found themselves lost in their belief that all things could be explained by science and equations, but Thurman had always maintained the ability to see the shadows flitting behind the curtain. No matter what equation or postulation came up, he always believed that someone or something had to be just one step in front of it. Harmonicum was no different. While he knew there may come a day when people would know all there is to know about it, the how or why was a whole different ballgame.

He sipped his tea as his mind ran wild at the possibilities. His mind drifted to stories he read as a boy. Stories of robots, distant alien races that came to invade Earth, space explorers outfitted with computers in their brains to compensate for the stresses of deep space travel. He recalled how he marveled at those ideas as a boy. Using machines to extend the reach of humans. Thurman sat and reminisced about how potent those feelings of awe were to him so many years ago. And yet he felt exactly the same way now—filled with awe and wonder about the possibilities that lay before him. He felt connected to that young boy again.

As he let the nostalgia wash over him, it soon began to ebb, changing into something that he was not prepared for. As a boy, Thurman also saw in those stories the evils that people could propagate. In almost every story, there was some villain using the same technology, or one far superior, for their own nefarious ends. Molecular disruption devices, cyborgs with hive minds more insect than human, mind control, mechanical implants to control their subjects...

Thurman's gut froze. Perhaps it was the cumulative effect of weeks of frustration or the result of strong emotional memories, but Thurman suddenly felt a sense of fear grip him. Something about those sci-fi stories touched a nerve inside him, something that had been creeping in the back of his mind, waiting for its opportunity to bubble to the forefront —which was now. Why had MESA been limiting his scope of research? *Because they want a foundation of research to be established before branching out into its possible uses,* Thurman told himself. But that creeping itch in the back of his mind called him out. That might have been what Thurman had told himself, but deep down did he really believe it?

No, thought Thurman. *No, I am a scientist. I look at things objectively. I have been trained to set aside bias.* Yet the more evidence he threw at the argument, the feebler it became. The itch continued to creep forward, eroding his frail excuse of a position on the matter. Thurman slumped in the chair. What was he doing? What lies had he conned himself into accepting as justifications? How far had he rationalized his principles? Was he first doing no harm?

Thurman's mind started to race as the feeling of dread grew stronger. Perhaps it was the trip down memory lane, but Thurman felt just as he had when his father had caught him lying or disobeying. That same knot was tying itself taut in his gut as the itch revealed things as they were.

MESA was limiting his scope of research, but why? The answer floated up. It was not because they wanted a foundation they could build on prior to branching out. That was just the comforting lie Thurman had been telling himself in an attempt to not quell his excitement about limitless resources, a highly qualified staff, and what seemed to be an infinite supply of Harmonicum. The rose-colored glasses were falling away from his eyes. MESA was limiting his research to align with their personal agenda. All of those labs Thurman had never seen. All of the pies that MESA's fingers were in. Thurman's mind replayed his first day at MESA, something that Kingston mentioned in CJ's lab when Thurman had asked about their funding.

"Mostly pharmaceutical companies. Although we do have large contracts with various defense departments from across the collective, and a large part of our research is self-funded as well."

Defense contracts, self-funded research, pharmaceutical companies. Thurman now wondered why he hadn't seen it before. Defense contracts meant weapons. Pharmaceutical companies—

Wait, thought Thurman. *Why would MESA need pharma companies to ante up funding? MESA is one of the largest manufacturers of medical and pharmacological equipment in the collective.* Was it possible that MESA's funding actually occurred through companies that they owned or at least had a controlling stake in? How deep could MESA's pockets run?

They are bottomless, it seems, thought Thurman. So if their funding was not controlled by outside interests, aside from government defense contracts, that left self-funded research. Research that would be governed and directed by MESA...for MESA.

A chill ran down Thurman's spine. Suddenly those villains seemed to come to life in his mind's eye. Thurman looked at his leather-bound notebook. His eyes wandered over the last entry about a seamless integration of Harmonicum into a human being. The world's first bio-mechanical computer capable of not only lossless interfacing but made of what was, in all aspects, the ambrosia of the gods. What could MESA do with a fully integrated user? Thurman's hand trembled as his mind took the natural next step in this line of thought. *What has MESA already accomplished?*

This was all too much for him. Thurman reached for the cup of tea, now probably cold. He needed to calm down. He needed his hands to stop shaking. The ceramic cup clacked against the saucer as Thurman lifted it towards his lips.

"Professor?"

The cup shattered on the ground as Thurman recoiled in fright. His heart raced as adrenaline pumped through his system.

"Professor, I'm so sorry to have startled you."

Thurman, hands still shaking, looked up at the man

standing at his table. A kind pair of eyes looked down at him. There was a look of concern and worry on the man's face.

"I am terribly sorry, Professor. I thought it was you sitting over here by yourself, so I came to say hello. Please, let me help you clean this up." The man waved for the waiter to come and clean up the spilled tea. Soon another young waiter joined him in picking up the shattered pieces of ceramic.

"Could you bring another cup for my friend here, and an espresso for me, please?"

The two waiters mopped up the last of the spilled tea and went to retrieve the cup and coffee.

Thurman's heart had slowed considerably, but that was not what was bothering him now. The feeling of gut-wrenching tightness had taken over his chest. If he had lied to himself about MESA, had he lied to himself about MESA's employees?

"Again I am so sorry, Professor. I really did not mean to sneak up on you like that." The look of concern had changed into a soft regret as the kind eyes remained fixed on Thurman.

"I hope you don't mind if I join you. We haven't been able to make our schedules line up, so I thought I would share a few minutes of relaxation with you."

Thurman's throat was suddenly dry. An effect from the adrenaline, no doubt, but still, his words came out cracked.

"CJ...what are—I mean, how nice of you. Of—of course, have a seat."

CHAPTER 4
RETURNING TO THE ROOT

Time: Mid-morning
Scene: Sacred temple deep in the Burning Plains

"Dirk, are you sure you know where you're going?"

Dirk stood on the edge of a cliff-side road, remembering the past in highlight reel fashion. The last time he was here was one of those narrow escapes that led to his two near-death experiences in the mansion of the governor of Sanzarubi. The guards, the loss of the Golden Sword, and getting shot at with the ever-so-classic AK-47s; there were some things he really regretted about that week. Dirk remembered the governor's eldest daughter. Then again, there were some things he certainly did *not* regret.

"Dirk, when are you going to stop ignoring me?" Rona stomped her foot in an uncharacteristically childish way that Dirk found adorable.

"Calm down, Rona," he said, coming back to reality and trying to get his bearings. "It's been some time since I've been here, and I don't have the map anymore."

Rona perked up. "A map? You actually had a map to this location?"

Dirk returned to the gas-powered jeep. "Yes, it was a...gift from a local shaman. He was a nice fellow, though he was responsible for getting me caught and almost killed."

Rona raised an eyebrow. "I sense a story there."

He nodded. "And you'd be right, but not one we have time for right now. Perhaps I could tell you about it over dinner."

She laughed. "Who am I to refuse my fiancé? Oh, and that was a lame segue, just so you know."

Dirk shrugged. "You said yes, didn't you?"

She laughed again. "Can't argue with that."

Dirk winked at her. "Come on. We've got some caves to explore."

————

"Dirk? DIRK! Are you alright?"

Dirk flipped on his flashlight and cursed inwardly. Rona was a beautiful girl, but if she didn't keep her mouth shut, she was going to get them both killed—the locals were patrolling this area more frequently since his last visit.

Dirk simultaneously tried to whisper and yell at the same time. It didn't work well.

"Yes, I'm alright. Now shut up! Do you want to alert every local on the planet that we're down here?"

Dirk's skin started to tingle. Rona was complaining about him. He just knew it.

"Rona, get down here already or I'm going on without you."

Twenty minutes later, Rona finally stepped into the passage. Dirk, who was sitting on a lip in the rock playing Raging Pigeons on his handheld, gave her a condescending look.

"Seriously?" he said, standing up and putting his mini-tablet in his pack. "What were you doing, waiting for the mountain to erode around you?"

"Har, har, har," answered Rona spitefully, "you're hilarious. I've never been very good with heights."

Dirk cocked his head to the left. "Can I ask what exactly you were expecting?"

"Not this," said Rona, looking around the narrow space. "Do all ancient catacombs smell like this?"

Dirk let out a burst of mirth. "You don't have much practical experience, do ya, Rona?"

The dark hardly stifled the death glare Rona leveled at Dirk. She changed the subject instead of commenting, as the look was all the discourse she needed. "So is this chamber far?"

Dirk took a few steps deeper into the mountain. "Oh yeah, we've got a ways. This is where it could get dangerous."

Rona cast a sharp glare. "Why dangerous? Haven't you been here before?"

Dirk grinned and pulled out a roll of yarn. "That's when I knew where I was going, darling. This time we're going to have to do this the old-fashioned way."

Rona groaned. This was going to take a lot longer than she had expected.

———

Just as Dirk started to lose hope and Rona's whining became unbearable, the walls of the tunnel widened. Dirk grinned boyishly as he saw scattered and broken rays of light illuminating unsettled dust particles.

"Rona."

Rona's voice came out irritated. "What?"

"We're here."

"Really," she said with a hint of surprise. "How do you know?"

He pointed at the memorable cracked rock formations; there was just enough natural light to see clear across the cavern. On the far side, he said, just like he had seen it so long ago, was the same large outcropping of stone and the carved imprint of a massive blade. The sword obviously wasn't there any longer, but Dirk's nerves still did a little dance as he remembered this particular conquest. His was a beautiful one. If only they hadn't lost his finds in the city.

"Dirk, have you seen these?"

Rona was examining some hieroglyphics. There were many more than Dirk remembered, literally hundreds scattered around the space. Rona was studying a particularly large one that sort of jumped out. "Fascinating."

Dirk joined her. "Mind sharing with the rest of the class, my dear?"

Rona pointed to the hieroglyphic. "You've probably seen this before even if you don't have any experience treasure hunting for Egyptian artifacts. This is a common one. The Eye of Horus is actually the basis of the Egyptian—"

Dirk interrupted her. "Fractional system. They used it to keep track of grain, land prescriptions. Yeah, I know."

Rona glared at him. It was totally cute. "You get a kick out of pretending you don't know things."

Dirk shrugged. "I'm a funny guy. What can I say? Here's what I'm not understanding—look at these."

Dirk took Rona to another space of wall. "What do you think of these?"

Rona studied the markings, which were far different from the Egyptian hieroglyphics. "These aren't Egyptian."

"No, they're Sumerian."

"How do you think that happened?"

"Your guess is as good as mine. The two empires did exist around the same time."

Dirk took her to the other side of the chamber, closer to the stone pedestal where the sword once sat. From that viewpoint, the chamber's unique layout was more readily visible. Still, the darkness and shadow from the limited light made it difficult.

Dirk had had enough. He pulled out his emergency flat disc, touched a large button in the center of it, and threw it to the middle of the floor. The disc shot a light beam up and out that lit up the cave like a spotlight.

"We've got twenty minutes before that burns out."

Rona grinned her approval.

Dirk pointed to right above the entrance. "Now those I remember. Take a look at that."

Huge groupings of designs and symbols, intricately cut, ran along the top of the ceiling, stretching the length of the room. There were stark differences in the style and general feel of the groups Dirk recognized, but many he did not. He had no idea what this meant and was hoping that Rona did.

"Did you see what I'm seeing here?" he asked, pointing at the different symbols.

Rona pulled out some sort of strap-on goggles. They reminded Dirk of the twentieth-century night vision goggles he used to play with as a child.

"Adams gave these to me," she said in response to the look on Dirk's face. "They're called Spectros; I'm not sure what their real name is."

She looked through the Spectros and studied the wall for

a few minutes while turning dials and pushing buttons on them. Finally, she pulled them off, exclaiming, "Unbelievable! Dirk, do you know what this is?"

Dirk felt a witty comment coming on but just said, "I've no idea, but I'm glad you're so excited."

Rona pointed to the far upper left corner of the chamber, which was completely out of reach for a normal person. "Start there."

Her index finger slowly dragged across the top of the wall. "Are you seeing the difference between, say, the left corner and the right?"

"Of course," answered Dirk, wheels turning, trying to determine what Rona was playing at. "Different groups of symbols. Why?"

"Exactly!" said Rona, her excitement steadily rising.

"So what's so great about that?"

"It means that different societies used this room. It wasn't just the Egyptians!"

Dirk cocked his head to the left. "Rona, I hate to do this, really I do, seeing as you're having some sort of epiphany, but I already came to that conclusion, you know, when we saw both Sumerian script and Egyptian hieroglyphics over there. Not gonna lie, that was kind of a giveaway."

Rona laughed; she seemed uncharacteristically giddy. "You don't understand, Dirk, there are many different societies represented here: Egyptian, Sumerian, Akkadian, Eblaite, Elamite, and a handful of other dead languages including something close to ancient Greek and Chinese. It was like someone went around the world just collecting the fundamentals of as many languages as possible—wait, no way!"

Rona ran to an obscure corner of the chamber. "Dirk, I recognize some of these. These types of markings were only recently found by one of my old professors at Candlebridge."

She pointed to some curving markings. "These three symbols here are pieces of the Norte Chico alphabet. That's the oldest recorded society to come out of the Southern UWC, around 2500 B.C."

She ran her fingers along the wall, studying the remaining markings. "Dirk—I could be wrong, but this appears to be a complete list of alphabet symbols and sample writings of the Norte Chico...this—this is impossible. Who could have done this?"

Dirk didn't answer.

"Dirk, are you even listening to me?"

"Rona, come here for a moment."

"Why, what's up?"

"We need to radio the extraction team, the one going after the sword. We've got major problems."

———

Harrison loved his job. Mostly it was the gadgets, but the travel perks were pretty sweet, too. He never thought in a million years he would be in Sanzarubi, let alone skulking around a seriously old palace looking for cool stuff. He had been itching to try out some new equipment, and this operation gave him just that opportunity. Harrison held the GRI— or Gamma-ray Imager—out in front of him. While the walls of the palace were old and thick, they were no match for the highly energized photons Harrison beamed around in front of him. The GRI's display rendered an image of the hallway. Harrison dialed up the output, and the hallway walls gave way to the contents behind them. He searched the rooms as he swept back and forth, but nothing of interest caught his eye.

"You done playing with your toys?" asked a gruff man behind Harrison. "I gotta piss, so ya mind not taking all day?"

That was the one downside of fieldwork. He never got to go anywhere by himself. Always with him were the ever-present grunts and their guns. "It's not like we can just blast our way through," Harrison said with as much courage as he could muster. "So, let me do my work, so you can do yours."

The gruff soldier made a rude gesture and replied, "Sure we can, watch." He raised a hollow tube to his side and squeezed off a round. The small grenade flew into a door ten meters down the hall and turned it into tiny splinters. The explosive round was designed to be highly contained, but the loud burst was still unsettling.

"See? Much faster." Harrison dusted the debris from his clothes, scowled at the gruff man, who was now laughing raucously, and returned to the GRI display. Trying to ignore the fact that the laughter was at his expense, Harrison continued down the hallway, checking rooms and offshoots.

At the end of one hallway, the GRI's screen produced only static as Harrison passed it over a particular wall. He swept it to the left, and the image cleared to show the wall and some of the space behind it. Coming back around, the image once again dissolved into static.

"What's the matter, your toy get broke?"

Harrison could hardly contain his frustration.

"No, you oaf. I believe the spot we're looking for is behind this wall." Harrison tried to put as much authority into his voice as he could, but he still wasn't sure it had worked.

"Well then, what are we waiting for?" Harrison saw the hollow tube come up.

"No!" he screamed. "No, don't!"

The gruff soldier looked at him with a disapproving smirk. "What is it now, Nancy?" A few of the others gave a slight chuckle at the derogatory nickname.

Harrison, relieved that the buffoon hadn't just killed them all, took a deep breath to shed some of the frustration welling up inside him.

"The reason I know that this is the spot is because the GRI cannot see behind it. That means there are at least two meters of rock in this wall. If you wanted to hide something from everyone else, you'd do it in a thick-walled room. So before your little pea-shooter rebounds like a small marble and kills us all, how about I find a way to get inside that doesn't call for death by moron?"

Harrison walked away from the group, partially because he had to radio in their find, but mostly because he was much smaller than anyone he was with. He wasn't sure where his assertiveness had come from, but it felt really good. Still, he didn't want to stick around for the reaction. He sent a small message off to the ops server detailing where they were, his suspicions about the thick-walled room, and that they were going to attempt to breach it. Now he just had to figure out how.

More than an hour and several high-density plasma torches later, Harrison and the small crew poked through the hole they had made in the thick rock. What lay on the other side was a mix of history and technology. The thick walls of a cata-comb-like structure spread out in multiple tunnels, all lined with what looked like state-of-the-art detection and moni-toring systems.

"No one move," said Harrison quietly. No doubt, they had tripped a few alarms with their entry, but aside from a possible silent alarm somewhere, Harrison couldn't see anything that would pose a threat. Still, he had to be sure.

"Pass me my case." A black case was passed from person to person up to Harrison. He carefully set it down, opened it, and began examining its contents. He selected a passive Electromagnetic Frequency detector, powered it on, and swept the room in front of him. Just as he expected, the walls were alive with electricity feeding the detection equipment. As he spun around, he spotted a small line close to the crew. Stowing the device away, he retrieved a small readout display attached to some cables. Walking over to the wall, he carefully attached each of the cables to the rock along the line where the detector showed the EM field. When the last cable was affixed, the readout came to life. Harrison sat watching the data scroll across.

"Hey, gadget-boy," he heard. He was growing tired of the nicknames. "You gotta have some cool stuff in that case of yours. Why don't you just break some of it out and we can get on with things?"

Harrison ignored the request. He was here because he had a brain, not because he was some bellhop carrying a box full of gadgets. He continued to watch the data flow across the screen when something caught his eye. He scrubbed the data feed back and then forward. Something about it seemed off. Again, he pulled the data feed back and then forward, studying a specific section and the sections before and after it.

"It couldn't be that," Harrison mumbled. "That wouldn't make any sense."

"Hey, tablet-monkey. None of us are getting any younger here."

Harrison barely heard him as he did the calculations. "It would work...," he muttered, "but where would the...?" He trailed off as he looked up from the readout and started looking around the room. He stopped at a small box mounted on a wall across from him. "Couldn't be...."

Harrison retrieved the EMF detector and scanned the floor. Nothing. He set it down, grabbed a small pen-like device, disconnected the cables from the readout, and carefully walked across the room. Once at the box, he moved what looked like a penlight over it. Instantly, the readout showed a GRI-rendered display of the box and its hidden contents. Harrison took a minute to look for trips or triggers but found none. "Low levels. Interesting...."

"Pinhead, care to cut the geek-speak and tell us what's going on?" asked the gruff soldier.

"Not really," replied Harrison. He set down the readout and tucked the pen into a pocket. He found a latch on the side of the box, popped it open, took a quick look at the wires inside, then, grabbing a pair of wire cutters from his belt, snipped a small green wire. Instantly, a humming that was present moments before died. The room seemed less...alive.

Harrison strode easily back to his case, double-checked that all the EMFs were no longer powered, packed up his gear, then closed the case. "Grab that for me," he said offhandedly as he made his way across the room and into one of the tunnels.

———

Fifteen minutes later, the crew was standing in front of what appeared to be a large high-security vault. There was a brief argument about just blowing up the vault; thankfully, Harrison's calmer mind prevailed, and he set to work cracking the vault's security measures. Blowing through most of his diagnostic and passive monitoring equipment, it took him another forty-five minutes to successfully navigate the failsafes built into the vault. Unfortunately, it was also forty-five minutes of enduring jeers from his simian-brained coworkers. Just when he thought he would snap at the next reference to his lack of manhood, a comm sounded an incoming message. Harrison quickly spun around.

"Don't answer that!" he yelled.

The large man holding the ringing comm smirked at Harrison. "What, you gonna tell on us...gonna tattle on us for calling you names?" he said in a mocking whiny voice.

"No, but if you answer that comm and the connection frequency interferes with one of the failsafes, you could blow us all up. So, whoever it is, we'll call them back after the vault is disabled." The large man looked at Harrison and then to the squad leader.

"Better do what Nancy says." With that, the large man holstered the comm and motioned for Harrison to continue.

Ten minutes and two failsafes later, Harrison let out a deep breath. "OK, done. Now we just need to carefully extract whatever is inside, and we should be good. But I do have to warn you—"

"Yeah, yeah, *carefully*. We get it, Nancy. Now step aside." With that, the gruff soldier scooted Harrison aside with his beefy arm and stepped up to the vault.

"Wait, I really think you should—"

"Look, screen jockey, you did your thing. Now let the big boys handle it," said the man over his shoulder. He cocked his head to one side as he grabbed the latch on the vault. Slowly, he turned it until it thunked loudly. Leaning to the side, he peered into the small opening crack as he swung the door slowly open. His eyes reflected the glint of shiny metal as he pulled the door wide, and the crew exchanged high fives, whoops, and hollers as they got their first look at the gleaming gold hilt, jewel-encrusted guard, and polished blade of a large scimitar.

"Now that's what we came for!" yelled the gruff soldier. "Radio into base. We got it." The soldier reached into the vault, grasped the handle, and was blown back by the wave of fire that erupted from the vault. The blazing inferno engulfed the small, enclosed space in under a second, barbecuing everything in its path. As the fireball retreated, all that remained was the smell of burnt flesh and the sparking of charred electronic gadgets.

CHAPTER 5
GŌNG ZHǓ

Time: Evening

Scene: Sam's quarters inside the Jadian airship

"Are you two just pretending not to speak English? Because I think you can understand. You're just staying silent to annoy me."

The two Jadian soldiers standing to either side of her door ignored Sam, maintaining silence and strict posture. Sam glared at them from one of the plush chairs in the massive room, trying to remain cross in the midst of the opulence surrounding her. In the far corner sat a rosewood four-poster bed with ash and walnut credenzas on either side. Next to one of the credenzas was a black wood armoire and a king-wood vanity, all resting on hickory paneling. All the luxury made Sam uncomfortable. She tried not to think about it too much and, alternatively, tried to mess with the two guards standing inside her room.

Sam stepped up to one of them. He was a handsome devil with deep blue eyes, a short stocky frame, and a total baby face. He was disciplined as well, refusing to even look at her, let alone converse or answer any of her questions. Sam was doing her best to wear him down, though. This was the third time the powers that be, whoever they were, had placed this particular set of guards to watch over her, and without knowing exactly why, Sam recognized the signs that she was wearing on the handsome soldier. He seemed intimidated by her for some reason despite her being the one held captive. She didn't question it, only tried to take advantage. She had already tried several different strategies to no avail, but she was getting closer. Her next tactic was rudeness. She was going to try insulting the soldier and see if he reacted. Sam put her strategy to work, letting out a string of insults culminating with, "Your mother was a UWC Bollywood starlet."

She took a breath and watched the soldier. Nothing. She checked insults off her mental list. The soldiers continued to stare forward as if Sam were not there.

Sam started to pace back and forth in the room. "You two are worse than Richard. He didn't answer my questions either, but at least he actually talked to me. Aren't you two bored? Curious? Annoyed? Anything?"

She stopped her pacing, practically yelling, "You can talk,

right? Would you react if I stripped here and now? Then would you say something?"

The two soldiers' eyes shifted ever so slightly. They looked at each other with indiscernible expressions. The look was insubstantial, just a little shift and communication. She saw the opportunity. Sam once more walked right up to the handsome soldier. His eyes were facing forward again in a blatant attempt to ignore her.

Sam narrowed her eyes. "You know, you're awfully handsome. What would you do if I kissed you right on the mouth?"

The soldier's eyes bulged, and he turned his gaze to her. Now that was interesting. Why of all things did that get a reaction? Sam knew it was impossible. The only person she had ever kissed was Richard, and now he was dead. Sam felt a twinge of sadness sprinkled with guilt. Poor Richard. Without realizing it, Sam inched closer to the handsome soldier.

"Gōng Zhǔ."

Sam refocused, just now recognizing that she had zoned out. The handsome soldier was looking at her with concern and a bit of fear.

Sam took a step back from him, her face reddening. "So you can talk. Good."

To her surprise, both soldiers bowed, but it was the handsome one who spoke. "I apologize if we seemed rude, but we were told not to speak to you before the Da Xiao has had the opportunity to return. We know he is anxious to do so."

"Da Xiao?" asked Sam, trying to get him to continue talking. She had played this game with Richard. If she got him talking....

The soldier nodded. "Yes—uh—the colonel. Da Xiao is the colonel and is in charge of the mission and this ship. He is anxious to meet with you, but he has been away for some time and must return to his duties. He's not just a Da Xiao, so his other duties keep him busier than most."

Just then, a door opened, and two lovely young ladies entered wearing fanciful clothing that Sam had never seen before. One wore a body-hugging red dress that hit just above the knee and reflected ample amounts of light from gold-embroidered dragons. The other wore a straight, T-shaped robe that fell to the ankle, with a thick collar and long, wide sleeves that almost completely covered the girl; only her face and hands were visible. She wore a strange sort of sandal and sock with it. Sam was at a loss; the styles were completely unknown to her.

The soldier straightened and returned to his former rigidity. Peeling her eyes from the two girls, Sam scoffed openly as the soldiers replaced their masks of formality. She swore internally, trying hard not to let the frustration show too much on her face. She was finally making headway with that soldier, and the two little Jadian dolls just had to come and interrupt the most informative conversation she had participated in since being picked up by Adam and the soldiers. She felt like hitting someone, but fought the impulse; instead, she faced the two strangely dressed Jadian girls.

"Gōng Zhǔ," said the two girls in unison while bowing. The one in the dress stepped forward. She spoke with a heavy accent. "We apologize for our lateness; you are to dine with the Da Xiao tonight, and he has asked us to attend to your needs."

The girl in the dress bowed again. "I am Chen, and this is Misaka, and we are your handmaidens."

They both smiled expectantly, though they politely refused to meet Sam's eyes. Sam was speechless by the appearance and demeanor of the girls. Days of nothing but this room and statue-like soldiers watching her every move. Hours of her attempting to force any type of information out of her captors, who simply stared forward like inanimate objects. She wasn't sure how to take this change in circumstance. It was then that the weight of Chen's words struck her.

"Chen, was it?"

The young lady in the shiny dress bowed again. "Yes, my lady."

"Did you say handmaidens?"

Chen nodded in a confused way. "Yes, my lady. We are here to serve you."

Sam's bafflement reached a whole new level. Now she was *really* confused.

Chen and Misaka bowed again. "I'm sorry if we've displeased you, my lady. Your arrival was unexpected, and it was forbidden to have direct contact with you unless the—"

"Wait just one brickin' second, what do you mean direct contact with me is forbidden? Why forbid contact with me?"

Chen wasn't listening, or appeared as if she wasn't, but was instead staring at a timepiece pulled from seemingly nowhere. The appearance of the old-fashioned pocket watch was quite a feat, as her tight dress didn't appear to have room for pockets. "I am sorry, Gōng Zhǔ, but we must prepare."

Chen touched a button on her timepiece, and a hollow projected interface popped out in front of her. Chen pressed a series of buttons and then quickly closed the timepiece.

Immediately, a rumbling right underneath Sam's feet forced her to take a couple of steps back just as sections of the floor shifted open, folding, turning, and bending. Aside from the rumbling vibrations, the room was transformed with little noise. It happened quickly, and Sam had no idea what she was supposed to be looking at when it was over. Chen ushered out the guards. Sam started to protest but was distracted by Misaka, who slid in behind her and, before she knew it, had undressed Sam to her undergarments.

"Mi-Misaka, what are you doing?" Sam, feeling quite exposed, attempted to cover herself in front of the two young ladies.

Chen rolled her eyes but bowed slightly. "We are getting

you ready for dinner, my dear. The Da Xiao is expecting you. We must properly prepare you."

Sam's eyebrow shot up. "What does that mean exactly?"

Misaka and Chen simply giggled.

———

Sam quickly came to the conclusion that Misaka and Chen were not messing around. The transformation of Sam's room and their sudden appearance were all for the purposes of getting Sam "ready" to eat dinner with this mysterious "Da Xiao." This individual must have had some heavy clout because Misaka and Chen spared no effort in their preparations. Sam's quarters had been converted into a steel-frame spa complete with a soaking tub, waterfall facets, and silver ion misting sprays. Low, soothing music played as Sam soaked in the tub. Meanwhile, Misaka and Chen fussed with her hair. She didn't care, though. She felt the worry and tension drain from her body, allowing her to almost forget where she was. She could get used to this.

She suddenly tensed as the image of Richard came to her mind. He was dead, and she was sitting in an enemy's plane enjoying a bath. She should be ashamed of herself and probably a great deal more worried. Back in Academy City, the Jadian soldiers would have done some pretty horrible things to her if Richard had not put them in their place. Now they were treating her like some government VIP. It didn't make sense. If she let her guard down, bad things were going to happen, and after Richard's sacrifice, that was unacceptable.

Sam's eyes popped open as the spray from the silver misters lapsed. She tried to shrink back when she became aware of Chen's face mere centimeters away as she applied some sort of scrub to her neck and upper chest. As soon as Sam noticed what she was doing, her face flared red.

Chen smiled at her. Sam tried to smile back but found it difficult. "Little close there, Chen."

She glanced down at the scrub. "I hope you're planning on buying me dinner after this."

Chen stared, obviously confused. "No, Gōng Zhǔ, you will be dining with the Da Xiao tonight. You do not want to eat dinner with us. We are handmaidens—our role is to prepare and support. We are not allowed to associate with you outside our preparations."

Obviously, sarcasm was wasted on Chen. Sam sighed. She didn't like the sound of dining with this Da Xiao guy, and there was that title again: Gōng Zhǔ. Why did people keep calling her that?

She closed her eyes again as Misaka placed a strong but sweet-smelling substance on her head and began massaging her scalp. Boy, did she have magical fingers. Sam literally felt her resistance melt away as her breathing deepened and became more steady, patterned, and even. She found her mind turning and clearing. Suddenly, an idea struck Sam. If the soldiers were unwilling to talk to her, then maybe....

She opened her eyes to find Chen still uncomfortably close. Her heart began beating faster. She wanted answers, but she needed to ease into this. "What exactly do the handmaidens do here, Chen?"

"We are attendants to the Gōng Zhǔ, of course." Chen gave a little bow and ironic smile. She continued to wipe at Sam's neck and shoulders and did not elaborate. Sam's eyes narrowed.

An awkward silence followed. Well—Sam felt it was awkward; she had no idea what the handmaidens were thinking. They both continued their work with vapid smiles on their faces. It was time to be a bit more forward.

"Chen, Misaka, do either of you have any idea where we are?"

Chen was the one to answer. "Of course we do, mistress. We are nearing the western solar power grid of the UWC, the Valley of Death."

Sam chanced a follow-up question. "And why are we going there?"

Chen paused, allowing hot soapy water to drip from a sponge. "Because the UWC's Gamma Star Detection Platform is very thorough, and although this ship has been fitted to avoid detection, the sea lines of the UWC are jealously guarded, much like those of our great empire."

Sam did not like the sound of that. "So why are we going to the sea line? What will we be doing there?"

Chen raised an eyebrow. "Do you really not know, Gōng Zhǔ, or are you jesting?"

Sam's confusion was evident. "I'm afraid I don't know what you mean."

Chen and Misaka exchanged looks. "Gōng Zhǔ, it seems that it is even worse than the Da Xiao feared. You know nothing."

Misaka covered her mouth, apparently scandalized.

Chen put up her hands. "You need not fear now. We are making the long trip back from whence we came. We are leaving this uncultured and uncivilized place and returning to the Jade Empire, your home."

———

Chen and Misaka refused to answer any of Sam's other questions, and their work turned from spa treatment to borderline prison treatment. Sam did not understand their behavior.

The questions and whatever information the girls gleaned from Sam's questions supposedly startled them enough that they wanted nothing more than to remove themselves from her presence as quickly as possible. They did finish their work, however. They brought out an assortment of robes and dresses not unlike the ones that they were wearing when they entered her room. Chen offered Sam a less risqué version of the silky dress she had been wearing, calling it a Chinese qipao, a traditional piece of clothing that originated with the Qing Dynasty of seventeenth-century Imperial China. The robe-like outfit worn and presented by Misaka was a Japanese kimono, traditional ceremonial garb from inland Japan, a province of the Modern Day Jade Empire.

Sam went with the more comfortable of the two, deciding to wear an ankle-length red qipao with thigh-high slits. Misaka was surprisingly disappointed, as if what Sam wore was a matter of pride for her. Regardless of Misaka's disappointment, the girls arranged her hair in an elegant updo and applied expensive makeup to her face. By the time they were finished, Sam hardly recognized her own reflection.

She barely had a chance to utter a thank you. Chen and Misaka ushered her to the hall outside her room, where four soldiers, including the handsome one, waited for her. They escorted her deeper and deeper into the ship, during which Sam arrived at a conclusion or two. The main one being that the ship she was on was absolutely massive. She wasn't exactly sure how long they had been walking, but it was long enough that the heeled shoes she was wearing were really irritating her feet. The second conclusion was that the borders of the UWC weren't as difficult to penetrate as school and the national media had led her to believe if this massive flying stadium could get past all those orbiting satellites. The thought was not a comforting one.

The soldiers, and because she was sandwiched in between them, Sam, too, came to an abrupt stop in front of a massive and stunning dragon head. Wrought in the famous Jadian gold, the detail was so exquisite that the dragon looked real. Large ruby eyes gazed down at Sam and sent a chill up her spine as if the dragon was just waiting to bite down on her.

"You enter here," said the handsome soldier, pointing to the open maw of the dragon. "He is waiting for you."

He shifted uncomfortably. "A word of advice, Gōng Zhǔ."

He bowed. Sam raised an eyebrow. This was the first time he had initiated conversation with her.

"Tread lightly with the Da Xiao. He is an up-and-coming mystic with...strong political connections. You should not trifle with him."

The other soldiers nodded their heads. They all bowed and then retreated with a certain amount of haste. Sam watched them go. She did not like the way this was shaping out.

She turned her attention back to the dragon. She was entering the belly of the beast, literally in this circumstance. Sam smoothed down her dress and entered the mouth of the dragon.

———

Walking through the door of the dragon's mouth, Sam had frightful visions of running headlong into a digestive tract. Was it silly to be afraid of the stomach of a fictional creature? Of course, but she was a little anxious all the same. It took much longer to navigate the dragon's head and throat than expected—not because it was difficult, as the hall was lighted; it was simply that long. At the end of the hall was an intricate and beautifully carved door. Sam walked right up to the door and tried to open it. It was locked. At a loss as to what to do, Sam did the only thing that came to mind. She knocked.

Immediately, the door slowly opened inward to reveal a room that was one part dining area and one part cozy den complete with a fireplace. To the far left, huge fish swam lazily in a backlit, humongous aquarium, which sent watery reflections onto a long black wood dining table. To the right, couches were arranged in a half-circle around an oversized wood-burning fireplace, where an individual stood in silhouette; the darkness of the room coupled with the light from the fireplace made it difficult for Sam to make out any details aside from the military uniform.

"Sam, it's so nice of you to join me."

Sam recognized the voice. As her eyes adjusted to the darkness, she could see Adam smiling at her invitingly. "I hope all has been well."

Sam pushed a strand of hair out of her face. "I guess I'm not really sure how to answer that question."

Adam cocked his head inquiringly. "You could start with the truth."

Sam rolled her eyes. "I've been kidnapped; you don't want to hear the truth."

Adam gestured to the dining table. Sam walked cautiously towards it and sat down. Seeing Adam brought mixed emotions. Lingering affection made her heart pitter-patter even now, but circumstances of which she was clearly unaware had brought Adam into her life. She no more trusted him now than anyone else. She could not let her guard down.

Adam sat down opposite her. He adjusted in his chair, apparently finding a sweet spot, and clapped his hands twice. A door, hidden by the aquarium, opened, and servants flooded into the room carrying tray upon tray of fragrant sweet and savory dishes. Sam instantly started to salivate.

She shook her head. She needed to stay focused. The servants placed the trays along the table and then retreated, standing uniformly at attention.

Adam wasted no time. He stood and picked up his plate; he called to Sam, who was a good distance away at the other end of the table. "When I am at home, I am forced to go by protocol, but on this ship, my word is law, and I hate to stand on tradition. Please help yourself. I know you must be—"

"Why am I here, Adam?" Sam yelled, unable to control herself. She was tired of waiting, tired of the games. It was time for some answers.

Adam's carefree demeanor changed at the question. Still,

he spoke softly. "Is that really the question you want to ask, Samantha?"

Sam hesitated ever so slightly but answered affirmatively. "Yes, but it's not the only one."

Adam smiled. "Well, why don't we start with your questions? It might make this easier."

Sam hesitated again. She voiced the concern. "Just like that? You're going to answer my questions? No games? Straight answers?"

His smile grew wide. "To the best of my ability."

Sam was unable to conceal how pleased she was. She racked her brain, which had suddenly gone blank. She settled on her first question: "Why am I here?"

Adam sighed as he turned his gaze to the huge fish swimming about in the aquarium. "Alas, that *would* be the first question you ask me. You're here because I was commanded to bring you here—because you're a very special person."

His voice was almost sorrowful.

Sam started to ask her next question, but Adam cut her off.

"I can't tell you details as I don't know them myself. I was ordered to bring you here by someone who isn't used to hearing 'no.'"

Sam didn't like the sound of that but was too irritated by

the situation to think rationally. "So you just ran off to Academy City 676 to find me? No one has that much clout."

Sam got out of her seat and walked right up to Adam. "So what is it, Adam? What do the Jadians want with me?"

His laugh was unpleasant and at odds with his soft, musical voice. "Clout? Clout, you say? You are incorrect on that point, my dear—you do not understand. I'm taking you to someone with much clout—the most clout. Sam, I am taking you to see the Emperor of the Jade Empire."

CHAPTER 6
ADVANCEMENT

Time: Late evening
Scene: Courtyard of the governor's mansion

"Gingrich, come on, kick that Dem up."

Gingrich leveled a high kick at the head of Coda, a.k.a. Teddy, as the group of Republicans cheered on the sparring match. The kick missed horribly. Coda didn't really dodge, either. He took half a step back and simply leaned. Gingrich's momentum did the rest.

"Come on, Teddy, make 'em dance for me," Palin, a.k.a. Lacey, screamed from the sidelines. "Teach him how he should talk to a superior."

Coda rolled his eyes as another wayward kick, this one aimed at his hip/midsection, missed its target. Coda figured it was time to fight back. Gingrich attacked again but proffered a different tactic, moving in close in a traditional forward stance. He attacked with sharp hand movements, throat thrusts, and sword chops that were a bit more difficult to defend. This time, Coda countered, delivering a breaking knuckle punch to the solar plexus of Gingrich. Gingrich dropped like a bloated Gangan.

The cheering stopped immediately, all except Lacey, who was whooping it up with the best of the drunken soldiers. It made Coda chuckle.

Coda returned his attention to Gingrich and offered him a hand. "Are we done there, Newt?"

"I—told—you—not to call me that," coughed Gingrich through huge gasping breaths.

"Bro-haas, you can't be that upset. The guy was called Newt Gingrich, right? Fifty-second president? Any of this ringin' a bell?"

"It's not what you said," wheezed Gingrich, "it's how you said it."

Gingrich looked like he was about to cry as his eyes wandered towards a rowdy Palin. Coda felt his heart soften. He knew what this was really about. "Gingrich, if you want to get Palin's attention that badly, there are easier ways to do it."

Gingrich flushed as much from embarrassment as from pain. "Easy for you to say, Teddy. You could have any girl here, any girl you wanted!"

Coda exhaled deeply and ran a hand through his hair. "Not any girl, Newt."

Just then, Palin stumbled over and started to speak. She hadn't gotten more than half a word out of her mouth when....

Hiccup!

She began giggling uncontrollably.

Coda stood up. "I think that's my cue."

Palin latched onto him. "Come on, Co-dah, I mean Teddieee, heh heh. Just stay with me a why-elll."

Coda sighed again and steadied the girl. "Why do you always do this?"

He picked her up, carrying her like a baby. She nestled her way into his shirt. "You know why," whispered Palin.

Coda looked down. "What was that, Palin?"

Palin didn't answer.

Coda took Lacey to an old-fashioned leather couch where he set her down to sleep it off. Lacey was a cheap drunk. It took almost nothing to get her totally blitzed out of her mind. And Coda knew from experience that the strong drink loosened up the inhibitions of more than a few of their more unscrupulous allies. It didn't help that Lacey lost all sense of decency when she was drinking. Coda was barely able to keep her from completely removing her clothes because it was "hot"—and forget about Lacey's kissing games; that's where it got a bit hard. On more than one occasion, Coda had been the victim of one of Lacey's drunken smooches. But they weren't so bad; he had experienced worse. Her main problem was the abundance of alcohol. Several years previously, one of the other Republican captains found a barrel of twentieth-century wine as well as instructions on how to make the perfect batch for this region. It had been downhill for her ever since.

Coda sat down next to Lacey, who, groggy and drunk, snuggled up next to him and fell asleep. It was probably her plan the entire time. Coda shook his head, remembering from experience that there were worse ways to sleep.

An authoritative voice jarred Coda out of it. It was Coolidge. "Come on, Teddy, you too, Palin. This concerns both of you."

Lacey was instantly up and looking quite alert for someone who just minutes ago was too laced to function. Coda didn't say anything but followed Lacey, Coolidge, and about twelve others through a series of halls into the main briefing room. A man was already on the screen. Coda and Lacey stopped abruptly; he was wearing the oddest assortment of clothing.

Coda leaned into Lacey. "Is that who I think it is?"

Lacey was apparently too shocked to answer.

The man on the screen smiled. Coda tried not to gawk, but his outfit was outrageous: He wore a pleated coat, waistcoat, breeches, and a shirt with gathered sleeves, topped off with a good old-fashioned powdered wig. It was quite the sight.

In any other situation, at any other time, they might have laughed, but the soldiers understood who they were looking at: John Adams, the number two of the Republican movement and the world's greatest hacker. Most of the soldiers in the room, including Coda and Lacey, had never spoken directly to Adams. They had all received orders or equipment from him at one time or another, but now...now they were going to talk to him?

"Please be seated, everyone." Adams' voice was even and smooth, but authoritative. They all listened and took a seat in the circle.

Adams waited for them to take their seats before he said, "Mr. Coolidge, if you please."

Coolidge tapped a couple of buttons on his tablet. The floor inside their circle opened up, and a virtual theater board came up through the floor. The soldiers watched with anticipation.

The theater board came to life, and once it did, the screen version of Adams disappeared, and a half-size, full-colored hologram of him appeared on the virtual theater board. The group stared openly.

Adams smiled. "I've modified this board so you can see me, and I can see you. I wanted this to be as much like a face-to-face conversation as possible. I apologize I can't be there in person. My own mission objectives make it difficult."

Nobody said anything.

"You are all probably wondering why I brought you here."

A couple of the soldiers stirred; still, no one said anything.

"It's really quite simple. You are some of the best shock

troops in this region of the UWC. All of you have extensive combat experience. You're going to need that experience because, ladies and gentlemen, we are going to war."

Low mutters broke out. Coda leaned into Lacey. "And here I thought we were already at war."

Lacey smiled. "Smart apple."

Coda shrugged. "If the shoe fits...."

A grin stretched across Coda's face as the sour expression of a Latina girl with crunchy hair popped into his head. "Next time we're around 676, we should see what Cammie is up to."

"And what do you think, Teddy?"

Coda's code name played across Adams' lips with a distinct ping. Coda looked around the room. Everyone was looking at him, and Adams scowled with disapproval. Coda decided to just come clean. "I'm sorry, sir. I wasn't paying attention."

Adams' gaze softened. "I'm glad that you and Palin are getting along so well, Teddy, but you'd better pay attention to this, seeing as you're one of the assault captains."

Coda's ears perked up. Did Adams just say assault captain?

"Not all of you will be familiar with this target," said Adams as his holo-projection flicked out of view. "So I need to give you a visual to really see what we are up against."

A projection of Adams, this one life-size, hit the floor, no longer confined to the top of the virtual theater board. He had a clicker in his hand that he pointed at the virtual board. "Some of you may recognize this, but most of you won't."

The board set out a projection of a massive facility. The representation was highly detailed, three-dimensional, and in color. A couple of different versions of the scale floated in front of the group of soldiers, each representation providing a bit more information on the venue of this target. The first helped Coda appreciate the location. It was situated deep within a lush valley surrounded by high snow-covered mountains. The facility was big, too, if the panoramic view and measured miniature mountains were any indication, literally stretching across the whole of the valley. A second representation was a much closer look at the facility itself. Kilometers of fence surrounded groups of buildings in which a single road and hover pad marked the only visible means of entrance, giving it an ominous feel. Gunships on the roof and free electron defensive platforms at every guard tower, which were placed strategically around the perimeter, showed potentially unwanted visitors that whoever owned the building meant business.

No one said anything. Adams laughed at their confusion and then spoke with understanding. "You are all much younger than I expected. No matter. Ladies and gentlemen, you are looking at the main research facility for MESA Labs."

This announcement brought mixed reactions. One or two of the more dramatic gasped and whispered in hushed, worried tones, while others were more stoic and simply looked on in amazement. Only Coolidge had no reaction at all.

"Mr. Coolidge, your brief on MESA, if you please."

Coolidge stepped to the virtual theater board, put on a conductor's glove, and started to talk.

The brief was fascinating. Coolidge went into everything MESA while the onlookers took notes. The information was borderline manic, covering everything from corporate structure to suspected clandestine activities. MESA was an entity as complex as any country, with a yearly revenue to match the GDPs of most smaller states. Finally, they came to—

"Harold Hughes," said Coolidge, snapping his fingers, "the founder and CEO of MESA Corporation and one of the richest men in history. This son-of-a-one-eyed Gangan founded MESA when he was only fourteen and went on to create one of the most successful enterprises in the world."

A full-sized, lifelike projection materialized from the holo-board. The little old man walked around smiling sweetly.

Lacey giggled. "Ahh, he's cute!"

Coolidge scowled. "That 'cute' little old man is a ruthless imperialist and believer in social Darwinism, Palin."

"That ain't the half of it," interrupted a young black man at the end of the row. He nodded to Coolidge. "Permission to speak, sir."

Coolidge nodded. "Go ahead, Jackson."

Jackson took a deep breath. "Hughes is cold as ice even to

his own people. Do you all remember that earthquake and blackout near New Reno seven or eight years ago?"

Some nodded; some didn't.

"I was living among the Smithies near that massive salt lake there. My dad worked in the salt reserves. Anyway, my brother left the UWC special ops and got on with MESA. He wasn't supposed to, but he told me something that I've never told anyone."

The announcement was so unexpected. No one spoke.

Jackson continued his story, sounding a little more confident. Even Adams was listening intently. "About eight years ago, my older brother was working at a secret underground facility deep within the mountains. He didn't tell me what they were doing out there, but what he did say was that there was a special place in hell for people like him because of the things that they did."

Jackson paused. He sniffed a little, clearly identifying the emotions. "I got sidetracked a bit. I apologize. The reason I say this is because apparently that base was MESA's brain center, housing some of their most sensitive and dangerous breakthroughs. My brother came back often and told me he was worried—he was worried that whatever it was they were working on there, the mega-geniuses at MESA would complete it soon."

Coolidge interrupted. "I hate to stop you, Jackson. But is this going somewhere?"

"I was just getting there, sir."

Jackson took a deep breath and continued. "Eight years ago, Hughes was spending billions in research and development on a two-part project that was supposedly a game changer. The expense, however, subjected Hughes to a hostile takeover of his company. They almost succeeded, too. Until—"

Jackson's voice broke slightly.

"Until what, Jackson?" Coda asked.

"Until most of the higher-ups in MESA died when their secret underground desert facility was blown sky-high. Hughes did it. He blew up his own facility to prevent his board from pushing him out."

"Jackson, where are you getting this intel from?" asked Adams, sounding intrigued.

"My brother and I were on the cloud when the chaos started."

"You had a brother on the inside, and we are just now finding out about it?"

"No, sir, all this information should be in my file."

Adams grimaced. "I will check into that gap later. Continue, Jackson."

"I was only twelve at the time, sir, but my memory is quite good. The scientists were working on something. Something big, revolutionary in the world of weaponry. And the last message I got from my brother was that whatever they were working on had gone missing. It was stolen. The base blew up not long after."

Adams nodded to Coolidge, who took a step away from the virtual theater board. "Thanks for the segue, Jackson. You have given us much-needed context."

Adams made swiping motions, and screens of information jumped to the surrounding windows. "What I am about to share with you is beyond classified. Do not ask questions. Many of the extraneous details are on a need-to-know basis, so I will tell you if you need to know."

The attendees all sat up a little straighter.

Adams swiped again, and a picture materialized on the screens. "Do any of you know who this man is?"

No one answered in the affirmative.

"Not surprising," said Adams, turning his holo-body to the picture. "This is Doctor Eli Thurman. A leading physicist in the particle, theoretical, and condensed matter fields, he's essentially the second-smartest person on the planet..."

Jackson spoke aloud. "Who's the smartest, sir?"

Adams turned his attention to Jackson. "I'm sorry?"

"You said that Eli Thurman was the second smartest person on the planet. Who was the first?"

Adams gave Jackson a withering look and continued as if uninterrupted. "Until last year, he was working with the Ivy League's education system as a professor and lecturer."

The holo-projection of MESA's headquarters reappeared.

"Now he works here, at MESA's headquarters, as head researcher in their developments division."

A section of the MESA headquarters lit up.

"We, ladies and gentlemen, are going to break him out."

Lacey raised her hand.

Adams raised an eyebrow. "We are not in school, Palin. Ask your question."

Lacey put her hand down. "Sir, why would MESA put an academic in as head of the developments research lab?"

"I'll top ya on that one, Palin," said Coda. "Why is he important enough that we need to break him out and take on MESA in the process?"

"Classified, Teddy. Suffice it to say that for this mission, strike team one will be going after Thurman. Failure is not an option. MESA needs Thurman to complete a very specific project, literally a project that could have dire consequences for the rest of the world. Thurman has to be extracted—at all costs."

"Sir," asked Roosevelt, "did you just say strike team one?"

Adams nodded. "Yes, Roosevelt. That is exactly what I said. This is a two-team job with one primary and two secondary objectives. Teddy is on point for Red team. Harding is leading Blue team. This is a surgical strike that is going to cross over into all-out war. I need you all to be focused."

Palin started to raise her hand then thought better of it. "Sir, what's the second mission objective?"

Adams smiled and winked at Palin. "Destruction, Palin. There is a particular section of MESA that I want you to utterly destroy, from the people to the information. This objective is only slightly less important than getting Thurman out and will push back MESA's timeline another seven years."

Coda looked at Palin. Seven years seemed like a strange number.

Harding spoke up. "What's in the second lab, sir? I understand that whatever it is may be classified, but I'll need to know if I'm to prepare a demolition skid and attack plan."

Adams considered this statement. It was obvious that he was really weighing his options. "Feedbackers, Harding. MESA is working on a lab of advanced-level feedbackers and has developed a system that can identify the DNA markers in potential candidates."

Coda's hand shot into the air. He grinned at Lacey. "Sir, I'm afraid I'm not familiar with the term feed—"

"Sorry, Teddy—but I need to say this." It was Ford, one of Coolidge's shock troops. "Sir, attacking MESA when they're out in the open is insanity. But attacking their base of operations is brickin' suicide. MESA headquarters is home to Containment and S&D, two weapons divisions that we have approximately zero intel on. Hell, I can't even name someone who has survived an encounter with them, let alone been able to gather intel."

"That is not entirely true," replied Adams.

The silence of overwhelming disbelief descended upon the room. The soldiers glanced around at each other, wordlessly asking the same question: *Did Adams just imply what we think he implied?*

Adams rolled his eyes and flicked his wrist. "Ladies and gentlemen, I want to introduce to you the last remaining member of Washington's Culper Ring: Code Name - Richard."

CHAPTER 7
FIBONACCI'S FORTUNE

Time: Afternoon

Scene: MESA's Harmonics lab

Thurman sat in his office, staring at his leather-bound notebook. It, in turn, sat quietly staring back at him. He had barely made a scribble in it since that chance encounter with CJ outside the café. While that was weeks ago now, he couldn't shake the feeling of anxiety that constantly accompanied him. What had he gotten himself into, and why had it taken him so long to break through his self-imposed blinders? Despite his feelings of remorse and frustration with himself, he had bigger problems. Much bigger.

MESA was not what he had led himself to believe. He had set aside his scientific principles and his morals for nothing more than money, recognition, and the possibility of furthering his life's work. Now he feared he had become the

Oppenheimer of his time. *I have become Death, the destroyer of worlds.* What would MESA do with this research? More alarmingly, what had they already done?

Since the day CJ had surprised him, Thurman had been struggling to dam his emotions and keep them from spilling out into the open. That whole event seemed to rattle him good. He knew Warrick had noticed. The little man's incessant probing had, if possible, become more incessant. Thurman felt he had played it off successfully, throwing out things like being tired, working long hours, and the like. It seemed to have worked, as Warrick had backed down just a bit. Yet Thurman still felt like he was being watched. More closely watched than just the regular big-brother stuff he was sure had been going on since he stepped foot into MESA. Absentmindedly, he traced the small scar on his wrist where a *harmless* RFID chip sat just below his skin. *What have I done?* he thought.

A knock at his door made him jump ever so slightly.

"Good morning, Professor," said Kingston in a very cordial voice. "I haven't been down to see you in a while and thought I would pop in before you got underway today."

Thurman steeled himself and rose to shake Kingston's outstretched hand. "Good morning, Mr. Kingston. Yes, it has been some time, hasn't it?" He motioned for Kingston to sit down, as if the man weren't already moving toward the chair.

"From the reports I've seen, it looks like you're accomplishing some great things down here," remarked Kingston. Thurman put on his best humble-acceptance face.

"Yes, well, it would be difficult not to produce at least something with what you have given me to work with. I know I've said this before, but the resources you have put at my disposal are truly remarkable."

Kingston responded with a snake oil salesman's smile; at least that's what it now looked like to Thurman.

"It is our pleasure, Professor. Say, speaking of resources, I remember you asking about some of our other projects here at MESA."

On the inside, Thurman's blood seemed to freeze. On the outside, however, he forced his face into an innocently curious scrunch.

"Oh, well, as you know, I'm always interested in Dr. Jameson's—I mean CJ's—lab." Thurman added a gentle smile. "But I am sure you have a number of other fascinating projects here."

"That is a fact, Professor. *Many* interesting projects. In fact, one of them just came online on the other side of your wing." Kingston leaned closer to Thurman's desk and jokingly added, "I figured you may have seen some new faces in the hallways around here."

"Oh, Mr. Kingston, I'm terrible with faces. Most of my time is spent here, and truth be told, I am a little awkward when it comes to meeting new people. I usually just fumble over words and such." Thurman looked away, a little embarrassed. He hoped Kingston was buying it.

"Well, that's what I wanted to come offer you. A little social interaction with a fellow researcher. If you have a minute, I'd love to show you the new lab and have you meet some of its staff." Kingston looked inquiringly at him.

Thurman looked up, a little surprised. "You mean right now? Oh, well sure, I mean I suppose if it's OK with, you know, whoever is running the...or the head of the...what lab is it exactly?"

Kingston flashed that salesman smile again. "Oh, I don't want to ruin the surprise. Come on, walk with me."

Thurman's mind was racing. Another lab? What was this all about? He had been isolated ever since he arrived, and now they wanted him to tour another lab? Thurman didn't have time to sort through his emotions. Quickly he centered himself and then got up, acting as if he was searching for his glasses by patting his pockets. He touched them on his face, laughed, and threw in a self-deprecating head shake. He started around his desk, raised a finger, turned back around, and reached over to lock his terminal. Kingston, now standing, watched with a simple grin on his face. "Ready, Professor?"

"Yes, I think so. A little frazzled, I suppose," he replied in an even voice.

Kingston smiled and led the way out of the office and out of the lab.

Thurman watched as Kingston opened the last biometric lock on the lab door. During the five minutes on their way to the lab, Thurman had done his best to compose himself. He tried to set aside his fears about MESA and his analyses of Kingston and Jameson. He ignored his mind's yearning to apply this same friend-or-foe analysis to each person they passed along the way. He instead let the feelings of anticipation and excitement bloom within him. He recalled his birthdays as a child, the first day of school, his first teaching job. He pulled at anything and everything that would aid him in masking his fear.

Kingston entered the lab with Thurman just behind him. Thurman looked around as they made their way to the offices. Its appearance was very similar to the Harmonics lab when he first arrived. Equipment was still being unpacked and set up, maintenance and network technicians were intermingled with what appeared to be the laboratory staff, and systems were running through diagnostics. A large set of observation bays, similar to those in the Interface lab, or that were in the Interface lab, lined one side of the space. Technicians were busy installing an array of vid monitors and a number of other devices that Thurman didn't immediately recognize. Yet despite its normal appearance, something tugged at his mind. Something was different about this lab, and he couldn't quite articulate what the difference was. Thurman finished counting to five and quietly let out a deep cleansing breath. An inter-departmental shipping label told him how vital the deep breath would become. It read: East wing - Feedbacker Lab.

Kingston's voice brought Thurman back around to the offices. "Ah, Dr. Rai, I would like you to meet your neighbor across the way. This is Dr. Eli Thurman."

A curvy caramel-skinned woman turned towards Thurman and Kingston. Her jet-black hair floated easily past her shoulders, and a smile reached from her white teeth to her chocolate brown eyes. Thurman immediately let his mind go blank. So blank that the beauty of Dr. Rai did not even register.

"Dr. Thurman runs our Harmonics lab on the other side of the wing. I figured since the two of you would probably bump into each other in the hallway, I would make the formal introductions."

Dr. Rai smiled sweetly at Kingston and placed an affectionate hand on his arm. "Oh, that is so kind of you. You are so very thoughtful." Her accent placed her somewhere in the southeast of the Empire, but it was crisp enough to suggest northeastern schooling. She turned towards Thurman and offered her hand in a similarly affectionate manner. "Dr. Thurman, is it? I am Dr. Rai, but please call me Sati. It is very nice to meet you."

Thurman's blank mind told him to shake the outstretched hand and reply with something polite. He did so, almost without thought. "Dr. Rai—Sati. It is nice to meet you as well."

In his peripheral vision, Thurman noticed the slight smirk on Kingston's face. Thurman gave it no heed and focused on Dr. Rai, willing himself to make small talk. "I see you are getting settled in your new home, so to speak. If you are anything like I was a short time ago, you must be itching to get started on...well, to start...what is it exactly you do here, Dr. Rai?"

Dr. Rai smiled warmly. "Dr. Thurman, please. So formal. I told you, call me Sati." Thurman could almost feel the warm emotions float from her. He smiled.

"Of course, Sati. Then you must call me Professor. I was in academia so long, I can't say that you'll get a prompt response with 'Dr. Thurman,'" he replied with as much good humor as he could pack into the sentences.

Dr. Rai hooked her arm around Thurman's and started towards the observation bays. "Well, *Professor*," she said with a genial laugh, "I will be running MESA's new Feedbacker lab. Do you know the science?"

Thurman put on his best curious face. "Feedbacker...you mean like clairvoyants or fortune tellers?"

Again, the kind laugh. "Well, that is what feedbackers are referred to in the secular circles, but my research has proved that to be a very inadequate label."

They stopped in front of a bay where it appeared all the equipment had been installed. "Feedbackers," Dr. Rai continued, "are individuals with a proclivity to understand the world around them in terms of emotions and feelings as opposed to the tangible or physical. It is often this lack of grounding to the material world that gets feedbackers the 'psychic' branding. That and the leftover stigmas from fortune tellers and gypsies." Dr. Rai gave another amiable laugh.

"Most interesting. And so these feedbackers, they have what—just heightened emotional awareness?" asked Thurman, keeping the conversation going.

"At first, yes," replied Dr. Rai, "but my research shows that with help and training, that awareness can lead to incredible things. We are focusing on three types of feedbackers in my lab, namely t-kines, precogs, and emoticons."

Thurman's puzzled look prompted her to continue. "Well, for example." Dr. Rai pointed to the bay they were standing in front of. "This observation bay allows us to monitor the physiological and mental changes that occur when a feedbacker is engaged. We have cameras that pick up micro-emotions, thermal readings, and small electromagnetic shifts." She pointed to some other sensors in the bay. "These produce a constant non-invasive MRI output of the subject's brain activity and blood consumption, while other sensors monitor the subject's vitals."

Thurman added some curiosity to his tone. "So, a person would sit here in the bay and...do what exactly?"

"That depends on what type is currently being observed.

T-kines...," Dr. Rai paused. "Telekinetics would attempt to manipulate an object or part of the environment. Moving a small cube, or lifting a ball—things of that nature. Precogs anticipate the outcomes of certain actions—like guessing which box contains a marble, or giving the next line of a speech without hearing it first. Emoticons push and pull the emotional fabric around them. These, of course, are just the preliminary exercises that we administer. As a feedbacker develops his or her talents, we push their abilities to expand and advance."

They continued to tour the lab, looking at various bays and equipment racks. Thurman kept the conversation going by asking minor questions here and there. Yet his mind was solely focused on the task at hand. Never once did his concentration waver.

"Tell me, Sati, this all seems so new. How long have you been at this?" Thurman asked cordially.

"Well, the UWC has just recently gotten into the feed-backer arena. For decades, the Empire has held the most advanced programs for feedbackers. It has only been in the last two or three years that the UWC program has started producing favorable results. When I was—"

Kingston coughed and put his hand on Dr. Rai's shoulder. "Excuse me! Must be all the dust in here from setting up."

Dr. Rai turned to him. "Oh Kingston, a little dust won't kill you," she said with a smile on her face.

"Yes, well, I think it's time we were leaving. Thank you for the tour, Dr. Rai. If you need anything, just ask." Kingston shook her hand and started for the door.

"Well, I guess we're leaving," said Thurman amicably. "Thank you so much, Doctor—I mean Sati. This has been truly enlightening. Don't be a stranger now. We are, after all, hall mates, if you will." Thurman let out a small chuckle as he shook Dr. Rai's hand as well.

Dr. Rai smiled at Thurman as he turned to leave. "Thank you so much for coming. I shall see you soon."

Kingston turned to Thurman as they walked back to the Harmonics lab. "Pretty neat stuff, eh Professor?"

"Oh, yes indeed, Mr. Kingston. Quite fascinating." They continued down the hall. "I assume that this new project will be occupying a large portion of your focus once they're up on their feet?"

"Yes, but as you saw, they are still a ways off from a full production cycle. Don't worry, Professor, we're still very interested in your work even with the new kid on the street." Kingston smiled as they reached Thurman's lab.

"Of course, Mr. Kingston. And thank you so much for asking me along. That was a real treat." He shook Kingston's hand as he entered his lab.

A little taken aback by Thurman's dismissal, Kingston watched the door close on the lab before continuing down the hall.

"We are changing out the system security backup nets later this month. The redundancy servers will be in use for twelve to fourteen hours while the calibration sequences compile. No labs should be affected, but I wanted people aware in case something comes up."

Ms. Green stood at the side of the boardroom table, finishing her weekly briefing with the old man and Kingston.

"Very good, Ms. Green. If there is nothing else, that will be all for today," Kingston nodded as the elevator doors opened. Dr. Rai entered the boardroom, and Green walked right past her, never acknowledging her presence. Dr. Rai took a seat a few chairs down from the end of the table as the elevator doors shut.

"Well, I have certainly made an impression on a few of MESA's employees, haven't I?" commented Dr. Rai.

"You don't exactly have to be a psychic to realize that Ms. Green is less than happy that you are now in our employ," replied Kingston sarcastically. "Besides, most of the psychics I have met were more intuition and less psychic."

Dr. Rai smiled at him playfully. "Well then, I suppose that using my woman's *intuition*, I could tell you that the reason Ms. Green does not like me here has little to do with where I come from, and much more to do with the fact that I have a larger bra size. Of course, she also is not too keen on you overseeing my lab, but I am sure you already knew of her *crush* on you, Kingston." Dr. Rai smiled sweetly as Kingston took the smallest of pauses before looking up from his interface.

"Yes, well, as you said. Intuition." Kingston glanced back down at the interface before looking back at Dr. Rai. "So, Doctor. Would you be so kind as to enlighten us? What did you think of our resident Professor?"

Dr. Rai rolled her eyes as if she found Kingston's lack of belief comical. "He is a sweet man. So gentle and kind. Very engaging once you get him talking. He reminds me of a favorite uncle from home. Based on our short time together earlier, he is very bright and—"

"Yes, Dr. Rai. I am well aware of the kind of man Thurman is. He has been working here for quite some time now. However, the reason you are in his wing is so you can tell us what we can't see."

"Right to business then," Dr. Rai smirked. "Well, at first I felt how incredibly intelligent the man is. I felt a deep sense of wonder and creativity. His mind seems capable of processing large amounts of complex data with ease. Yet at the same time, when I processed his output, the majority of his reflection was beta waves. He was very calm and relaxed. His mind at times felt very...well, simple."

The old man raised an eyebrow. "Simple-minded is probably the last descriptor I would use for Dr. Thurman."

"Yes, that came out wrong, didn't it?" Dr. Rai bit her thumbnail in thought. "Not simple-minded, but rather constantly occupied with thought. While we were touring my lab, there were only small flares of alpha waves. He took in everything I explained to him in a very thoughtful manner. I sensed very little engaged wave activity."

Both the old man and Kingston sat staring at Dr. Rai. She smiled again. "To put it another way, if someone is trying to deceive you, their brain will be constantly engaged in analysis and creative processes as they craft their lies. Those that have no deception in mind are more passive in their patterns. They have moments of active thought but take things in more easily. Basically, what I am telling you is that I don't believe he was hiding anything from me. Like I said, his mind was constantly occupied with his thoughts, but he wasn't trying to create things at those moments."

The old man sat tapping his fingers on the table for a few moments. Unlike most of the people who sat in the boardroom, Dr. Rai seemed perfectly at ease.

"Very well. Dr. Rai," said the old man. "Please keep us informed if that changes as your interactions with Thurman proceed. Now, while you are here, how about an update on your lab's preliminary progress."

————

Once again, Thurman found himself sitting at his desk, staring at his notebook. He was very calm despite his inner turmoil, and his breathing was slow and consistent. He was sure MESA would be able to hear anything he said aloud, but he believed, or rather, seriously hoped, that what he spoke in his mind was still safe. He had been at this for almost thirty minutes now. The numbers were getting very large, but he continued to recite them.

One million, three hundred forty-six thousand, two hundred sixty-nine and eight hundred thirty-two thousand forty, is two million, one hundred seventy-eight thousand, three hundred nine.

Two million, one hundred seventy-eight thousand, three hundred nine, and one million, three hundred forty-six thousand, two hundred sixty-nine is three million, five hundred twenty-four thousand, five hundred seventy-eight.

Three million, five hundred twenty-four thousand, five hundred seventy-eight and...

CHAPTER 8
ESCAPE

Time: Late afternoon
Scene: Jadian airship, just off the west coast of the UWC

"Gōng Zhǔ, why do you look so sad?" Chen and Misaka sat on either side of Sam, Chen wearing her traditional Chinese qipao and Misaka her Japanese kimono. Sam sat in short shorts and a flimsy tank top. She wasn't trying to be immodest; it was just so hot! Where the blazes were they, and what happened to the air conditioning?

"Chen, please go tell the idiot in charge that if he is going to leave me here, then he should at least keep me comfortable," said Sam, frantically fanning herself. "What's happening to the temperature control? I think I might actually be cooking alive."

Misaka attempted an awkward sort of bow while sitting. Chen grimaced. "I apologize for your discomfort, Gōng Zhǔ, but we are nearing the western coast of the Collective, and the ship's cold fusion reactors will be spotted if we rise above fifteen percent output. It takes thirteen and a half percent just to power the engines and navigation systems. Most of the ship's other functions will spike the power output, temperature control especially. Please endure, Gōng Zhǔ. We will be landing soon."

Sam had resumed her self-fanning and was only half-listening. It took a second for the words to sink in.

"Wait a second." She opened her eyes and put down her fan. "Did you just say that we're landing?"

A voice sounded from behind the girls. "The ship can't get past the border patrol satellites."

The three girls jumped, startled by the sudden appearance of Adam, who stood rigidly just inside Sam's room. His presence made Chen and Misaka go into grovel mode, all while trying to properly cover up Sam. Sam let them, though she did not feel the least bit embarrassed. Maybe she was turning over a new leaf.

"Da Xiao," said Sam patronizingly, bowing from her sitting position less than gracefully. "How kind of you to join us."

She glared as Adam sighed. "Are we going to go through this every time we talk, Samantha?"

"Gōng Zhǔ, please," whispered Misaka, "might you be just a little more respectful—"

"Kidnappers don't get my respect," declared Sam, cutting

off Misaka, "especially ones who refuse to explain themselves."

"We have discussed this, Sam. I—"

"You can call me Samantha. Only my friends call me Sam."

Adam bowed. "Ms. Montgomery. I assure you the situation you have envisioned is not the case. I am simply not cleared to explain the details to you."

"You aren't cleared to tell me about it. And I'm just supposed to accept that explanation? You've no justification for bringing me here. I know nothing about you or why I would need to go with you. You might be anybody, taking me anywhere. You could be a slaver from the Burning Plains planning to sell me for a bottle of eighteenth-century whiskey. Why whiskey? I have no idea. But you probably have a perfectly good explanation for why you'd sell me for whiskey. But I don't know and have no way of finding out. So it just leaves me to wonder."

Sam was speaking in anger, rambling on about whatever came to her, but in truth, the thought had crossed her mind in the time spent alone in her quarters. Rob, the slaver who tried to capture Cammie and her back at MegaLots, was a Jadian. He used the light shiv and boasted obvious competency with it from the way he swung it from side to side. The weeks on the ship and her infrequent trips around the craft gave her the opportunity to witness similar displays from the soldiers on board. Sam had no doubt: Rob, at some point in the past, had been a Jadian soldier, and since making that connection, the fact that she and Cammie had come so close to living as slave girls festered within her. Perhaps if she came out of this latest predicament unscathed, she would try and figure out what happened that night.

She covertly studied Adam. Her heart still fluttered slightly at the sight of him. This reaction made her angry, but his effect on her was wearing off with each subsequent visit, as the reality of her situation really set in.

Her situation was not an encouraging one. She was in a Jadian aircraft with a Jadian military leader who had posed as a classmate and supposedly came specifically to a nondescript Academy City in search of her. Now she was being treated as something between royalty and a prisoner of war while they transported her to gods knew where. Besides simply not making sense, it was scary. She was more scared than she wanted to admit.

"Chen. Misaka. Please. Leave us." It was a command. He commanded them. Chen and Misaka did as they were told without objection.

"Samantha," said Adam, his voice warm and inviting. "You trusted me once. I know this has all come as a shock, but please understand. You belong with us."

"I belong with my family and my friends, in my country," she replied. "You want me to trust blindly? Who does that? You've given me no reason to trust you. Trust is earned, not given. If you want my trust, you need to show me that you're trustworthy. And you don't have much working for you. I know nothing about you except you've got some connection to the Jadian Horde, and like I said, you could be a slaver, mind you a really well-funded slaver, but a slaver nonetheless."

Unexpectedly, Adam came straight over to her and took her hand. She did not have time to protest, but his closeness made her very aware of how little clothing she had on. He took a knee. "I assure you, Samantha. I am no slaver, and when I tell you that it is with good reason that I do not explain my actions, I mean it. But I understand your hesitancy. The only thing I can offer you to alleviate your fear is my oath. The strongest one I can make. I, Michael Hunang Sun, swear on the Jadian Sun that I mean you no harm and all your questions will be answered in due time. And as sure as the glorious sunrise over the Emerald House, the burning in your heart will subside, and you will be made whole."

Silence followed his declaration. Adam released her hand, though the heat of it lingered mockingly. He then stood, bowed, and exited, but not before saying:

"We disembark within the hour. Have Misaka and Chen help you prepare, and try to be in good spirits. It's a long way to the Seven Cities."

"At one point," said Chen, her voice low and respectful, "this land was a territorial province or a 'state' in the old United States of America. It was called California."

Sam walked arm-in-arm with Chen and Misaka while Jadian soldiers used their utility belts to remain hidden. Chen was keeping up a low, almost unending chatter about the landscape, people, climate, and history. Apparently, she had majored in Californian history in her advanced education.

"What happened here?" asked Sam, trying to take in everything from the cinder block shacks to the deformed beggars on the street.

"We are in the outskirts of Angels. This place was once one of America's largest cities. It was huge in both sprawl and population. It was one of the first places destroyed in the Great War."

That much was obvious. The war was years ago, but the place was still half a breath away from being a straight-up wasteland. Sam didn't like it here. It was a grim reminder of their bloody history that wasn't quite far enough in the past.

"Chen," Sam asked as she dodged locals, "where are we going, and why are we walking there?"

Chen gripped Sam all the more tightly. "There is an international water port here. It's one of the only ways that undesirables like us can get in and out of the UWC. The Empire has a similar or perhaps greater weakness to infiltration by boat travel."

Sam did not like the sound of that. "We're taking a boat

all the way to the Jadian Empire? Isn't that, like, a really long time on a boat?"

"It's just until we get beyond the UWC border patrol and their satellite detection. Once we do, the Empire will do the rest."

Misaka nodded her head. "Just follow our lead, Gōng Zhǔ, and we will guide you."

Sam sighed. That was what she was afraid of.

Sam, Misaka, and Chen spent hours navigating the streets, if they could even be called streets, of Angels. The poverty, desperation, and pure hopelessness got worse as the day went on. It was more than relief that assaulted Sam when they finally arrived at the waterport; it was downright salvation. The port sat properly on the water in an amalgamation of salvaged cement, metal, and wood. In any other situation, the strange building would have been humorous, but not now. Sam just wanted to get inside of it. The three girls entered the building, pushing alongside hundreds of other travelers. Sam looked over her shoulder at the slums and people left behind. Her eyes moistened as she looked away.

"It's different when the suffering is right in front of you, is it not, Gōng Zhǔ?"

The pain in Misaka's voice was palpable. It caught Sam off-guard. "What do you mean, Misaka?"

"The aftereffects of the war." Misaka continued, "Did you know the Great War was not the first time mass destruction weapons were used? The United States dropped two atomic bombs on my mother country in the twentieth century during the last great war. Two Japanese cities, Nagasaki and Hiroshima, suffered the wrath of the United States on August 6, 1945, and again on August ninth. It was the only time in a hundred-year period that nuclear weapons were used. They changed the landscape—the field of war—forever."

Sam's voice went dry. She wasn't sure what to say to this. It was true that Academy Cities talked about the arsenals of the UWC and the Jade Empire, but it was only in the theoretical, the abstract, a concept that the students of Academy City 676 understood.

Misaka smoothed her hair. "If we don't learn our lesson, Gōng Zhǔ, it might one day be too late."

"Misaka," interrupted Chen, "enough of your doom and gloom. You're going to upset the—"

Sam interrupted. "Will you two stop calling me Gōng Zhǔ! I've got a name: Sam or Samantha. That's an order."

Sam surprised herself. She did not know where that last part came from. The two girls exchanged slightly startled expressions but smiled.

"As you wish, Samantha," said Chen. Misaka merely bowed.

"Good. Now what's the deal here? What are we doing?"

"This is where we board the ship that will take us to the Atlantic Islands. We will be retrieved by another Mogui team when we land."

Sam perked up. "We're going to Atlantis?"

Chen and Misaka nodded their heads.

Atlantis was an artificially created port in the near-middle of the Pacific Ocean. The founder of the island was supposedly one of the most brilliant engineers to have ever lived. Now self-sustaining, Atlantis boasted the wealthiest population per capita in the world.

Able to stay outside the military influence of both the Jade Empire and UWC, Atlantis was also a safe haven for the politically active from both the Empire and UWC. It was strictly neutral in that cold war; it did not allow any outside military action within its air and water space. Any violation of this rule was met with swift and decisive action from the island's Parliament, which had come close to starting World War Four on more than one occasion. It was the only place to make a transition to a Jadian vessel without the UWC knowing. It was a perfect plan. Not only that, but Sam really wanted to visit there. Their beaches were supposed to be insane.

"With its own standing military, highly evolved political structure, a booming population, and technology to rival the Seven Cities, Atlantis stands on its own and is a ruby in the blue of the Pacific Ocean." Adam appeared behind them.

"I hate it when you do that," snapped Sam, turning to face Adam. "Just popping out of nowhere like that. Where have you been?"

"Securing our passage." Adam handed Sam, Misaka, and Chen their tickets. "This is a Josephite establishment, so—"

"Men and women will be separated. I know. I was in world cultures, too," interrupted Sam.

Adam smiled. "Try to stay out of trouble, Samantha, and enjoy the trip. Before the end of next week, you'll make your debut in the Seven Cities of the Jade Empire."

Sam's breath caught in her throat. Next week....

"I will see you in two days." He turned and walked away without another word.

———

Josephites weren't as bad as everyone made them out to be. Sure, they had their old-school traditions and outdated viewpoints, but regardless of who you were, where you came from, or what you believed, they treated you with love and respect, and that was not something very prevalent in modern society.

It had been three days since Adam, Sam, and the other Jadians boarded the boat, and ocean travel was surprisingly...

"Boring." Sam nudged a groggy Chen. "I wish something would happen. I think I might lose it."

"What were you expecting, Gōng Zhǔ? Fireworkers?"

Sam smiled affectionately. "It's fireworks, Chen. Not fireworkers."

"Umm," grunted Chen. Silence settled, and her breathing grew heavy. When she did not answer, Sam knew Chen was asleep. Sam got up from her bed. Chen and Misaka occupied one of the two queen-size mattresses in the room, while Sam took the other near the window. She was tired but found it difficult to sleep in the monstrous moving hunk of metal. She had to get up; she had to get out.

Sam dressed and moved gingerly to the door. She opened it quietly and slipped out, knowing if Chen and Misaka woke up, she would be hard-pressed to stop them from accompanying her. She accomplished her exit with little more than a click of the door. The hallway of the ship's female quarters was dimly lit and way too quiet, to be expected with the lateness of the hour. Sam stepped quickly out of the hallway to the outer corridors of the ship and to the upper balconies where the group rooms were located. Chen and Misaka did not like it when Sam ventured into this area of the ship—it was for the commoners; it was inappropriate for the Gōng Zhǔ to venture there—but with all the people, it was one of the few places she felt comfortable. The calm atmosphere of the group rooms enabled her to think, and she really needed to think right now.

Sam smiled as she entered a room. Even at this hour, it was alive with activity. Josephite women taught various crafts from water purification to organic solar cell construction, all sprinkled with bits of Josephite doctrine. Sam wandered a bit and stopped periodically to listen and observe as one topic or another caught her interest until the sound of her own name startled her.

"Samantha!" called the shrill voice, "You get back here this instant!"

Sam put her head down and was just about to shuffle away, absolutely sure that Chen or Misaka was about to make a scene. They did not. Neither Chen nor Misaka appeared to scold her and escort her back to her room. Instead, a child darted between her legs to hide, playfully using her legs for cover.

"Oh my dear, I'm so sorry," said a haggard-looking woman who walked up to Sam, forcing a smile. "Little Samantha there is a bit overexcited—too much sugar, I'm afraid."

Sam glanced downward to stare directly into the eyes of the child peeking her head through her legs. A beautiful little girl, with big blue eyes and artfully curled hair, little Samantha smiled brightly and squeezed Sam's legs with her small arms.

Sam disentangled little Samantha from her legs and handed the child back to the woman. She asked the question before she was fully aware of her own curiosity.

"Is she yours?" asked Sam, pulling softly on one of little Samantha's curls.

"Granddaughter," answered the woman, "the youngest in a long line of little girls."

Sam was surprised at this. The woman did not look to be very old. She grinned as if she were reading Sam's mind.

"Chinese restorative techniques work wonders, my dear."

Sam's confusion only heightened; restorative techniques were expensive. And when was the last time Sam heard someone mention the Empire's mother heritage?

"Where are you heading, my dear?" the woman asked absentmindedly.

Sam hesitated, then answered simply, "The Seven Cities."

It was the young-looking grandmother's turn to appear surprised. "The Seven Cities? You don't say. Have you ever been?"

Sam shook her head.

She smiled. "You are in for a treat, my dear. The Seven Cities is one of the eight wonders of the world, especially the three inner rings. Amazing. Absolutely amazing."

Sam did not have an answer for this.

The woman was unfazed. "But why the Seven Cities? If you don't mind me asking, what brings you to the Capital of the Jade Empire?"

Sam thought about her predicament. The question caught her off-guard. *What indeed?*

"Nana, I'm hungry." Little Sam pulled at the hem of her grandmother's shirt.

"Hush, Nana is talking."

Nana looked at little Sam with utmost affection, a brightness and sparkle in her expression. The corners of Sam's eyes watered.

"My dear child," said Nana, "what is wrong?"

Sam wiped at her eyes. "No—I'm sorry—you just reminded me of my mother."

"You're not with your mother, my dear girl?"

Sam shook her head. She was not traveling with her mother. She had not seen her mother in months, and there was no foreseeable time when that would be remedied. Involuntarily, Sam lost control; she started sobbing.

"My goodness, dear, I am sorry—"

"Nana," said Sam, wiping at her tears. "I need your help."

———

"I think I understand now." Nana and Sam sat at a small table in Nana's room, little Samantha sleeping quietly on one of the two beds in the room. Sam had just finished telling Nana her story. She relayed the whole of the events that landed her on a Josephite ship heading to the Atlantic Islands. It was strange, Sam sitting in this room with a woman she had just met, spilling her life story like word vomit. It was stupid and possibly dangerous, but she was compelled, unable to stop speaking until her story had run its course. A half-hour passed before Sam finished her narrative. Nana looked like she had been punched in the gut.

Sam didn't even know Nana's true name, but Sam was confiding in her like Nana was *her* grandmother and not little Sam's.

"What do you think, Nana?" prodded Sam. "Can you help me get out of here?"

Nana ran a hand through her dark hair as she contemplated the question. She looked almost disappointed as she answered.

"Yes." Nana suddenly stood up. "I think I can, but—"

"But...," Sam prompted her.

Nana pressed her lips contemplatively, like she wanted to say something important but was at a loss as to how to express herself. "Are you not the least bit curious, my child?"

Sam blinked. Did she hear that wrong? "I'm afraid I don't understand, Nana."

Nana's contemplative expression deepened, becoming all the more serious. "Aren't you curious as to why you're really here?"

Nana continued before Sam could answer. "Think about it, my child. Obviously, these soldiers have no desire to hurt you. Or they would have done so by now. Actually, it's the exact opposite. They've treated you with something close to reverence. Do you not wonder why?"

Sam blinked again, unsure as to how to answer. "Of course I am curious—it's just—"

"You are scared, my child." Nana touched her nose knowingly. "I understand, but it is always—"

"Nana, I don't mean to be rude, but it sounds like you're agreeing with the Empire, like you're just fine with them kidnapping me."

Nana sighed. The conversation wasn't going the way she wanted. "I'm sorry if you feel that way, Samantha. It is not my intent. I simply cannot help but wonder."

Sam was about to answer but stopped. Honestly, it was not like the question had never crossed her mind, but with so much happening.... Sam realized she hadn't really considered, really mulled over the actual reason for her kidnapping, even with the information she gained in her conversations with Chen, Misaka, and Adam. Strange. Sam involuntarily spoke aloud the title used by most of the Jadians when referring to her.

"Gōng Zhǔ."

Nana's eyes grew wide, and her voice sounded panicked as she repeated the name. "Gōng Zhǔ? Are you sure, my child?"

Sam found herself nodding without meaning to.

"We must leave immediately. You won't have time to return to your room. Do you have all that you need?"

Sam's head dipped down once. "There isn't anything back in my room that I can't live without."

Nana returned the nod. "Then we leave in a few moments."

Nana picked up a cell phone and started speaking almost immediately. She spoke Mandarin.

"OK, let's go. I will take you to the survival pods."

"Survival pods?" asked Sam. "Why not just go to the Josephite security force?"

Nana patiently explained. "My dear child, these Jadians have to believe that you are far away. Because if they surmise, even falsely, that anyone on the ship is hiding you... we might as well slaughter the ship's passengers and crew right now and save them the additional horror."

Sam's face went pale. "But why, Nana? Why react in such a manner?"

Nana smiled. "Child. My dear, dear child, do you have an inkling what *Gōng Zhǔ* means in your tongue?"

Sam had not the foggiest, and it was evident on her face.

Nana bowed her head like she was going to cry. "I am sorry, Gōng Zhǔ. But I cannot tell you. For now, it's better you do not know."

Nana stood and ushered Sam out the door. Sam stole a glance back at little Sam sleeping innocently on the bed.

———

"That was easier than I thought," whispered Sam as she and Nana took refuge in a room just off the hallway.

"Yes," answered Nana, looking up and down the hallway. "It is just a bit farther to the emergency room. You should be able to make it from there."

Sam looked around. Something was off. They had been sneaking around for twenty minutes already, and they only seemed to be going up. They dodged groups of guards, mostly the easily recognizable, white-robed Josephite sentinels, but there were also pockets of patrolling Jadian Mogui in normal non-military clothing. Still, something about the whole situation didn't seem right.

"Are you ready, Gōng Zhǔ?" Nana had taken to using the term the moment Sam told her. "This is the final corridor before the pods."

Sam and Nana continued to navigate the Josephites' huge ship. It was totally disorienting. Coming from the bottom three floors to the seventeenth floor, they were making their way further and further into the belly. The patrols increased in frequency, and Sam and Nana had to hide more often. Nana spoke less and less.

"We are almost there, child. Be patient." Nana moved down the hall.

Sam followed, but her mind raced. It really did not make sense for the escape pods to be located here. This was where all the rich people stayed on the ship; did the affluent really have a private passage to the survival pods? The second she asked herself the question, things clicked for Sam. It actually made plenty of sense.

This is where *all* the rich people are.

Allowing them easy access to the escape pods, should calamity ensue, seemed quite logical. They were the big spenders. Ocean travel by speed liner had become popular since the war, as the effects on air travel left over from the major naval powers' use of nuclear and disassembled warheads still made it difficult for commercial planes to navigate the Pacific Ocean. Speed liners were safer, and of course, rich people who needed to travel would pay more for an extra layer of protection. The more she thought about it, the more sense it made—even if it left a sour taste in Samantha's mouth.

Sam reconsidered her conclusion. No. There was no way the pods were up here. To launch them into the ocean would be almost impossible from this height, given the other moving portions of the ship. It was much more likely that the escape pods were on the bottom floor. They had to be.

Sam paused at her logic and conclusion. Where did that train of thought come from?

Sam looked back the way they came. Something was just not right here.

"Nana? Are you sure that this—"

Sam turned completely around. Nana was nowhere to be seen. She chanced another call, this one a little bit louder.

Still nothing. Sam peered down the length of the hall. At the end of the hall, three or five meters away, a door was slightly ajar, but closing.

It was then that Sam heard the scream. She stopped thinking. "Nana! What happened to you?"

She ran and kicked in the door, not thinking about what might lay beyond it.

CHAPTER 9

PLASTIC SURGERY

Time: Dusk
Scene: Upscale Jadian residential complex

A nondescript man walks casually through a neighborhood just after dusk. The dog he has with him seems eager to be out, sniffing plants and trees along the way. The man appears relaxed as he patiently waits for the dog to explore the new scents she encounters. He glances around at the stately homes that line the block of the neighborhood located a few kilometers from the city. Lights inside various homes illuminate the domestic activities occurring within. The man seems to give no particular house any more interest than another as he continues down the block. He has made this trip several times over the past few weeks. Each time, the path he has taken has been slightly different, but generally along the same block of homes. If someone could see into his mind, they would find that this man is particularly interested in the third house from the end of the block. Without so much as a telling stare, he has reconned this house and the comings and goings of its occupants. This is the last time he will be walking this dog down this block past this house. His mental notes complete, he and the dog round the corner and finish their walk out of the neighborhood.

———

Eva Vilaró groaned as she slowly lifted her head. Everything felt fuzzy and disjointed. Her body ached like she had the flu, and she had a bitter taste in her mouth. Her throat was dry and scratchy, and for some reason, her brain could not tell her eyes to open, as if the signals it was sending out were all muddled. Her neck was incredibly stiff, and the muscles pulled taut as she continued to move her head around. Eventually, her brain and eyes sorted out their issues, and a hazy darkness filled her field of vision. Groggily, she looked around, blinking, trying to get her eyes to focus on any one of the blurry objects she could make out. Slowly, her vision sharpened bit by bit as the familiar surroundings of her home came into view.

She told her fingers to rub her throbbing temples, but it seemed they were having issues with her brain as well. She looked down at them to give them the encouragement to soothe her aching head—and it was then that she saw the restraints. At first, they didn't register. Something that out of place should have immediately set her on alert, but her brain seemed to work very slowly as she processed what she was looking at. As clarity seeped back into her consciousness, a tumbler in her brain clicked over, and she actually *understood* what she was looking at.

Restraints? Why was she in restraints? She looked around again and saw the furniture and paintings of her study. Her desktop interface was asleep, but she could see the soft blinking of the power indicator. She tried to adjust her legs and found that they too were in restraints. Somewhere deep in the limbic part of her brain, signals were sent to her adrenaline glands to pour on the juice, because something was not right. The increase of hormones seemed to cut through her mental fog. Eva turned her head to look around the room. Her mind was able to place her in the center of her study, restrained to a chair facing her desk. Other than that, there was little information it could feed her, as everything else seemed normal.

A tablet sitting in a dock to her left woke up as the screen flared to life. Its optical camera blinked as she saw her image appear on the tablet's face. Her vital signs soon appeared in the upper left-hand corner of the screen: heart rate, skin temperature, respiration rate, and O_2 saturation. While the heart rate seemed to tick up every few seconds, all the other numbers were in green. Her image faded and was replaced by a log window. A script started running, connecting the tablet to a one-time-use secure server on a Darkcloud outside of the DragonNet. Eva shifted uncomfortably as the script continued to run sweeps and checks against passive and active monitoring systems within her home network and the connection she had to DragonNet. At each challenge, the script loaded additional commands that circumvented the security protocols. Eva recognized the level of skill required to program those commands, let alone build an app that could apply them with a frighteningly intuitive efficiency. Eva called out to her husband, Carlos. She yelled his name again and was about to yell louder when the script caught her attention.

Once the script confirmed that all security protocols had been sidestepped, the last command launched a vid that was stored on the cloud server. Eva recognized the outside of her home at once. This faded as a picture of her husband on his last fishing trip came to the forefront, followed closely by pics of her two kids at their last birthday parties. If the heart rate figure was still visible, it would have shown a significant uptick at the sight of those images.

These stills faded as a vid of her husband and her two children boarding a private transport, followed closely by a rough-looking Gangan, filled the screen. The transport accelerated into the distance as the vid faded. Next was a view from the security monitor in her kitchen. From the ceiling corner angle, she could see the entire kitchen. At least she thought it was her kitchen. This room had the same layout, except it was covered in what looked like plastic drop cloths. A man in black entered the frame with a small case, which he set down and opened at the far end of the kitchen table. He exited the field of vision and returned, pushing a leather chair into the kitchen. Eva's spine went cold as she saw a limp version of herself being wheeled into her kitchen. The man in black gently, and without any appearance of effort, picked her out of the chair and placed her on the table. Eva felt her stomach drop as a hard fear set in.

The camera view changed, and all Eva could see was a green square of fabric draped over a body. In the center of the square was an open partition in which she could see exposed skin. The man in black had on synthetic surgical gloves and was busy arranging a host of surgical instruments. Choosing a scalpel, the man made a small incision in the exposed skin. Eva looked away at the sight of blood. She felt like she was going to be sick.

When she finally made herself look back at the vid, the man in black held a small square cube-shaped device in a pair of forceps. He looked at the device intently and then, using a skin retractor, inserted the device into the incision. Again, Eva could not stand watching. She closed her eyes tightly for the next few seconds. Her heart was racing now. She had no idea what was going on, but she had to get out of these restraints. She had to find her children and her husband and make sure they were okay. She started to pull at the restraints on her arms and legs, but they wouldn't budge. She caught the screen in her vision just as the vid faded to black. The blank screen soon filled with the live image it started with. Eva could see herself sitting in the chair with the restraints. Again, her vitals popped onto the screen. As she sat staring at her racing heartbeat, the camera started to zoom in. First, her legs were out of view, then her head and waist. The camera settled on a spot just inside the neckline of her blouse. A command script popped onto the screen and ran a few lines. The last line reported a successful activation, and then the command window faded out. Right behind it, Eva saw a soft blinking light at the edge of her neckline. She stared at the tablet, at the soft light, trying to figure out—suddenly, an all-encompassing fear gripped her.

The screen split as a new vid started to play to the side of the live image. An extreme close-up of what looked like the small device implanted in the surgery filled the partition. A small LED started to blink as the camera zoomed out, widening the field of vision to eventually show the device hundreds of meters away. The seconds ticked by as nothing happened. Then, without warning, a huge fireball erupted where the small cube was. Eva jumped in her restraints. Once the fireball had dissipated, the camera panned to the left to show the man in black holding a small remote. While he did not speak, the meaning to Eva was very clear.

The live image once again filled the entire screen as Eva watched the soft blinking light emanating from her chest. She started to look down, to see with her own eyes what the camera was showing her. The tears that now filled her eyes made everything blurry. As she blinked them away, her heart pounded at the sight of the soft blinking light. There was no scar, only a faint discoloration right above the small light. The tears flowed freely now. She looked back at the tablet in time to see the camera zoom back out and the screen go black. Words started to appear on the screen. Eva blinked away the tears again and tried to stem their flow as she read the message. The instructions listed what she was to do and the events that would take place over the next sixteen hours. It never mentioned what would happen if Eva were to fail or if she decided to alert anyone—that part of the message had already been clearly communicated to her.

The instructions told her to repeat back what she had been told to do. She looked around, confused, and then saw a waveform on-screen; it was picking up the ambient sounds in the room. She started to speak, and her voice cracked. She saw the peaks and valleys of the waveform move as she repeated back the instructions. Once she finished, the waveform disappeared, only to be replaced by more text. It assured her that as long as she did exactly as she was asked, everything would be fine. It told her that she was going to sleep now and that when she woke up, she was to carry out her instructions.

Eva laughed aloud. There was no way she was going to sleep. She was way too keyed up to even think about sleep. The tablet wished her good night and then faded to black.

Eva looked around the study and then back at the restraints. She was at a complete loss as to what she should do. Her mind was racing. Thoughts of her children, her husband, the pain in her chest and arms, the heaviness of her legs. Wait, when did her legs start to feel heavy? Yet, as she noticed the sensation, it seemed to spread. Next, her arms felt like they were surrounded by wet concrete. Her neck muscles seemed to grow weak, and her head felt like it weighed several kilos. As her whole body felt heavier and heavier, Eva slowly closed her eyes. In just under a minute, she was fast asleep.

———

Eva sat staring at her interface. She had been staring at it for the majority of the last twenty minutes. The entire morning was a complete blur. It started with her waking up in bed, no restraints, with a note to get up, shower, and get dressed for work. Thankfully, whoever was torturing her was smart enough to replace her normal low-cut blouse with a more conservative top. Having a blinking chest would certainly attract unwanted attention. She couldn't eat, and her stomach felt acidic as she made her way on the train to the datapost she managed.

Her heart was pounding as she passed through the security line, but none of the detectors flagged her as she passed through them. The rest of the morning was uneventful. Yet Eva could not focus on her work. In her head, she counted down the minutes, reviewing the instructions she had read the night before. The task was simple enough—if she set aside the possibility of being caught, found guilty of treason, and executed.

A small window popped onto her desktop interface. It said, "Greetings from the doctor."

Eva felt a wave of heat wash over her. It was time.

Just as she was instructed, she logged in with her admin authority to the maintenance servers. As soon as she was through the initial protocols, the small window executed a script. A remote session started and proceeded to open a back door into the maintenance subroutines log. Eva nervously looked around for anyone who could be watching. Periodically, the window would launch supplemental scripts that would halt all activity on the interface. Eva noticed that these times coincided with the random security sweeps she knew occurred on the network. Other times, the window would launch a command line to block the logging of any activity and replace it with bogus timestamps of events. Again, Eva was impressed at the skill of the programmer who orchestrated this whole hack—aside from the whole twisted psychopathic murderous intent bit.

At times, the window asked Eva to contribute certain credentials to the hack. Yet each time it did so, it blanketed her activity with false time trails and random events. It took a few minutes to see what the script was hunting, and with each level, Eva grew more and more confused. Eventually, the script located a transport ship req log. Specifically, the script dug down into the provisions and fuel requests and also seemed to settle on a request to replace the ship's GPS unit. The script continued to search for the logs associated with the GPS req but only found ones pertaining to the removal of the unit. It appeared that the ship sailed prior to the installation of the replacement GPS unit. The script poked around in a few more logs that didn't make any sense to Eva. In fact, none of this made any sense. The script basically ignored the databases she thought would contain valuable information. The defense grid and fly routes were located just a few servers over. Yet the script made no attempt to go anywhere near them.

The script backed out of the req logs and added some command lines to the cache sweep to clear out all of the recent activity and to purge it from the system, but masking it as a test of the cache purge.

Eva let out a small sigh of relief. It was finished, and nobody—the script started up again. Eva's heart sank. The req servers were just a prelim to try out the security protocols. She was sure the script would start to hack the defense grid servers.

But to her surprise, the script backed out of the high-security network and transferred itself over to a low-level administration database. Eva's curiosity was piqued as she wondered what could possibly be in there to warrant hacking into it.

Fear struck her again as the script pulled up the site's

personnel records. It flew to the bottom of the list and high-
lighted her name. Her resource record opened up as the script
flew past the security protocols. Eva froze as she watched the
script make one final adjustment to the network. The script
accessed her salary portfolio and added a seventeen percent
meritorious bonus to her compensation plan. It then did as
before, covering its tracks as it backed out of the server and
closed off all of the open connection ports. Soon, just the
black window remained at the top of Eva's interface. A name
and an address popped into the window. It remained there as
Eva saw the remote connection terminate.

Eva felt torn. She was almost positive that not even the
best investigators could recompile the script's activities. She
was slightly less confident that her workstation could not be
traced and tied to whatever the script was after. At the
bottom of her confidence list was her ability to not be impli-
cated, at the very least as an accomplice. That bonus would
look pretty suspicious if she were to report any of this. Eva
felt a small twinge of pain in her chest. Her hand jumped to
the spot where the small device was buried beneath her skin
as her heart rate escalated.

Eva glanced at the name and address on the small
window. She looked up the information on the public net and
was surprised to find a business listing for a plastic surgeon.
Transferring the information to her personal tablet, Eva
contacted her secretary and told the man she was not feeling
well and was taking the rest of the day off.

———

Eva felt incredibly anxious as she lay on the cold patient bed. Her husband had left her a message thanking her for the surprise gift of a day with the kids at a local amusement park. He reported that the VIP treatment with the private transport and guide was absolutely magical. He let her know that the three of them would be back later that night and not to worry about them. Nothing was making any sense.

The plastic surgeon finished his preparations as his assistant fitted the anti-microbial plastic shield around the soft blinking area of Eva's chest. The doctor turned to her and asked if she was ready. Eva nodded hesitantly. She had failed to tell him about the possibility of her being a bomb, but he seemed to be expecting her when she entered his office.

The surgeon took up the laser scalpel and was just about to make contact with her skin when he stopped. Eva's expression darkened at the hesitation. Thoughts of fake doctors harvesting organs raced through her mind. The surgeon brought his head closer to her skin to examine the prepped area. He swung a large magnifier over the area and peered through it at Eva's chest. He set the scalpel back down on the tray and began poking and prodding with a gloved finger at the exposed skin.

The surgeon removed the glove from one of his hands and again felt the area. Then he began scratching at Eva's skin. All of this did nothing to settle Eva's nerves. She was just about to ask what the surgeon was doing when she felt a small tug. She looked down and almost did not believe her eyes. The surgeon's fingernail had lifted a tiny edge of what looked like a sticker from her skin. He grabbed a set of tweezers from the tray and began peeling back the circular sticker. Moments later, he held up a blinking disc that was the exact skin tone of Eva's chest. It even had a small incision line running down the front of it.

Eva stared at it in disbelief. The object was impossibly thin and contained intricate circuitry on the back that all seemed to center on a minuscule blinking LED at the center. This looked nothing like the cube that was on the vid. Rather, this seemed more like something used by the makeup department in a high-end holo-vid. There was absolutely no possible way that this device could explode. There was just too little material to do anything. Eva couldn't believe that it was actually capable of blinking, let alone causing any kind of damage.

Just as Eva peered more closely at the disc, the edges of it started to crumble. Oxidation streaks appeared across the entire disc, and the LED went dark. In a matter of seconds, the doctor's forceps were empty, save a bit of fine dust. Eva flopped back against the headrest, closed her eyes, and wept.

———

A nondescript man walks casually from the ticket counter to the train platform. He glances at the signs and proceeds to the platform for an outbound express destined for Sanzarubi. He settles into his first-class compartment and calls up various documents on his personal tablet. He methodically peruses shipping manifests, provision logs, fuel consumption charts, and transport lanes as the train starts to pull out of the station. The confidential data stream continues to analyze and cross-check each document against a database of information. The man makes a few adjustments to the data-mining algorithm as the train heads off towards the famed province.

CHAPTER 10
THE D-LIST

Time: Late at night
Scene: Governor's palace, Sanzarubi

"Is there anything else I can get for you, sir?" asked the servant as he set the tray down on the nightstand.

Dirk looked up from the bed where he had been brooding most of the night. "No—John, was it?" John? Really?

The clearly Arabic servant smiled. "Does my name bother you, sir?"

Dirk shook his head. "No—well—of course not…it's just— yeah, never mind. That will be all, John. I'll call you if I need you."

Dirk stood up and started to pace back and forth. Under normal circumstances, he would have considered his current situation heavenly. He was in Sanzarubi and occupying the governor's personal quarters, no less. He did not have to hide from the local muscle, and he had all the wine any man could ever hope for. He should be happy. Elated, joyful, brickin' ecstatic!

He was so not happy.

Not happy? He was downright pissed. How had he missed it? Him? Missed something as important...as critical...it just didn't make any sense!

Dirk continued to pace. He was not in his element, and perhaps that was throwing him off. His mind reviewed the facts. The sword, the location, the preventative measures...they had been so elaborate. Yet, it was all wrong. How had he missed it the first time?

Dirk walked over to the sword and picked it up, examining the blade in all its golden glory. It bore the same exact symbols that he and Adams had seen in the DragonNet not so long ago. Dirk touched the blade of the sword. It drew blood. Such a fascinating weapon, so many years ahead of its time, but still just a blade...just a weapon.

Dirk's skin started to tingle.

Could you be something else? wondered Dirk as the hair on his arms stood on end. *Could you play some other part in all this?*

There was simply no way of knowing without more information.

Dirk needed relief. If he were anywhere else in the world, relief would be found at the nearest pub. He especially liked the ones in Nihon...such pretty little girlies always hanging around.... Dirk smiled to himself. But there was no need to visit a pub in Sanzarubi. All he needed to do was go visit the former governor's daughter, Delilah. The eldest daughter of the former governor had a soft spot for Dirk. And she was a beauty. Dumber than a Gangan house pet, but a pretty little thing.

Dirk smiled and walked towards the door, forgetting the sword was still in his hands. He was going to find Delilah and work out some of his frustrations.

———

Dirk stepped down another hallway. This had to be the right one. As the world's premier treasure hunter, he had an acute sense of direction.

Dirk stopped in the middle of the hallway. OK, he was seriously guessing now. He had no idea where Delilah's room was. Shoot, he wasn't sure if Delilah was even still around. The governor had met a gruesome death courtesy of the man in black—the Magician. Dirk needed to remember: The man in black was the Magician.

The Magician had wiped out half the household during his little visit, and from what Dirk remembered from the stories, the Magician had no problem dealing a whole lot of death to just about anyone—including women and kids.

Dirk was going to be really sad if Delilah was dead. She sure was a looker.

"Dirk, what are you doing with Gilgamesh's sword?"

"By Tarturs! Rona!" Dirk exclaimed. "You scared the decency out of me."

Rona rolled her eyes, and her tone was sharp. "You'd need decency first, *Dirk*."

She sounded angry. Dirk's face remained passive. He hoped she didn't realize what he was doing in *this* particular hall.

"You didn't answer me, Dirk. What are you doing here, and with the sword no less?"

Dirk had a funny feeling he was already busted. "No reason. I was just following up on a hunch and thought that the sword might help."

"You've had that thing since we went back to get it. You're just now having a hunch?"

He attempted a calming smile.

"And the fact that the governor's daughters live on the floor just above has nothing to do with it."

Dirk tried to act surprised. It was tough. Rona's female intuition seemed to operate at godlike levels.

"Rona, oh mighty and wise ruler, it's nothing like that. I was just taking a stroll with a meter-and-a-half-long sword made out of an incredible gold alloy. For self-protection, of course. One can't be too careful. Sanzarubi can be a dangerous place."

Dirk paused. At least he thought it was gold. But after what happened to Riker and the others, he wasn't so sure.

"Yes, Sanzarubi *is* a dangerous place, Dirk. You almost died here."

"Yes—yes, I—"

"Twice. Because of indiscretions with the governor's daughter."

"How could you possibly know—"

"It doesn't matter. Come. Adams wants to brief us."

Johnny boy. Dirk had almost forgotten about him. "And what does Adams want with us?"

Rona glared at him, disgusted. "He wants to know what happened to Riker and the team. He wants to know why the sword blew up."

"You haven't told him?"

Rona shook her head. "I thought it might be better coming from you."

Dirk winced. "You've made preparations."

"Of course."

Dirk shifted uncomfortably and then exhaled deeply. "It's show time, then. Shall we go?"

Rona was already several paces up the hall and continued walking like she couldn't hear him.

———

Dirk and Rona entered the main ballroom. It was very different from the first time he had seen it, just a few days ago. None of the decorating motif from the Magician's visit remained. No dead bodies or blood. The place was clean and divided into cubicles, holo-boards, and conductor's terminals, plus a host of other techie thingamajigs Dirk didn't care to attempt to recognize. There *was* one odd thing that he noticed.

"Rona," said Dirk, louder than he intended, "who is the old guy ordering everyone around?"

Rona shot Dirk a sharp, borderline-murderous look. "Dirk! Keep your voice down."

Dirk raised an eyebrow. "Who might hear me?"

"I would, Mr. Garrett."

The man they had just been discussing, who was more than a little bit burly, materialized out of nowhere in front of them. His sudden appearance surprised Dirk. He started to comment but stopped as he noticed Rona's reaction. She shied away from the man like a child about to be punished. Intrigued, Dirk put out a hand.

"You know my name, sir...." Dirk left it hanging.

The old man smiled. Dirk couldn't help but smile back. The man reminded him of his father, except this guy wasn't noticeably drunk and hitting Dirk. Ahh...got to love childhood memories.

The man took Dirk's hand. "You can call me Washington, Mr. Garrett. I've followed your career with relish. It's a pleasure to meet you."

They shook hands. Washington's grip was not unlike a clamp, a meaty, sweaty clamp. "So you're Washington, huh?

What part do you play in this little revolution, Mr. Washington?"

Grandpa Washington laughed. "To the point. I like that, Dirk. May I call you Dirk?"

He did not wait for an answer.

"So you want to know my part, eh? Basically, I'm in charge here. All the operations are funded by me. It's awfully expensive to run a revolution, Dirk."

Dirk studied Washington's face. He had seen the man before. But where?

"We should sit. Adams is about to contact us. Pay specific attention, Rona. Something is wrong—Adams is never in contact this much."

Washington motioned for Rona and Dirk to follow him, which they did without comment. The older man veered off towards the front of the room while Dirk and Rona lingered. Dirk's mind raced as he watched him walk away with a confident, steady stride.

"Rona." Dirk shifted his body close to Rona, whispering as best he could. "Did Grandpa Washington just say that he was in charge? I thought that Adams was running this little hoedown."

Rona's answer was confused. "What's a hoedown?"

Dirk chuckled. "Never mind that. An explanation is needed."

"Washington started the movement, funds the operations, and manages the people, including recruiting. He's the heart here, Dirk, and the bulk of the Republicans are intensely loyal to him. Adams is much more secretive and selective about whom he lets in his inner circle. Ironically, Adams and Washington have a similar relationship to their founding father counterparts. Adams organizes the larger operations, gathers intel, and spearheads the clandestine activities. Basically, he does all the dirty work, makes the hard choices. They are really two sides to the same giant golden coin—an infinitely large, famously valuable coin. The organization wouldn't work without both."

Two sides of the same giant golden coin...Rona sure was sexy when she was making gold references. Dirk forced himself to snap out of it. He needed to focus. "If Washington is really the one in charge, why isn't he wearing a costume?"

Rona's eyebrow rose. "You lost me there, Dirk."

Dirk rolled his eyes. "Every time I see Adams, he's wearing some ridiculous get-up. If this is Washington's show, why is he gitty-witty with his identity?"

"Gitty-witty?"

Dirk smiled. "I have a certain flair for expression."

Rona snorted. "I'll take your word for it."

Dirk's voice turned serious. "Careless. That's what Washington is doing. He is being careless."

Rona didn't answer.

Dirk categorized this information for later examination, as it wasn't what really piqued his interest. Dirk's skin was lit up like the sun itself, burning with warning. The impression was clear: Rona was holding back. "Rona, what aren't you telling me about him?"

Rona looked from side to side, surprise evident on her face. "I'm not—"

Dirk grabbed her arm, shocking both of them. "Don't give me that hullabaloo; you're hiding something from me, and I want to know why."

At the front of the room, Washington clapped his hands together. "Ladies. Gents. The briefing is about to start. Please be seated."

Rona, looking relieved, motioned towards a seat. Dirk did not let her go. "This isn't done yet, Rona. Not by a long shot."

"It's not what you think."

Dirk's eyes narrowed. That was a strange response.

Rona pulled her arm out of Dirk's grip. "We'd better find seats."

They found seats just as a materialization of Adams appeared. "Washington. What the hell happened to my team?"

"Calm down, Adams—"

"Do not tell me to be calm! I want to know what happened to my guys, and I want to know now."

Washington seemed taken aback by Adams. Oddly, Dirk understood his shock; the few moments he and Adams had spent talking were calm and steady. Adams was controlled and systematically tore down Dirk's defenses in the space of a few breaths. For him to explode like that was out of the ordinary. Dirk might even say extraordinary.

"We've a lead, sir," said a goofy-looking man-child seated several meters in front of Dirk and Rona. The man-child spoke in a nasal voice.

"Wait," interrupted Washington. "This isn't the time, Reid. I understand your anger, but we won't be discussing those things here. Let's get on with the briefing."

Adams didn't seem to like being ordered around. But he listened to Washington just the same. "Let's get to the agenda then, shall we?"

———

Dirk zoned in and out of lustful daydreams and steady problem-solving. His mind couldn't help but wander, especially with Rona sitting next to him. She was wearing just a tank top and old-fashioned camo pants, both of which were too small and, to Dirk's delight, did not leave much to the imagination. Really, in that circumstance, how could he not stare?

The attendance of the meeting slowly diminished as agenda items were introduced and discussed, orders were given, and specific soldiers were dismissed. By the time Dirk heard his name, there were fewer than ten people in the room, not including the holographic Adams.

"Dirk," said Adams, his voice echoing slightly. "I am hoping that you have some answers for me."

"It's good to see you too, John." Dirk stood, his skin literally on fire. Why was he so uneasy?

He walked to the front of the room and placed the monstrous golden sword on the table just in front of Adams' holoboard.

"This, ladies and gentlemen, is the Golden Sword of Gilgamesh. Rona and I found the sword in an antechamber just off the original location. I wanted to explore the location a bit more after our conversation, John, so we headed in that direction."

"In the meantime," cut in Washington, "I sent the guys to the dungeons under the palace complex. We knew that there were going to be pockets of servants and soldiers still loyal to the governor. I wasn't sure where the sword was being kept, and we didn't want to take any chances."

"So my guys go after the fake while Dirk and Rona go back to the dig site. Continue, Dirk."

Dirk picked up his narrative. "I didn't have a map this time; I lost it some time ago, so it was much more difficult to find the sword chamber. But once we did, there were several things we noticed that I missed the first time in my haste to escape the authorities. Namely, the markings that you brought to my attention, John, during our oh-so-wonderful time together underground. That wasn't all; we found writings and the alphabets of more than twenty other ancient languages, most of which are almost totally wiped out. After a bit of digging and the use of some strategic, low-grade explosives, we found the antechamber and the real sword."

"Never mind the obvious," interrupted Adams. "What happened to our guys? Was the fake sword a trap by the governor?"

"Oh, it was a governor, alright," replied Dirk, "just not one that has been alive in the last five thousand years. I'm not sure what to think here, John—I feel like the sword has a far more defining purpose. I just don't know what it is."

Adams' voice rose in frustration. "So we've got nothing, is that what you're telling me? One of my best teams is dead, and we've got no idea why."

The silence was almost unbearable. It was clear that the other people in the room found Adams intimidating. Only Washington looked loose and relaxed.

Dirk spoke up. "I never said we didn't have a lead, John. Don't get all worked up. I found something else that I think explains the situation clearly. Rona, dear, do you have your tablet?"

Rona stood without looking at Adams, her face sullen, even scared. Her movements were sharp and awkward. Her expression and actions surprised Dirk, though he suddenly realized why he was feeling so uneasy.

Rona was scared of Adams.

Dirk filed another piece of information away for later examination. Thanking Rona, Dirk took the tablet and pulled up the pictures and lab report. "Now where is that blasted—here it is. A little history for you all: the Sword of Gilgamesh is from, or so the legend says, the Gate of Mara, the proper name for Gilgamesh's vault in ancient Samaria. The vault was one of the wonders of the world, claiming to possess the 'magical' items of unparalleled power collected by Gilgamesh over the years. The legend states that the Golden Sword of Gilgamesh had the destructive capacity to literally rend creation itself when wielded by the proper person—"

"Mr. Garrett." The room's attention shifted to Washington, who was rubbing his chin skeptically. "I think you lost me there. I am pretty well versed in old civilizations, and specifically ancient Samaria. I happen to be familiar with the Epic of Gilgamesh, its origins and major points. Case in point, I don't recall any mention of a golden sword."

Dirk winked and pointed at Washington. "Or a vault for that matter."

Silence followed this statement.

"Dirk, are you really hinting at what I think you're hinting at?" muttered Adams.

"If you think that I'm implying that everything I just told you was completely and utterly untrue, then yes. That is exactly what I'm hinting at."

More silence.

"Master Dirk." It was Coolidge. His voice was low and dangerous. "Are you telling us that the very thing we invaded this bloody country for doesn't actually exist?"

The tone was civil but accusatory. Not shocking in the least. Coolidge was a soldier who had just lost some good men for no apparent reason. Dirk recognized Coolidge's tone and guessed his issue; he would need to resolve this quickly. He picked up the golden sword.

"Does this look like it doesn't exist?" Dirk's eyes never left Coolidge's. This little presentation wasn't going the way he wanted. He needed to clarify things so the old soldier would understand.

Dirk held the giant sword in both hands. He adjusted it so everyone in the room could see it. "Gentlemen, you're looking at a figment—something that is not *supposed* to exist."

Dirk brandished the sword. "In layman's terms, you're looking at an example of Dr. Jones's D-List."

"Ahhh," said Rona, comprehension finding its way onto her face. Everyone else looked on in confusion.

Rona picked up the thread. "Dr. Jones's D-List, or The Delusive List, refers to a relic hunter code for unclassified, mostly fictional items—things that come up over and over again in history, in various forms across cultures and legends, but that have never been found nor had their source story verified."

"Like the Holy Grail or the Ark of the Covenant?" asked Adams, sounding genuinely curious.

Dirk shook his head. "Not quite. The Holy Grail or Ark of the Covenant legends came from a specific culture, and while the consistency, content, and details of the legend have changed over time, the source of the legend is known. And, point of fact, the Holy Grail has been found and lost a number of times."

"The Delusive List refers to items that theoretically have a basis in history," explained Rona, "but have never been found or had their source legend traced. The Sword of Gilgamesh, the tablet of Ra, the Burning Bush Dictation, God's Banner—some of these you might recognize, some you won't. These are all examples from the D-List."

Dirk cut in. "So, Coolidge, I am literally holding something in front of you that shouldn't exist. And that, Mr. Adams, is why your soldiers died."

CHAPTER 11

BACK IN BLACK

Time: Late at night

Scene: Briefing room, governor's mansion

Adams seemed to have had enough. "Dirk, not that this isn't fascinating, but what does this D-List and the sword have to do with what happened to my guys?"

Washington gave Adams a sharp look. Apparently, he did not appreciate the phrase "my guys."

Dirk nodded to Rona, who gestured to a couple of soldiers holding a case in the back of the room. He then addressed both Washington and Adams. "I don't know if the D-list is connected, and I'm still not sure what the symbols mean. I don't know if we'll run into legendary, make-believe items that shouldn't exist. I can tell you, though, with a certain amount of confidence, that things are far more complicated than we thought. So in answer to your inquiry, sir, I believe that the D-list has **everything** to do with why your guys died."

The soldiers moved to the front and placed the case on the table. Dirk gestured to a lab coat in the back. The lab coat, a.k.a. Madison, walked forward, tablet in hand.

"Mr. Adams, General Washington," he dipped his head once to each of them, "I've uploaded my findings onto the interlink. Allow me to summarize the events that led to the deaths of Riker and his team."

Adams and Washington looked on without a word. Madison continued. "Sergeant Riker's team ran into the remnants of the Governor's Elite Palace Guard in the catacombs under the city. The firefight went well, as Riker and the others were fortunate enough to get the drop on the guards..."

Madison spoke uninterrupted for several minutes, perhaps fifteen or twenty; Dirk was unsure. He explained to Adams and Washington about the value, the treasures, and the podium. He detailed the dimensions and layout of the underground vault and complex, the display where the sword was kept, and the sword itself. Finally, Madison described the explosion.

Adams snapped a second time. "Damn it, Madison, get on with it."

"Sweat, sir," blurted out Madison. "Sweat caused the sword to explode."

There it was. Dirk would have laughed if he could have

picked out anything funny about the situation. Adams looked murderous.

"Explain," was all he said.

Dirk, despite an inclination to the contrary, interjected. "I've found something that I think explains this."

Dirk walked over to the now-forgotten case. He flipped it open and pulled out a single shiny golden brick, a third of a meter long.

Adams's eyes narrowed. "I've seen one of those—"

Dirk put his hand up. "No, John, I don't think you have."

Dirk handed Madison the brick. "You know what to do."

Madison eyed it, replying, "You understand that this changes everything, right?"

Dirk turned to face Washington and Adams. "You've no idea, Doctor."

"Harmonicum?" Adams exclaimed after a moment.

"Harmonicum," confirmed Dirk. "Dr. Madison, who apparently is the Republican's premier smart guy on the stuff, came to the conclusion just this morning."

Madison picked up the thread. "Sergeant Riker's team triggered the bomb by the simple act of picking it up. We discovered this quite by accident. The small samples of the original sword of Gilgamesh we were able to preserve were also made out of Harmonicum."

Adams interlocked his fingers. "How did you come to this conclusion, Madison?"

Madison made a few quick movements on his tablet, and

images appeared on the holo-board. "It was quite by accident, actually. The sample reacted when a solution of sodium, potassium, calcium, and magnesium—the main ingredients in sweat—accidentally came into contact with it."

"We had a mini-explosion as a result," added Rona. "It was Dirk who came up with the idea that the sword was a Harmonicum booby trap."

Adams and Washington exchanged looks of surprise. Dirk glowered. "Hey now, fellas. Good old Dirk isn't such a dumb one."

"Then tell me, I pray thee, Dirk," replied Adams. "How did you come to that conclusion?"

He shrugged. "My skin told me."

Silence followed that little confession. Dirk sighed. Would anyone ever really understand how valuable his skin was? Probably not.

"I just had a hunch. That was one of the things we talked about, right? Why the Empire and UWC are after me. They want me for some unknown reason, but they also have an interest in the symbols from those dig sites—my dig sites—you were so kind to share with me way back, John. The dig sites and the symbols held some independent importance but should ultimately lead to the same goal. And if that ultimate goal is Harmonicum—like you said, Adams—then it makes sense that any place or object bearing those symbols might be connected to Harmonicum."

Adams and Washington both looked like they had been slapped.

"Brilliant," uttered Adams.

"Genius," agreed Washington.

"Dirk came to the conclusion," said Rona, beaming, "and Dr. Madison and I worked backwards using Dr. Thurman's recognition method. We knew almost immediately that the fake sword was made at least partially of Harmonicum."

Washington stood and started to pace. "Well, that certainly answers the question of why the UWC and the Empire are looking for Mr. Garrett. Unfortunately, it opens the door to a great many more questions, I think the most obvious being—"

"Why the sword blew up when Riker touched it," Adams said, finishing the sentence, "and equally important, why didn't it blow up when *you* grabbed it, Dirk?"

"I'm overly cautious," answered Dirk without hesitation. "I always wear gloves when I'm hunting, and I always wrap my findings—for a couple of reasons. One, the wrapping hides my acquisitions from the prying eyes of those who—uh, might not like what I'm doing. And two, far more important, the wrapping is a special poly-cloth of my own invention. Not only does it protect the item, but it also protects me from anything that might be on the item—poison, for example."

Silence greeted this statement. Dirk continued. "Rich people in ancient times were just as stingy as rich people now. Even dead, they don't want others attempting to borrow their belongings. They put a lot of effort into guarding their property. Early in my career, I was poisoned on more than one occasion. I make a habit of cleanly wrapping my finds until I can make sure they aren't dangerous. The governor's henchmen must have kept my wrapping on the sword until it was put to rest on that podium where Riker and his boys found it."

Dirk glanced at Adams and noticed he was barely listening. "Hey, John," commented Dirk, "you look a little preoccupied."

Adams looked up from whatever he was attending to off-board. "Yes, I'm trying to keep a certain someone from crashing the party, but—"

Three knocks directly to Dirk's left captured the attendant's attention. Dirk lazily searched for the source of the sound and saw...the man in black standing in front of him.

Dirk and most of the others jumped back, startled by his sudden appearance. Adams addressed him casually with a hint of anger.

"You couldn't have waited until we were done here?"

The Magician shook his head slowly. Dirk had seen this gesture before. It was calm and deliberate and in no way aggressive. Nevertheless, Dirk felt his fear of this man rise and surface. But as scared as he was, he still stepped forward and greeted the Magician. "Hey there, my friend, it's been too long. Where were you when I was strapped to that silly chair? No worries. I have to say you didn't tell me you were the world's famous Magician. If I'd known, I would have asked for an autograph. Do you even know how much money your autograph would fetch? I mean, if I were you, I would stop all this assassin business and just sell my autograph. You'd make a killing."

Dirk tried to shut up, but he couldn't. "There was no pun intended there. Ya know, we could even do autographed pictures of you, though you'd have to stop doing that ninja vanishing act long enough for us to *take* your picture; I can't imagine anyone wanting to buy a picture of a black wall—"

"Dirk—"

"You wouldn't have to worry about marketing either—"

"Dirk!"

Dirk desisted his rambling and innocently looked at Adams. Adams glared back. "Dirk, I want to ask you a pointed question."

Dirk's forehead furrowed. "It seems like an odd time for Twenty Questions, John."

"I don't need twenty, just one. I want to ask you who allowed you to enter Sanzarubi totally unmolested?"

Dirk chanced a glance at the Magician, who stood like a statue, completely unmoving. Dirk pointed his pinky finger at the Magician. "Him, of course. What's your point exactly?"

"My point is simple, Dirk: If the legendary assassin decides to kill here and now in front of all of us, there is nothing I or anyone else in here can do to stop him."

Dirk cringed inwardly as his skin stood up and danced

the hula. "Point taken. Mr. Magician, let me start with my three-part apology."

A hand clamped over his mouth. It was Rona's. She nodded at the Magician as she pulled Dirk away. Strangely enough, the Magician nodded back.

It was hard to tell, but it appeared that the Magician had turned his attention back to Adams. His hands lit up, and a strange hovering holograph appeared in front of him—a computer interface in the sky. The fingertips of the Magician's gloves grew brighter and turned a mesmerizing red color. The Magician interacted with his floating computer terminal, his fingers moving with such speed that it was totally impossible to keep up with what he was doing. No one talked for several minutes while the Magician did his work, until abruptly he finished. He used his built-in conductor glove, gathered whatever information he was sorting, and flicked his wrist towards Adams.

Adams's gaze refocused off-screen to where Dirk could only assume he was looking at a holoboard. They didn't have to wait long.

Adams addressed the Magician. "You're sure?"

The Magician nodded.

Adams swore. "I knew as much. If you do not have a plan, I'm holding you personally responsible."

The Magician flicked his wrist a second time in Adams's direction. Adams took much longer to review the information the Magician had sent him this time.

"You're serious?"

The Magician nodded a second time.

Adams rubbed at his chin. "And how do you propose to accomplish such a task? I don't think you'd have any problems with the first couple of cities maybe, but the inner three? It's impossible. We've had this conversation before, I believe. There is too much risk to the collateral for an all-out war."

The Magician reengaged his holo-board, sending over info once again. Adams immediately resumed his reading, his expression becoming genuinely surprised. "You understand that if you proceed, there's no halfway, right?"

The Magician stood completely still. His third nod was delayed and even forced.

Adams sighed. "If you think it will work, then I agree. It's interesting that you pick now of all times to get out of your comfort zone."

"I don't mean to interrupt this strange reunion," said Washington, though he didn't sound remotely sorry for the interruption. "Could you two tell us just what the hell it is you're plotting?"

Adams was typing on his off-screen holo-board. "You'll know in a moment, Washington. I will explain when she gets here."

He addressed the Magician. "Send your plans and schematics, and I will brief the others."

Adams typed off-screen for a couple of very long minutes during which everyone in the room watched him. The quiet was killing Dirk. He desperately wanted to leave the room. Not that the Magician was doing anything inherently threatening. It was just that Dirk's skin was at total and complete attention. Conclusion? That this man wrapped in black from head to toe might be the single most dangerous thing he had ever come across. There was no denying it. No getting around it. And if Dirk made a wrong move around him, it might seriously be his last.

"He's not going to hurt you."

Rona sidled in next to Dirk. She appeared calm, even a little bored. Dirk did his best not to gape at her.

"You don't sound very convinced."

Rona smiled at him. "I am, trust me."

"How can you be sure? What if I accidentally make him mad?"

Dirk tried his best to make that last sentence sound as manly as possible. It so didn't.

"You worry too much. Trust me. You can't make him angry. Not as he is now."

"You're going to have to explain that one, Rona."

Rona pointed at the Magician. "That man is a professional among professionals, Dirk. Every action is planned, every kill is specified. When he puts on that mask, he is the world's most notorious assassin. A professional through and through. So trust me, you have nothing to worry about, least of all him getting angry."

Dirk was still skeptical. "Everyone gets angry, Rona; everyone has his breaking point. Even him."

Rona's eyes got a bit distant. "I hope to all the gods in heaven that is not the case, Dirk."

"Why?"

Rona turned a serious eye on Dirk. "Because if there is something that could happen to make that man mad enough that he actually strikes out in anger, then we are all in big, big trouble."

Dirk was unable to help himself. "And why is that?"

"Because the day that man loses control is the day that a whole lot of people are going to die."

The timing for some other people entering the room couldn't have been better. The not-so-subtle reference to widespread death was a little more than Dirk could handle in the immediate.

The newcomers, a handful of guards walking in formation around a short, completely covered individual, walked to the head of the room. Never breaking stride and without saying a word, they settled directly in front of Adams and Washington.

Washington nodded. "Thank you, Captain. At ease."

The soldiers did not move but visibly relaxed. Dirk stared at the individual with them. The coverings and wrappings of the woman—and yes, Dirk instinctively knew it was a woman —were expensive, remarkable, exquisite even. Some of the finest he had ever seen. Who was this person?

Adams spoke to the covered woman. "Gōng Zhǔ." He bowed respectfully. "Would you be so kind as to grace us with your presence and disregard your veil?"

It was hard to tell, especially with all the coverings, but Dirk knew that the "Gōng Zhǔ" was hesitating. Her hesitation seemed to melt away as she turned in the direction of the Magician, who Dirk had almost forgotten was still there. The Gōng Zhǔ stared in the Magician's direction. Then, in perfect English, said, "As you wish, Mr. Adams. I will join you."

The Gōng Zhǔ removed her dressing, and Dirk's eyeballs just about fell out of his head. The woman was so strikingly beautiful it was criminal! Long, shiny black hair and eyes, slightly slanted with full lips, clear olive skin, and slender legs and waist.

Adams didn't seem impressed. "Gentlemen and Rona, allow me to introduce you to the Sun of the Eastern Mountains, Second Daughter of the Emperor of Jade, Xui Li Fen Fang Sun."

CHAPTER 12

PREOCCUPATION

Time: Midafternoon
Scene: MESA's Harmonics lab

"The remaining cycles are either on track or ninety percent on schedule. All in all, we continue to meet our performance goals," Warrick said as the last chart faded to black and the lights in the boardroom came back on. "But despite our continued success, Thurman remains disconnected. He's going through the motions, but something is different."

"Different in what way, Warrick? Specifics, please," the Old Man said.

"I'm not sure I can put a label on it. He has been working just the same, and his insights about the work we are doing have certainly not let up. Yet, at times he seems completely preoccupied with something."

"Ms. Green had a similar report in her briefing," Kingston

mentioned. "From her monitoring data, Thurman has been wandering the halls more than usual and has taken to pacing regularly in his office. Has he mentioned anything to you about it?"

Warrick paused and looked down. "I asked him about it, and he got really defensive." He looked up at the board members. "Later he apologized and said he's still shaken up over the bombing. He started to talk about his decision to come and work for MESA instead of staying at the university, but stopped short of going into anything else."

Kingston glanced over at the Old Man, who was staring at Warrick intently.

"Most interesting," commented the Old Man. "Very good, Warrick. If there is nothing else, you may return to the lab. Thank you for your updates."

For a brief second, Warrick was hesitant to leave, thinking that there should be more discussion about Thurman's state of mind. Yet he knew when he had been dismissed. He and the other board members shuffled to the elevator, leaving Kingston and the Old Man alone.

Kingston spoke first. "I only see two options, neither of which I like."

The Old Man stood and took up his vantage point at the window. "I agree with you. A psych consult will do little to assuage whatever anxiety Thurman is carrying. Yet, do we really want to allow Thurman access to Jameson?"

Kingston sat in thought for a moment. He definitely had

his reservations about Jameson, especially after the bombing incident. But a psych eval would most definitely put more distance between them and Thurman. "Like I said, I don't like either option. But I suppose the only viable one is Jameson, even if putting them together is against protocol."

The Old Man continued to stare out the window. "We cannot lose Thurman, and second to that is we cannot let him feel that he is trapped here. Thurman emotionally shut down and uncooperative is just as bad as not having him here at all. I agree that protocol prevents us from using Jameson in that manner, but I do not see any other choice. It's what Thurman has been after for a long time now, and giving it to him just may be the boost he needs to shake whatever is clinging to him."

Kingston continued to sit silently. After a few moments, he looked up at the window. "Then I'll set it up. Would you like to brief Jameson on the parameters of his interaction, or should I?"

The Old Man turned from the window to look at Kingston. "I realize that you and Jameson are still experiencing friction. I may be old, but I am not blind. I don't want this adding to the tension between you two."

Kingston sat passively, knowing that despite his best efforts to hide his animosity towards Jameson, the Old Man didn't get to where he was by not knowing everything that went on at MESA. Especially those things that did not make it into any report or briefing.

"I think you two still need some distance. I will brief Jameson," continued the Old Man. Kingston nodded and returned to updating reports on his tablet. The Old Man continued to stare at Kingston for a moment before turning back to the window.

———

Professor Thurman sat at his large desk in his office in the Harmonics lab. The daily cycle reports sat scrolling slowly on his desk interface, but he was not even remotely paying attention to them. While he was staring out into the lab through his office window, he wasn't actually seeing anything. His mind was occupied elsewhere. His thoughts turned, as they had almost constantly lately, to his off-the-books research notes. Involuntarily, his gaze shifted to settle on the leather-bound notebook atop his desk. The notebook had not been opened for some time. Each time his hand made to reach for it to jot down an insight, it would always stop short. He would then do some routine mathematical problems in his head and try to distract himself with other mundane things. But a habit established over decades was not easily changed.

Thurman stood up and walked over to his office window. Anyone observing him would make the assumption that he was looking over the business of the lab. But his mind was not on his lab. In fact, his mind was almost constantly occupied with thoughts of the Feedbacker lab just down the hall.

While he forced himself to walk by it every so often just to keep up appearances, he did everything he could to stay away from it.

Part of him understood that he could not conceal this eccentric behavior for an extended time; while he could not prove it, he knew that MESA was constantly monitoring him. Yet, there was little he could do about that with his energies so focused on not being invaded by that siren in the Feedbacker lab. One problem at a time. That was all he could manage right now.

As Thurman continued to absentmindedly stare into his lab, a sudden noise startled him, and he whipped around.

"Professor, are you feeling all right?" asked Jameson concernedly.

It took Thurman a few seconds to piece together Jameson's presence in his office. Somewhere in the recesses of his brain, he recalled someone calling his name mere seconds ago, and he pieced it all together. How long had Jameson been standing there before he realized it?

"Oh, James—eh, CJ, no I'm not—I mean...ye—sorry, what was the question?" Thurman could not seem to get his brain to form a coherent thought. There were too many variables battling for his attention: Feedbackers, MESA, Harmonicum, CJ, Warrick...thoughts raced through his mind as he tried to compose himself.

"Professor, why don't you sit down? I didn't mean to startle you," replied Jameson. Fortunately, Thurman's social behavior center caught hold of the command and told his body to walk over to the chair and sit down.

"CJ, I am sorry. I just—well, I was...." Thurman took a deep breath. "My, it has been quite a week. I dare say that I am worn out," he commented congenially.

Jameson smiled warmly and nodded his head as he took a seat across from him and set his tablet on the edge of the desk. "I can certainly understand that. It's been some time since I lost my lab, and I still find myself with too much to do and not enough hours in the day."

Thurman's mind continued to race, trying to process the situation. Why was Jameson here? Who sent him? Was his supposed busy schedule all these months a result of MESA preventing Jameson from speaking to him? If so, why? What did they not want them to discuss? After all, their research was nowhere near related. Or was it? His mind jumped from one question to the next, never allowing time for an answer. Jameson continued with polite chitchat, and somehow Thurman answered, but never with any real thought to the matter.

"So, have they been keeping you busy here, Professor?" inquired Jameson.

"Oh, quite, CJ. Very busy indeed." Why was he asking about the lab? Was he trying to get information to pass on? But what information was there that MESA could not get from observing him or asking Warrick? Why, from out of the blue, was he even allowed to talk to Thurman? Thurman quickly stole glances at the corners of his office. There were no visible cameras there, but in his paranoia, he thought they would be the best spot for some.

"Look, Professor...I know—" Jameson started. *Here it comes*, thought Thurman.

"I know that I have been distant ever since you arrived here at MESA. There was very little I could do about it. I may have tenure here, but that doesn't change the fact that I report to someone, too. When they ask me to jump, I still have to answer how high...."

Of all the things that Jameson could have said to him, Thurman was not expecting that level of honesty. He realized that without coming out and saying it, Jameson had just told him that MESA had been keeping them apart. But why?

"I want you to know it has been no picnic for me either. There were—are—so many things that I want to work with you on and talk to you about. I think there is some real good we can accomplish together...."

Thurman heard the words coming out of Jameson's mouth, but he was still sorting through the myriad questions rolling around in his mind. The one he came back to again and again was *why?* What was MESA trying to prevent by keeping the two of them from working together?

"You see, Professor, I have been at MESA for a long time. I have seen this company grow and prosper, touching almost every field of science and technology. I understand that there are contracts we need to take from certain governmental

agencies that fund the rest of the research here, and I understand the politics that go into securing those funds...."

Was it something that Jameson was working on in the
Interface lab? Or was it the Harmonics research? What could
possibly be so important that MESA wouldn't want to further
their progress by allowing the collaboration? What were they
protecting...or hiding?

"It's just that recently, in the past few years or so, I have
seen a dramatic shift in this company's philosophy. It started
way before they became interested in helping you move your
research forward. At first, it was subtle. A policy change here,
less scrutiny on a contract there. Eventually, though, it
became brash; there was no attempt to hide it. MESA was
acquiring contracts for very large sums of money. And it
wasn't like we all didn't know where that money was coming
from."

Even if they were hiding something, where was the
danger in Thurman working with Jameson? What were they
afraid of Thurman discovering? Surely MESA could limit the
purview of the conversation to protect their interests, couldn't
they?

"Take a look at where they're taking the Interface lab. For
years, I had major say as to where the research was directed.
Now, not so much. I can't tell you how many board meetings
I've been to lately where the sole topic of discussion is that
new Feedbacker lab and how my lab can support their
research."

Thurman's questions ground to a halt at the mention of the Feedbacker lab. Apparently, he was not the only one concerned about their arrival.

"I mean, of all the pseudo-science we could fund, it has to be on people who can pick the three of diamonds out of a bunch of facedown cards?"

The momentary respite from Thurman's pondering helped him to see something else. Jameson was being extremely candid in his displeasure with MESA. Thurman thought about the things that Jameson brought up. There was no way that CJ was ignorant of MESA's monitoring abilities, especially when it had to do with Thurman. So why the candor? Why be so open about—

Then it clicked. Jameson was not stupid, nor was he ignorant. That left two possibilities. Either he was lying about all the things he was complaining about, or despite knowing that MESA was watching, he didn't care if they heard him.

"You must have felt something of that, haven't you, Professor?" asked Jameson. Thurman almost missed the question.

"Well, CJ, I believe every institution carries with it certain bureaucratic mazes." Thurman had no idea what CJ had just asked him, but he kept going anyway. If CJ really didn't care about MESA listening in, then his answers didn't need to add anything to the conversation. "At the university, my problem was always funding. Here that isn't even a remote concern."

CJ continued to nod as Thurman spoke of the differences between the university and MESA. Thurman had no idea if anything he was saying was even remotely related to CJ's comments.

"I suppose that's true, Professor. Each man has his own challenges to deal with." Jameson sat back in his chair and rubbed his face. Thurman thought he looked very tired all of a sudden.

"So, enough of my moping. What's cooking over here?" asked Jameson as he stood and wandered to the window overlooking the lab.

The question raised Thurman's hackles as his paranoia again took over.

"Oh, you know...a little of this, a little of that," he replied, staying seated.

Did Jameson really think that his poor excuse for small talk would be enough to get Thurman to open up about his research? *No*, thought Thurman. *He isn't that stupid. So what is he getting at?*

"I understand that you've met all of your goals for this production cycle," continued Jameson, "Congratulations. We're still only at eighty percent despite being rebuilt for a while now. I think people are still a little shaken up about the explosion. Very surprising and violent thing. I know it shook me up."

Thurman was at a loss. He honestly had no idea where Jameson was intending to take the conversation, nor what information he wanted. It seemed as if he was just passing the time.

"So have you been over to see the new lab and Dr. What's-her-name?" asked CJ.

"Yes, Mr. Kingston was nice enough to take me over there soon after they set up shop, so to speak," remarked Thurman.

"Fascinating work, that Feedbacker stuff. I was really intrigued by all the things they were setting up in there. I think they'll be able to turn out quite the product once they start cooking."

Thurman was momentarily taken aback by his words. Moments ago, CJ had called the lab "pseudo-science," and now he found it "fascinating?" Something was definitely going on, but Thurman had no idea what that something was.

"Well, it's been nice chatting with you, Professor," said CJ as he picked up his tablet from the desk. "I hope we aren't so removed from one another in the near future."

Thurman rose out of his seat to see CJ off. "Yes, well, thank you for stopping by. It was good to finally get to, er... talk."

It didn't appear that CJ was paying any attention as he frantically tapped away on his tablet. After a few moments, he looked up at him. As Thurman met his gaze, he noticed this was not the rambling CJ of a mere few seconds ago. This CJ had a hard, determined look in his eye. He extended his hand to Thurman. With a bit of apprehension, Thurman grasped it.

"You'll have fifteen seconds after I leave to read this. Fifteen. That's it," instructed CJ in a hushed, urgent voice.

"I'll what?" stumbled Thurman. "Fifteen sec—what are—"

"Fifteen seconds," repeated Jameson. Then he released Thurman's hand and left the office.

Thurman slowly looked down to his outstretched palm at the small square of thin paper pressed into it. Carefully, and with great reservation, Thurman took the scrap of paper and held it up to read its contents. He scanned the note quickly. Its instructions were simple and straightforward. He looked around, his eyes wandering to the corners of his office. Suddenly, a bright light drew his attention back to the scrap of paper. In the fraction of a second it took him to move his focus towards his hand, the last bit of paper flared up and blinked out of existence in a minuscule puff of smoke. Instinctively, he shook his hand away from the flare, but the paper had already disappeared, leaving no trace. Thurman's hand wasn't singed, and he could no longer see any trace of the small puff of smoke.

Thurman plopped down in his chair, his head in his hand. Of all the things that Jameson could have told him, why did he want him to stay away from the East wall next week?

CHAPTER 13
DILEMMA

Time: Early evening
Scene: Jungle on the borders of the main province of the Jade Empire

If Dirk ever got the chance, he was going to punch John Adams right in the throat. The man couldn't hide forever; eventually, he had to come out from his hiding place, wherever that was, and when that happened—POW, right in the pucker. Adams totally deserved it.

"Mr. Garrett, might we not take a break? I grow weary of this walking, and we shall meet him soon."

Dirk looked back over his shoulder at the two women following him. First was Xui Li, the absolutely delicious daughter of the Emperor. She was exquisite in voice and beauty. Dirk loved being around the girl—or at least he did during the first part of this idiotic venture. Xui Li was a princess in every sense of the word. Abducted from the Shangri-La, the Emperor's summer home, she was to have been sold by the slavers in Sanzarubi had it not been for the Magician. And Xui Li constantly reminded Rona and him of this, speaking of the world's most notorious assassin as if he were the dreamy captain of her school's combat tag team. The "Gōng Zhǔ," as she required them to call her, had developed a crush on the Magician. The situation was so bizarre it was almost comical.

Next came Rona, and she wasn't making the trip any easier on Dirk. Dirk liked Rona. He did. Even if she wasn't quite as beautiful as Xui Li, she was still a looker. It wasn't that she became annoying in the traditional sense either. Dirk got easily bored with women—their demands, their desires, their expectations. It was all so boring. Rona didn't do any of this. She didn't demand, desire, or expect anything from him. Their conversations were pleasant, and her real smile—the smile that crept across her face when she thought no one was watching and she was really into something—was about as fine a smile as he had come across. Dirk liked Rona just fine, but she was seriously impeding his progress with Xui Li, and he had a reputation and schedule to keep. By now, Dirk should have already rounded home with the little princess. Rona was seriously messing up his timetable.

Rounded home. What a great analogy. He had a couple of picture books called comics that dated back from before the Great War, and they used that particular phrase a lot.

Dirk found out later that the reference was to a popular game called "baseball," which people from the former United States went crazy for. They were an odd bunch.

Xui Li interrupted his thoughts. "Mr. Garrett, please. I desire to freshen up—"

Dirk glanced over his shoulder. "Yes, Gōng Zhǔ, we can stop for a few minutes."

They walked another fifty meters or so until they found a clearing among the thick trees of the jungle. Dirk didn't like to stop this far into the jungle. This part of the world hadn't been as affected by the fallout from the Great War, but even after all this time, there were some strange things that less-than-alert travelers could encounter. Dirk was not going to let anything happen. He scanned the area, scouting for potential threats. When none were found, he dropped his pack by a boulder and sat. He was dog-tired.

Dirk watched Xui Li do the same, but once she sat down, she was a flurry of activity. She worked on her hair, makeup, and nails, and then, for several inspired moments, she wiped the sweat off her body before she proceeded to arrange her hair into some sort of bun.

"A schoolgirl crush on an infamous assassin," said Rona, plopping down next to Dirk. "That is a virtual theater experience waiting to happen."

Dirk laughed. "Comedy or tragedy?"

Rona yawned. "I'm hoping comedy. I don't want to think of the alternative."

The minutes dragged on as Xui Li attempted to "freshen up," a task in which she obviously had absolutely no experience. Rona and Dirk tried really hard not to laugh. But Dirk's expression soured as he sat there. Xui Li had a crush on the brickin' assassin? Who honestly develops a crush on an assassin? She should have never come on this little mission.

"Remind me to punch Adams when we get back," said Rona, who suddenly sounded as angry as Dirk felt. It was an odd outburst from her. "This whole venture. We shouldn't be here, least of all with the little princess back there."

Wasn't that the truth! Dirk still couldn't figure out how they got here in the first place. He replayed the conversation and events leading up to this point.

"You're planning on doing what?" Dirk remembered saying, getting to his feet without realizing it, while his voice shot an octave higher than that of any twelve-year-old boy. Dirk had cleaned out his ear theatrically and then said, "John, I know I didn't hear you right. Because it sounded like you just said that you want us to go into the outer provinces of the Jade Empire."

A life-size holo-Adams spoke casually at that meeting, but he was haggard and came off as incredibly weary.

"We are working on a strict timeline here, Dirk," said Adams with almost none of his usual gusto. "I need you to get me as much data as possible on this particular site. The Jadians and UWC are talking about it almost nonstop. I need to know why."

Dirk looked at the location. It was in the middle of the jungle in the province of Shere Khan. "John, this jungle is almost entirely artificial. This area of the Empire was hit especially hard during the last Great War. If there was anything there, it was blown to Tartarus and back years ago. Not only that, the northern border of that jungle edges the second-biggest city in the Empire. It seems like a great deal of risk for some hunch."

"The entire western border of Shere Khan comprises one of the most rugged mountain ranges in the world. There are half a dozen groups living in total autonomy in those mountains just because the Emperor is too lazy to go in and actually subjugate them. You've nothing to worry about. Besides, I've ensured a bit of protection for you."

Dirk paused. He really hoped that didn't mean what he thought that meant. "You mean him?"

Adams nodded. "Of course I mean him. Who else could I mean?"

Traveling with the Magician. Dirk wasn't sure about that. Did he really want to sleep under the stars with the world's greatest assassin next to him? That would be a negatory. "John, I'm really—"

The doors of the meeting room were flung open just as Dirk was about to let Adams have it. There was absolutely no way he was going to go trucking halfway around the world with someone who could melt in and out of darkness like demon spawn. No chance. Dirk forgot his argument when he noticed who had entered the room. It was Xui Li.

Adams greeted her. "Gōng Zhǔ, to what do we owe the pleasure?"

Dirk tried not to stare at Xui Li, but he couldn't help himself. She was a sight. She wore a tight-fitting blue qipao with a high slit that showed off smooth, slender legs. Beautiful. Unfortunately, Xui Li caught him looking. "I submit to your proposal, Mr. Adams, but only if *he* is personally coming along. This is the Gōng Zhǔ's requirement."

Adams smiled. A real one, the first Dirk could ever remember seeing from him. "Excellent. You will not regret this, I assure you, and I wouldn't have it any other way. Dirk."

Dirk looked up from Xui Li's legs. "Yeah—um—what?"

"You were in the middle of rejecting the opportunity to travel with Xui Li and my associate—"

"I accept." Dirk shouted. "I think it's a wonderful idea."

Adams' smile widened as Xui Li stalked from the room.

That had been more than three weeks ago. In that time, Dirk had gotten nowhere with Xui Li, partly because of Rona, who at the last minute he learned would be tagging along, and partly because of Xui Li's unhealthy fascination with the Magician. Dirk was ready to leave the lot of them.

"Come on, Dirk," said Rona, stretching her arms straight in the air. "We need to get moving. We've got another couple of kilometers and only a couple of hours to do it. The Magician isn't exactly patient."

Dirk was not listening. He was staring at Rona's now-exposed midriff. He spoke without thinking. "Rona, you have a deceptively hot body."

Dirk didn't even realize he said it.

Rona pulled at the hem of her shirt and tucked it into her pants. This snapped Dirk out of it. "Come on, Romeo. We need to go."

"Who's Romeo?"

"Never mind."

Rona looked over her shoulder. "Gōng Zhǔ!"

Xui Li looked up from her primping. "Yes, what is it, Miss Rona?"

"We need to leave. We don't want to keep the Magician waiting."

Xui Li, in a shocking change from the norm, did as she was told without complaint. "Yes, he will have to answer to me! I have not seen him since we departed that awful province in the Land of Sand. I was promised he would be traveling with us."

Rona rolled her eyes. "He has been, Gōng Zhǔ. You just haven't seen him. Now hurry—we need to be off."

Rona started back up the trail, hacking at the excess vegetation when necessary. Dirk watched her backside as she moved up the path. It had been bothering him for a while now—not her backside; everything was in order there—the way that Rona talked about the Magician. It was like...it was like she knew him.

Dirk rushed after her. "You're quite mysterious, did you know that?"

Rona hacked at some tree branches impeding their path. "That's an odd thing to say."

Dirk lingered a little farther away than he normally would as Rona continued slashing at the branches. "It's true. As a matter of fact, I think you've been holding out on me."

Rona shot an inquisitive look over her shoulder. "You're gonna have to explain that one."

"The Magician," Dirk said simply.

"What about him?"

"I have this distinct impression that you know him much better than you let on."

Rona laughed. "Is that the impression you get?"

"Yes, it is, as a matter of fact. I think you're keeping me in the dark." Dirk left the implication hanging.

"We're in the dark. Funny. Do you always make such stupid jokes?"

Rona pushed forward, hacking away until the footpath became a bit more accessible. She did not pursue the conversation. Either she didn't understand the implication or she was ignoring it; regardless, Dirk didn't like it.

"Rona, I want to know about the Magician."

"Dirk, saying I know about the Magician is like an oceanographer saying he knows about the ocean. Definitely more than most, but compared to what is still unknown, it's hardly noticeable. The ocean is full of mysteries, many of which should never be explored. The Magician is similar."

Dirk started to protest, but Rona cut him off. "That doesn't mean...that I won't answer your questions. It just means that my knowledge is minimal."

This surprised Dirk, but he was not going to look a gift donkey in the honkey. That was another one of those old comic book sayings. He didn't really understand that one as well as the others. Dirk chose his words wisely.

"Does he have a name?"

"Sure, lots of them."

"That's not what I meant."

"I know."

"So that's how it's going to be?"

"That's how it is, Dirk."

"What do you mean?"

"Just what I said. He has lots of names."

"He doesn't have a real name?"

"Not that I know of."

Dirk cringed. He wasn't expecting that.

"What is his appearance like?" asked Xui Li, materializing out of nowhere. "I wish to know, is he handsome?"

Rona considered this. "Yeah, I think he's cute. He certainly cleans up well."

Dirk scowled at Xui Li's question, and then again at Rona's response. The assassin, *cute*. Unbelievable.

Xui Li smiled that gorgeous smile. "What is his favorite food? What does he like to eat?"

"He likes classic dishes. And he likes old things. He isn't one for technology. Not that he isn't completely comfortable using it."

Dirk sighed. Xui Li was going into fan girl mode. He had to break this up. "How do you know him well enough to know what kind of food he likes? What's his relationship with Adams?"

Rona hesitated at this, like she was sizing him up. Dirk thought she wasn't going to answer. "That's a long story, and most of it is classified. I don't think it's a—"

"If you do not explain, I shall go no further," stated Xui Li as she plopped on the ground like a dollop of pork fat. "If I am to make this man my husband, I must know him in greater detail."

Dirk and Rona gaped at her. She did not just say that!

"Yes, that was part of the bargain with Mr. Adams. If I lend my assistance, then Mr. Adams shall bless my betrothal to my Dark Angel."

"Dark Angel?" repeated Rona blankly.

"Yes," answered Xui Li with a dreamy expression on her face. "He came like a thief in the night to punish those who would do wrong to the Gōng Zhǔ. He held me gently as he removed me from harm's way and delivered justice to the men of the Sand."

Rona rolled her eyes. "I'm sure he's going to love that."

"As his future wife, I shall know more of my husband than some commoner from the western Empire. You shall tell me the story."

Rona's tone was exasperated. "Fine, but get up. We're losing daylight, and your husband-to-be isn't exactly patient."

They resumed their pace slowly so Rona could get her bearings. "How much do the two of you know about the Republican movement?" Dirk and Xui Li acknowledged their ignorance of the Republicans and their purpose.

"Washington is some big-shot billionaire. I don't know his story exactly, but he started this whole fight. I wanna say it had to do with the Cerbus Virus and internment camps, but I can't say for sure. He started the Republicans with Coolidge and a few others and built it from there."

"Where was Adams?" asked Dirk, listening closely.

"Adams didn't come on until way later." Rona sheathed her chopping blade. "So the Republicans operated for a number of years, created networks, recruited operatives, and started to push their agenda among the western coastal cities of the UWC."

The path opened up; Dirk fell in next to Rona. "Why the coastal cities?"

"No idea. I assume that was close to Washington's power base. So Washington started his revolution and was having some moderate success striking fear into the UWC lackeys. Then his group started having run-ins with the Magician."

"What does *run-ins* mean?" questioned Xui Li.

"They started knocking heads," stated Dirk. Xui Li looked at him blankly. "They got into fights, Gōng Zhǔ."

She nodded her understanding.

"This went on for a number of years," continued Rona like there had been no interruption. "Until Washington decided he'd had enough."

Dirk was getting into the story. "So what did Washington do?"

"He formed the Culper Ring," responded Rona. This statement was met with blank stares from Xui Li and Dirk.

Rona tried not to let her irritation show. "Some history trivia for the two of you. In the American Revolution, General Washington personally picked and trained a network of spies that helped him with important information-gathering and delivery operations. This spy network may have been the single most important factor in the colonists' winning that struggle against the British Empire."

Dirk scratched at his face. "Washington was trying to channel some good karma, huh?"

She shrugged. "Apparently he thought it was poetic, ironic, who knows. But that's what he called them. This unit trained for years under harsh conditions, and after that period of training, they were ready."

"To fight the Magician?"

"Yes."

"Did they ever get the chance to fight him?"

"Yes."

"I'm assuming that didn't go well."

"If you consider not a single member of the Culper Ring surviving 'not going well,' then yes. You can safely say that."

"Apparently they didn't train hard enough."

"Something like that."

Again Dirk scratched at his face. "So if the Magician wiped out the Culper Ring, how did he hook up with the Republicans?"

Rona grinned at Dirk like he was a zealous primary school student. "Excellent question. The answer is Adams."

Dirk and Xui Li waited for her to continue.

"After the Culper Ring incident, Washington realized that a particularly brilliant hacker was supporting the Magician."

"How did he know that?"

"No idea, but he did, and somehow Washington got ahold of the man now called Adams."

"And they joined up just like that?"

"Not exactly."

"Then what, exactly?"

"I don't know the whole story, and really, you can guess the rest. The Magician is a gun for hire. Adams is a handler of sorts, plain and simple."

"So if Adams didn't join for the cause, then what is his revolution? What is he fighting for?"

Rona pushed her hand through her hair. "You'd have to ask Adams. There isn't much more I can tell you."

Dirk looked to Xui Li, who looked as contemplative as Dirk had ever seen her. It was obvious that Rona's information had satisfied her curiosity.

Rona rounded a huge boulder and pulled out a mini tablet. "I think we're here."

"No way. If we are, shouldn't—"

The Magician walked out of the shadows of the boulder. They all jumped, even Xui Li, though she lit up like a Christmas tree as soon as she saw who it was.

The Magician held out his wrist, touching it where a timepiece would have been. His meaning was clear. "You're late."

Dirk sighed again. Out of the pan and into the fire. Wonderful. Just wonderful.

CHAPTER 14
THE SEVEN CITIES

Time: Dawn

Scene: The Seven Cities of the Jade Empire

"Welcome to the Seven Cities, Samantha." Adam's smile was as large as she had ever seen it, showcasing an array of dazzling white teeth. "Bear witness to one of the eight wonders of the world."

Sam harrumphed.

Adam gave her a look that was half-sympathetic, half-patronizing. "I told you it would be foolhardy to try and escape. It's unfair for you to be upset with Nana. She's a loyal subject of the Empire; she was merely doing her duty."

Sam still refused to speak or even glance in Adam's direction.

"Gōng Zhǔ," said Misaka tentatively. "At least look to the

horizon. The Valley of the Jadian Sun is a marvel that few, even those of the Empire, are privileged enough to see."

Sam exhaled deeply. She had to admit the silent treatment was getting old and only seemed to be having an effect on one person: herself. She leaned her head against the window, reliving the moment she ran after Nana back on the Josephites' ship. She knew it couldn't be that easy. The scream had sent her into a panic. The prospect that Nana was being attacked was too much to bear. Sam had burst through the door to see...Nana bowing respectfully in front of Adam and a group of his Mogui. Sam had come to a screeching halt, jaw dropped.

"It appears you are correct, my dear lady," said Adam, gazing down at the prone Nana. "It seems that I may have misjudged the validity of your story."

"Yes, my—"

"You deserve a reward for your show of loyalty," yelled Adam, making much more noise than was necessary.

Adam snapped his fingers, and a Mogui soldier dropped a gold bar in front of the woman. Nana gawked and picked up the gold.

"You are dismissed. Speak to no one about this."

Nana hurried from the room, catching Sam's eye as she left. She had the decency to look mildly guilty for her betrayal.

The travel over the next week was concurrently wondrous and obnoxious. Once they reached the Empire's airspace, there was less paranoia and fewer rules. The guards became more comfortable, regular soldiers weren't so rigid, and even Sam's handmaidens weren't so standoffish. The change was a pleasant one, and while Sam was still furious with Adam for his little ploy on the boat, she grew more contented with the time she was spending with the Mogui and the service staff. Sam allowed herself to relax a bit. Was she still scared? Of course. Was it still insane that she was there in the first place? Absolutely. Did she have any idea why she was there? Nope. But something about the Jadian landscape calmed her fears and steadied her nerves. Ultimately, she decided that, for the moment, she was along for the ride. So she might as well enjoy it.

That is when Sam stopped talking and started listening. She listened and learned.

For example, Sam learned about the subtle differences in the military rankings. The Mogui were one of the most elite units in the Jadian military. They were highly educated, highly trained, and Misaka hinted, highly altered through some sort of secret and dangerous means. Sam also learned from Chen that Mogui often traveled with lesser units for support. These units acted as computer, guard, and medic supports for the two main Mogui forces, Mogui Light Ops and Mogui Heavy Ops. The Mogui Mediums, as they were called, rank and prestige was above that of the regular military but were often looked down upon by the ranks of senior Mogui. The Mogui wasn't the only group she learned about, either. Detail on top of detail was given to her; Sam just soaked it in. In that week of traveling, she learned and took in more about the Jadian military than was in the databases of the UWC's head of military intelligence. And all Sam had to do was participate in girl talk. It did not last, however; after a while, Chen and Misaka caught on and refused to say more when Sam broached that particular subject again. She decided not to push her luck.

It wasn't like the handmaidens stopped talking to her, though. They talked of their home provinces, their education, and their ultimate desire to enter the Madam's formal mystic training. Sam was baffled by the mention of mystics but was too comfortable with the conversation at the time to ask. There was simply so much to see and take in.

There was another major change when Sam and her escorts entered the People's Republic, which was the main province of the Jade Empire. There, within the rolling hills and sprawling valleys, was the seat of the Empire, the Seven Cities. When it finally sunk in that they were going to the famed Capital of the Empire, she could hardly contain herself. She was way more excited than she would have liked to admit, especially to Adam. Her attempts to spite him, make him angry, or simply dissuade him from coming in proximity to her were all for naught. Adam was his regular super-calm, super-handsome self, and despite her anger with him, Sam found she was warming to his attempts to cozy up to her.

Adam, Sam, Misaka, and Chen all sat in the forward

observation chamber of a luxury hovercraft that floated soundlessly on the crest of a valley stretching for kilometers in all directions. There was nothing in the valley but greenery and forest barely visible in the pre-dawn light.

Sam finally answered Misaka's plea. "I'm not trying to be stubborn." She shot Adam a calculating dirty look. "I would look and behold the Seven Cities in all its greatness, Misaka. But the only things I see are trees and grass."

That wasn't entirely true. There were roads that meandered over the uneven terrain in strange and unnatural patterns with no real rhythm to the way they spread across the valley.

Misaka, Chen, and Adam just smiled and watched. Irritated, Sam started to ask why they were smirking when the darkness of night suddenly receded, and the first light of the yawning sun crept over the mountainside.

Then something incredible happened. The direct light of the sun touched the epicenter of the valley...and a city, a mystical, fantastical city appeared.

Sam's jaw dropped as Adam's smirk grew to epic widths.

"Samantha Montgomery, behold the most mystical city in the world. The center of industry, art, and forward thinking, the beacon of the east, the lighted candle of the mystics, the Capital of the Jade Empire and the home of the Jadian Sun. Let me be the first to welcome you, Sam. Welcome to the Seven Cities of Jade."

———

Sam remained speechless for the duration of the trek to the hill just outside the entrance of the first of the Seven Cities. It wasn't until they reached the city that her curiosity sufficiently overcame her awe, and she was able to ask: "How—"

"Does the city remain invisible?" finished Adam, as if he were simply waiting for Sam to ask the question. "Each of the Seven Cities has a specially designed displacement shield. The technology behind it is very advanced and highly secretive. There are only a few people within the Empire who know how the shield works. The oscillation shields that the Mogui wear are a scaled-down version of the technique, but not as advanced. After the Great War, the Sun dynasty had to come up with a way to protect the epicenter of the Empire or else be wiped out by a single disassemble warhead. Facing a similar problem, the UWC came up with its StarWar Initiative. The Empire's solution for the Seven Cities was the dome. There are seven domes, each with a displacement shield that runs with the concentric layers of the city—"

"Concentric?" questioned Sam, not following. "What do you mean the concentric layers of the city?"

Adam nodded in the direction of the city. "You'll see in just a moment."

It wasn't a moment. It wasn't even an hour; it was much longer than either a moment or an hour, though Sam could not have said how. As soon as the group cleared the hill, the road changed from desolate to chaotic. People by the bucketful flooded the neatly groomed streets, some moving away from the now-visible outer wall of the Seven Cities, but most walking towards a massive opening in the wall. They neared the outer wall and its gate after what seemed like hours of wading through the seas of people.

"We'll need to walk from here," said Adam, placing a green beret on his head. "The hovercraft will have to be searched by the Line Troopers before it can enter."

"Line Troopers?" Sam muttered through fabric drawn over her face. Misaka and Chen were trying to force some sort of veiled shawl over her head. "What are Line Troops?"

Adam examined a highly ornate plasma scimitar. He placed the weapon on his belt. "Yes, the Line Troops are a sort of city police for the outer four cities of the Seven Cities. They aren't on the best of terms with the Mogui, so they have a tendency to dominate each other whenever placed in a position of power over the other."

Sam sighed through the fabric. Perfect. Knowing her luck, she would get pulled into some sort of Jadian Special Forces pissing match. "You have no need to worry, Sam. The Line Troops will not detain us."

"And how do you know that?" Sam's head popped through the veiled shawl just in time to see Adam smirk.

"Because I'm here. Shall we?"

Without another word, Adam, with three of the hulking

Mogui behind him, exited the hovercraft and was swallowed up by the sun.

———

Adam was true to his word. The Line Troops didn't bother them. They barely looked at them and hardly made any attempt to search them. The gate of the outer wall should have taken hours to get through; there were hundreds, if not thousands, of people standing in line to get into the city. The hordes took one look at the Mogui and, more specifically, Adam, and moved immediately to one side, bowing and kneeling in an odd show of fealty. Sam tried to stop once or twice to talk to one of the citygoers out of a simple sense of curiosity but was urged rather forcefully to move along. Her annoyance with this behavior was short-lived. Once they entered the gate, it was a whole new world, the massive outer wall a backdrop for miles and miles of homes, shops, restaurants, stadiums, office buildings, and the like. The buildings, design, and urban planning were all normal enough, just as one might see in any affluent city in the UWC. There was a stark and obvious difference, however. Everything from the buildings to the road shimmered with a silvery white hue, like the whole city was built out of finely glossed steel.

"The Palladium Ring," whispered Adam as if reading Sam's mind, locating an incorrect assumption, and proceeding to correct that assumption. "It's not my favorite ring, but sheer magnitude does certainly impress."

"You can't be serious," announced Sam, cottoning on. "Are you trying to tell me that the whole city is—"

"Made out of palladium?" Adam smiled at her. "That was what you were going to say, was it not?"

Sam scowled at him through her veil as Adam's smile became disgustingly self-satisfied. "No, Sam, I'm not telling you that the whole city is made out of palladium. It's just covered in a palladium leaf. All the rings are."

Sam didn't know what to say to this.

"Wait until you see the blue silver of Osmium Ring, Gōng Zhǔ—"

"Misaka." Adam spoke sharply. "Be careful. We do not know who is listening."

Misaka's face looked like she was going to die of embarrassment. Sam didn't understand Adam's sharp tone. She started to ask, but just like before, as they prepared to exit the hovercraft, Adam was already in motion. At least this time he beckoned them to follow.

"We have to be prepared. The higher-ups know of our return, but the general populace does not. There will be much rejoicing. Still, we should proceed with caution. Your arrival indicates an upheaval of the status quo. This always upsets those in control of that status quo."

Adam looked back over his shoulder and leveled an eye at Sam.

Sam cocked an eyebrow in response. "If you say so."

Adam led Sam, Misaka, Chen, and their Mogui guards to a platform where hundreds of people stepped into and out of large, sleek carriers, which appeared to be a sort of monorail system. The multi-rail display above the cars lit up a stream of numbers, the number changing as people got on and off the cars, which then took off at high speed. Sam saw individual cars echoing the Palladium Ring's motif, with the same whitish silver metal coating the car and reflecting the noonday sun. Palladium was not the only coating, however. Sam asked the question.

"Do those—"

"Cars' plating correspond with their individual rings?" answered Adam, again anticipating her question. "Correct. The cars don't stay together once they leave the station—they go to their respective rings."

"Just to be clear, when you say ring, you mean city?"

Adam laughed. "Of course you're not familiar with the slang; yes, Ring and City are used interchangeably here."

Sam nodded. "Got ya."

Adam picked up his thought thread. "As I said, the cars don't stay together once they leave the station—they go to their respective rings, and the rail lines to different rings bypass the main traveling routes for faster and easier access."

Sam studied the cars. The different colors were fantastical, like she had stepped into a children's book. It was then that she noticed...

"Adam, what about those black cars?"

Adam turned to see at least twelve cars slow, many people disembarking, and many, many others getting on the black cars, which were noticeably less crowded.

Adam watched as one of the large black cars zoomed out of its stall. "The first four rings are open to the public. Anyone can move in and out of those rings with minimal security after their initial inspection at the outer gate of the Seven Cities."

Adam pointed to the black cars on a lone monorail just in front of them. "Those three cars go directly to the three center city rings—the Gold, Platinum, and Green Rhodium Rings. Those three rings are different. You have to go through vigorous screening to enter the Gold Ring, and through screening, background checks, and brain scanning to enter the Platinum. You can't get into the Green Rhodium Ring without a specific invite from the Emperor and a mystic's divination from the Madam herself."

A mystic's divination? Sam shuddered. That did not sound pleasant.

"So where are we going?" asked Sam apprehensively.

Adam smiled. "Right to the center of it all, Sam. We're going to the city of Green Rhodium, to the palace of the Emperor himself."

"I thought you said that we couldn't get through without an invite and a divination from a mystic?"

Adam's smile widened. "I did say that. Guess where we're going next?"

———

For the next hour or so, Sam, Adam, Misaka, and Chen zoomed through the seven cities in a mono-car plated in green rhodium and accented in gold and platinum. For the duration of the trip, Sam's mouth hung open like some sort of flytrap. The rumors that she had heard about the Seven Cities were not only true; they were an understatement.

Sam had dared not envision, even in her wildest fantasies, a place like the Seven Cities. Each straightaway in the mono-car was a wonder, each turn a giddy sensation. The place was simply magnificent. There was no other way to describe it. It wasn't simply the technology on display—of which, from security to shopping, there was plenty—that so amazed her. The Seven Cities were run on technological marvels like the DragonNet, a fully integrated Sentient Intelligence that policed, governed, served, and surveyed the citizens of the Seven Cities. But that wasn't it. And it wasn't the precious metal coating of the various rings, either. Palladium, Osmium, Indium, Ruthenium, Gold, Platinum, and Green Rhodium: the building material of each city was probably worth more than her entire province. What really caught Sam's attention, what really touched her center being, was the feeling of familiarity. Like she had been here before. But that was impossible. People didn't just come to the Seven Cities as if they were some sort of vacation spot. Yet Sam felt a connection; she couldn't lie to herself.

After an extended time on the mono-car, the group disembarked and proceeded to a sort of open carriage, which took them to a massive rhodium-covered temple surrounded by Japanese cypress.

Sam paused. Japanese cypress? Now how did she know that?

Sam looked down and found that she was gripping Misaka's hand. Misaka gently put her other hand over Sam's.

"A remnant of my country." Misaka gestured to the temple. "It was moved in full after the Seven Cities were founded. This is one of the grander shrines from Nihon."

Nihon, or Japan, another large, mostly homogenous country off the east coast of China.

Sam paused again. OK, that was weird.

"Sam, I'm sorry, but we'll have to part here."

Adam's touch on her shoulder pulled her attention back.

Her response was flustered, like she had done something wrong. "Um—yes—I would like—where are you going, Adam?"

"I have matters I have to attend to for the State. I've been away too long. I trust that Misaka and Chen can keep you company?"

Sam nodded.

"Then I will—"

Adam broke off at the look on Sam's face.

"Sam, I'd be interested to know what you were thinking."

Adam caressed her shoulder with a soft touch.

She managed a weak smile. "A penny for my thoughts?"

"What's a penny?"

Sam's smile faltered. "Nothing. It's an old saying that Richard and I used to have. Pennies were a part of the currency back in the old United States. 'A penny for your thoughts.' It was a saying, that's all."

"Ahh," answered Adam, apparently amused. "I would pay a penny for your thoughts."

Sam giggled. "Unfortunately, I don't have more than one to give."

"Well then, how about a Jadian Meydal? I can assure you it's worth more than your penny."

Sam laughed again. "I think I can take that deal."

Adam sat down next to her, dismissing Misaka and Chen with a flick of his wrist.

He adjusted his position. "Well, Sam. What do you got?"

Sam sighed. "I think you know, Adam."

"I could probably guess, yes."

"Adam," Sam almost pleaded. "What am I doing here?"

Adam stood up and flicked the Meydal into her hand. "I'll tell you. But not now. You're about to meet the Madam, and trust me—you won't want anything else to focus on."

Sam frowned at this pronouncement. "Sam, don't worry. We've got some exciting stuff. First the Madam, and then we go to the Jadian Sun—and trust me. That is not something you want to miss."

CHAPTER 15

PLAN OF ATTACK

Time: Late at night

Scene: An unknown location

"Red One, this is Red Leader. Are we a go?"

"Red Leader, we are a go."

"Red Two, this is Red Leader, are we a go?"

"Ready to boogie, Red Leader."

Teddy shook his head, irritated. "Boogie"? Seriously?

"Eye in the sky, this is Red Leader. Are we clear?"

"Red Leader, this is Eye, we are a go in ten."

Teddy turned back and gave the thumbs-up followed by a five-five on the same hand to his four-man team. They caught the meaning: *We are good to go in ten seconds. 10, 9, 8, 7, 6, 5, 4, 3, 2, 1…*

Teddy pulled down his infra-red. It was time to hunt.

———

Palin checked the guard on her combat bow and her stock of specialty arrows. The others were using kinetic round machine pistols, as the low-light rounds were less conspicuous than most other kinds of energy-based weaponry. But Palin liked the classics. The combat bow was completely silent and almost totally immune to energy detectors. In stealth situations, it was the ideal weapon, especially with her variety pack of utility arrows she always kept with her. She also had two old-fashioned machine pistols strapped to her upper thighs for when things got nasty. Old, loud, and hard to fire as they were, with the modifications Coolidge had made and the specialty exploding ammunition Adams had concocted, she was ready for this fight.

"I'm in, Teddy," said a voice from directly behind her. Palin glanced over her shoulder. Cain, the Red team's combat hacker, was typing furiously on a holo-interface superimposed in front of him. "I'm creating a thirty-second window. This is the only chance we'll get. I've never seen a firewall coding so advanced. I'll be locked out after this. So make it count. Move in ninety seconds...."

Cain went quiet as Teddy touched his comm. "Eye in the sky—are we clear? We move in ninety."

"Negative, Red Leader, negative, the path is not clear. Thermals in sight."

Teddy grabbed the tiny marble-sized ball cam from his

cargo pocket, twisted it on, and tossed it so it bounced around the corner and rolled to a stop.

"Count?"

"Three tangos."

Teddy swore as the three guards came into view on the small screen strapped to his arm.

Cain whispered, "Red Leader, we aren't going to get another shot. Window starts in forty-five seconds."

Just then, two of the guards walked out from around the building. At least they didn't have dogs with them.

Teddy swore again. What should he do? If they were seen, it was over. The guards would alert S&D and Containment, and they would all be dead. Creating the hole in the monitoring system was just as important. The door to the courtyard was their only chance to breach MESA's defenses and still have a chance of surviving. The impenetrable layer of technology that defended MESA was weakest in that courtyard. They had to get there without being seen and without tipping off the guards. Teddy slapped his comm.

"Eye in the sky, engage targets as they wrap the corner. You get the lead, Palin, and I'll mop up."

Teddy didn't have to ask her. She knew by instinct. Both her bow and his suppressed tournament-style .22-caliber magnetic round rifle had to be used. If all three shots could be timed before the window opened, they had a chance. But it was still a gamble. The cover fire was far enough away that the sound would melt into the nothingness of the valley, but the kinetic rounds Eye in the Sky used lit up like a narcotic-filled firefly when fired. The distance would diminish the trace, but would it be enough?

Luckily, the third guard just then emerged from around the corner. He was smoking an old-fashioned pipe with a strange substance that let out a sort of purple smoke.

"Palin, Eye in the Sky, fire on my mark...three, two, one!"

All three marksmen let loose as close together as could be expected. Even though the .832 kinetic round from the hovering SkyEagle was shot from over two kilometers away, the supersonic projectile connected first and made a huge mess as it tore apart its target. The other two guards did not have time to be shocked as both were impaled at the throat at nearly the same moment. Palin's arrow and Teddy's .22 caliber magnetic round were not as spectacular as the kinetic round, but they did the job effectively, dropping each of the guards with complete silence. It was actually quite amazing.

"Red Leader, the window is open. You got thirty seconds. Move!"

Teddy and his team sprinted to one of the outlying buildings in MESA's main complex, then proceeded to one of the few back doors in the complex. It was difficult to find; the exit blended into the stone of the building. A hidden keypad, a stolen passcode, and they were in. The intelligence Adams had gathered was dead-on, and they quickly found themselves in the reaches of a well-illuminated hall. Teddy threw up a fist, and the group immediately ceased moving. The fist changed to two fingers, which pointed to the right flank. Palin and Huntsman took up the covering position. When he was sure they were alone, Teddy touched his comm.

"Blue Leader, this is Red Leader. Do you copy?"

"Red Leader, this is Blue Leader, I copy."

"Are you and your team in position?"

"Affirmative."

"Then execute op protocol Three in t-minus two minutes. We need that much time to get to the courtyard."

"Heavy weapons are primed and ready to go. We'll bring the rain."

Teddy smiled at the old U.S. Army reference. "Bring it, Harding. Bring it hard."

"Hey, Teddy."

"Yeah, Harding?"

"We'll see you in hell."

"Yeah, I'll race ya."

The line went dead.

Teddy motioned to his team, who fell into line, ready to move down the hallway. They proceeded, stopping periodically to check the cross-sectional hallways in the seemingly endless facility. Slowly and quietly, though not as slowly or quietly as any of them would have liked, the team moved towards their goal in a precise and deliberate fashion.

The end of the hall was dark, and the only sound was the hum of some internal system not relevant to the op. The group took a sharp right, remaining in formation in case they encountered any guards or scientists. Down two more hall-ways and after another couple of right turns, they found their target, just as Adams said they would. Through a massive wall of very clear glass, Teddy saw a large, open courtyard stretching some two hundred meters through the heart of MESA's facility.

———

An explosion ripped through the air, sending tremors and vibrations through the entire facility. The battle outside had started. Teddy moved the water-tamping shape-charge strips into place, running them along the cracks of the door leading to the courtyard.

"Fan out. We've got about a hundred meters to move. Stagger the movement so we can avoid getting our position flanked. Protect Palin—she is to deliver payload, breach, and collect the package. Internal security will be on us, so stay sharp."

Teddy stepped back a good distance from where he placed the explosives. "We got ninety seconds. Go."

The alarm sounded, and they heard the clamor of foot-steps coming towards them. Teddy didn't waste any more time. He pushed the button to detonate the explosives. The windows shattered, sending shards of glass and chunks of metal into the courtyard, and a back blast of water into the hall. When the smoke cleared, they no longer heard footsteps.

They entered the courtyard, fanning out into flanking positions and scanning for any hostiles that might have been preemptively alerted to their presence. More alarms sounded after little more than a few meters into the yard. Teddy cursed. Laser trip wires—now MESA knew their exact location. He should have been more careful.

The Red team watched in horror as giant gun turrets rose from the ground, fixing menacingly in place.

"Grab some cover!" Teddy yelled as he slammed in a different set of rounds for his rifle and pulled on the action. Rolling for cover, he grabbed a cylinder from his belt and twisted the concave copper top. The high-pitched whine of an electromagnetic generator climbed until he could no longer hear it. Peeking around the corner, Teddy lobbed the device at the closest turret. His throw was inaccurate, but the device veered off its initial trajectory and slammed itself into the metal hull of the turret. A second later, the cylinder delivered its payload, melting the copper disc into a high-velocity molten slag of metal which proceeded to rip through the turret's innards. One down.

Palin calmly pulled and nocked an arrow, one of the specialty types that she always kept in reserve for such an occasion. This particular kind of arrow was her favorite, a nasty little concoction called Dragon's Breath. Palin drew and held the bowstring. She waited, adjusting for distance, and fired, letting loose the arrow at the remaining turret. The arrow remained silent until it touched tip to metal. Bright light accompanied the gushing flame, resulting in the complete meltdown of the target and most of the surrounding area.

Palin yelped as Teddy pushed her out of the way of a volley of plasma bolts fired from a group of MESA's internal security force.

"Shasta!" swore Teddy. "They are on us, boys—we need to move!"

He pulled out his fusion-round rifle and returned fire. The high-energy weapon vaporized everything in its path.

"Palin, to the package, it's now or never. We've got to move if we want any chance of getting out of here."

Palin didn't have to be told twice. She slung her bow and pulled out one of her machine pistols and a circular plastic disk. She ran, firing from the hip as often and as accurately as the machine pistol's heavy recoil permitted. She moved evasively, not allowing any machine to corner her and her comrades.

Palin ducked behind a bushel of thickly knotted trees as a gaggle of gunfire ravaged her chosen path.

Teddy and the rest of the Red team advanced, stepping into position to cover Palin's next move. She holstered her machine pistol and sprinted to the far side of the courtyard, ducking, rolling, and dancing as ionized rounds from the turrets and soldiers hailed down around her. She reached the wall and placed the plastic disk in the center of a wall. Quickly, she pulled the four pie-shaped sections of the disc a half meter away from the center, affixing them in an elongated "X" on the wall. She retreated and ducked behind a stone bench.

"Fire in the hole," she whispered. No one could hear her as she pressed the button. The section of the wall vaporized, sending hot steam and water through the wall and out into the courtyard. The moment seemed to last a lifetime for Palin. A giant hole appeared out of the smoking watery mess.

"Cover me," Palin yelled. She charged, running through the perfect oval in the wall.

Once inside, she swung her machine pistols, one in each hand, searching for potential enemies. She saw none, but neither did she see anything else. The place appeared to be empty. Palin's senses were on high alert. The package had to be here. Had their intel been wrong?

Then she saw him, cowering in the back room. Relieved, Palin walked cautiously towards her target. She pulled up a holographic image of Dr. Eli Thurman in her heads-up display while keeping one of her pistols trained on the man. He could be a double or impostor, and she had to make sure. As she neared him, her thumb slowly slid the switch on her pistol that loaded a Neuromuscular Incapacitation Round. If it came down to it, she'd have no qualms about slinging the old man over her shoulder to extract him. When she was little more than a meter from him, Dr. Thurman looked up. Their eyes connected, and their surroundings went quiet. The only emotion she could read in the large brown eyes of the rumpled but still handsome professor was...fear.

Just as she was about to speak, several more massive explosions went off, sending shock waves through the air. She looked back the way she came, realizing that Blue team had to be well into their assault. She had to get Thurman out of here before the fireworks spillover and trapped Red team in the crossfire. Palin returned her attention to Thurman, who was regarding her with fearful, strained eyes.

She did not notice the civilian-issue stun baton in his hand. Thurman stood, faster than she might have expected, and took a wild swing at Palin, whose quick reflexes saved her from what would have been an incapacitating discharge from the stun baton. His haymaker swing enabled Palin to sword-block the professor's blow and step inside of his guard. She maneuvered around him, taking his arm with her.

"I do not have time to explain," she said, wrenching his arm up and behind his back. "I need you to not attack me and listen: We're here to help you get away from MESA at the request of someone who doesn't want to see you used as a tool. You have three seconds to decide if you want to come with me or die right here and now."

For the briefest of moments, Palin thought he would resist her. The threat had been an idle one; she really didn't want to hurt him and did not think she could kill him in cold blood. Luckily, she did not have to, as she felt his body relax.

Palin unwrenched his arms and attempted a warm smile. "I know that this is hard to believe, but I'm here to help."

"My dear lady," he said, his voice calm. "You had me at 'get away from MESA.'"

Just then, three soldiers interrupted their tender moment, two entering the laboratory through Palin's self-made exit, and the other one from an adjacent door, which presumably led to the rest of the complex. Palin took aim, depressed the trigger, and developed a sick feeling as her ammunition found its mark. The soldiers did not stand a chance.

Palin tried to control her queasiness as she offered her hand to Thurman. "It's now or never, Professor. We won't get a second chance at this."

He hesitated slightly, but then thrust out his hand towards Palin's.

Two more soldiers entered the building through the gap in the wall, catching Palin out of position with her machine pistol hanging uselessly at her side. The MESA soldiers raised their guns to their shoulders and pointed them directly at Palin. She swiveled, raising her pistols in an attempt to meet the threat.

She could already tell...she wasn't going to make it.

But before either the soldiers or Palin could fire, there was a crash, and the highly recognizable echo of shattering glass flooded the space. Palin saw something drop at the feet of the soldiers and instantly, a strange purple gas formed and stretched out, as if it wanted nothing more than simply to envelop the soldiers with its purple embrace.

Unexpectedly, the soldiers did not fire; they did not even stay. At the first sight of smoke, they turned tail and ran, not even bothering to look back. Palin shot the man an inquiring look. He smiled.

"I'll explain later, I promise you."

They both stepped out into the courtyard, looked to the right...and saw the barrel of a gun. One of the internal security forces was pointing a plasma pistol directly at Palin's head. She tried to move out of the way, her arm raised instinctively in an attempt to deflect the trajectory. She was not going to make it. Palin watched as the security officer depressed the trigger. She felt searing pain, and everything went black.

———

I'm dead, I'm dead, I'm dead, I'm dead, was the only thing that ran through Palin's mind, but wait...that wasn't right...she... was....

Palin ripped off her Sensory Integration Unit as she realized she was holding her breath and was still able to exhale. Stupid visual training software was so real. She hated it.

"Sorry to say this, Palin, but you're dead."

The details of the scenario flooded Palin's mind. The deliberately altered thought patterns, neural simulators, and blockers returned to normal and allowed her thought processes to function uninhibited with perfect recollection. Palin was not happy with that training exercise.

"Oh, as if that was a fair variation of the conflict—a court-yard? You're not brickin' serious! There is no way that MESA has a courtyard in the middle of their headquarters. And even if I could possibly believe that they did, there is no way that they have automatic gun turrets. That was an unfair iteration."

Palin could see the operations officer trying to hold back his laughter. "Don't look at me, Palin. I just run the variants I'm told. If it makes you feel any better, you aren't the only one who died."

Palin glowered. It didn't make her feel better at all.

Teddy neared her. "We died just as you entered the lab. Got flanked by some of the soldiers—we didn't stand a chance."

Palin scratched at her nose. "I wasn't the first? I could have sworn I saw you still fighting as I made my run."

"No, Gingrich and Romney went down right after you entered. I died trying to pull them back. It happened so fast."

Palin, Teddy, and the rest of the Red team made their way to the debriefing room, running into Blue team just before the entrance.

Apparently, Blue team didn't fare any better.

Harding and Teddy were already deep in discussion. Teddy touched his nose. "We'll need to take more men in.

We've been completely wiped out in eighty percent of the variants we've tested—not odds that I'm particularly looking forward to."

Harding agreed. "I'll follow your lead. Maybe if we ask Washington and Adams together—"

"You don't need more men. You need better planning and a tighter time variable, and most of all, you and your teams need more discipline."

The voice, which was magnified, sounded soft but managed to carry across the room. Richard's holo-projected image stood waiting for them. "You're attacking the home base of MESA. They have large contingencies of both S&D and Containment there. If you don't execute mission protocol perfectly, you're all dead."

Harding shot Richard a nasty look and whispered to Teddy out of the side of his mouth, "I hate that guy."

Palin agreed. Richard was a friend of Teddy's and knew that Teddy had gone in under orders because of MESA's suspicious activity. Little did he know that the sole survivor of Washington's Culper Ring, the specialty unit handpicked and trained by Washington only to be almost completely wiped out by the Magician, was stationed at the Academy City as well. Palin had yet to figure out why.

She knew it had to do with that Sam girl. Teddy's odd behavior said as much, but Palin couldn't figure out what was so special about Samantha. Teddy was one of the greatest specialty fighters in the Republican Nation; he was brilliant and deadly—and handsome, like no one else she had ever met. And then there was Richard, who, or so the rumor went, had personally taken on a contingent of MESA's Containment and S&D forces and lived to tell about it—no small feat. He was also the only person from his unit to survive the encounter with the Magician. Palin didn't know a single person, hadn't even heard of a single person who could boast that particular accomplishment. It was a well-known fact: To encounter the Magician was to encounter death, no ifs, ands, or buts about it. But this Richard fellow...

"Palin, are you listening?"

Palin realized that she had zoned off in the middle of a debriefing. Not good.

"Sorry, sir, I wasn't paying—"

"Attention? Of course you weren't, Palin, and that's why you got your team killed in the last sim. You are reckless. You moved with little to no backup and without having the exit secured. You'd better shape up or you're going to be off this mission."

Palin felt her stomach lurch. "Yes, sir."

"Now let's review your point movement...."

Palin glared at Richard, a skinny no-nonsense killer, and thought, *I think I liked you better when you were fat.*

CHAPTER 16
DISTRACTION

Time: Late morning

Scene: Jungle in the Jade Empire

Dirk's dream world was a lovely place, filled with wine and women, tranquility and treasure, discordance and distraction. It was a world where Xui Li flirted with him in the morning and Rona hung on his every word in the evening. Rona making her way into his dream world actually surprised him. She was a beauty, with her dark hair, smoldering eyes, and old Scottish accent, but she was too smart for her own good. Dirk liked his women dumb; they were a lot easier that way. Xui Li, for example, was an eastern beauty of exquisite stock, seriously rich, pure and untouched by any man, and dumber than a Gangan house pet...every man's dream.

Yeah, right. Inexperienced women were generally just

exhausting. The learning curve until things actually got fun—or at least *interesting*—was astronomical.

Then again, training Xui Li in his way of doing things held certain possibilities but was inherently problematic. Despite her repeated, thoroughly welcome, and incredibly bold advances in his dreams, the real-life Xui Li maintained her absurd crush on the Magician of all people. The bone-chilling figure—and of course, Dirk knew him to be bone-chilling because the man wrapped in black oozed "assassin" like some sort of pheromone—had completely ignored the advances of the princess, who somehow envisioned some sort of fated, fairytale encounter of forbidden love, which was ridiculous. If there was such a thing as fate or gods, those cosmic entities had long forgotten this hellhole. More than likely, there never were such entities, nor any higher power or greater human purpose beyond existence. Anything else was just fantasy. That may have been part of the reason that Dirk was attracted to Xui Li; she still held those delusions of far-off places, daring sword fights, princes in disguise, and faith in a creator. Yes, it would be nice if he could believe again.

Pain erupted in his side and then soon passed. He didn't know where it came from, but it sure was obnoxious. The pain flared up on the other side, followed by the sensation of being in water. He was drowning. He was in the middle of the Yellow River and sinking to the bottom. What a way to go!

"Dirk, if you don't get up, I'm going to kick you again."

Dirk sat up and felt distinctly...wet. Apparently, in her haste to awaken him, Rona had liberally used the contents of her canteen. Perfect.

"Was that really necessary?" asked Dirk, holding up his hands in a questioning gesture. "I thought I was drowning in the Yellow River because of you."

Rona busied herself breaking down camp. "I know. You talk in your sleep."

He did not know that. He had never stayed with a woman long enough for her to comment. He wondered how much she had heard...

"Come on, Dirk," urged Rona, tossing him a breakfast bar, "we've got terrain to cover and the day ain't getting any younger."

"Sure. Are Xui Li and—" Dirk broke off. Xui Li and the Magician were nowhere to be seen. This wasn't out of the ordinary for the man in black; the assassin usually scouted ahead. But Xui Li missing too?

"Rona, where is Xui Li? We have to find her—"

"Relax, Dirk, Xui Li left with the Magician over an hour ago."

Dirk stopped his frantic search. "They what?"

"They left—"

"I know what you said, but why? Where did they go together?"

Rona shrugged. "Don't know—Adams' orders. You'll have to take it up with him."

Dirk cursed. Xui Li, his Xui Li, was gone, traveling with probably the most interesting person on the planet. How could he compete with that?

Dirk felt his anger flare. "Rona, get Adams on the sat com, now."

She didn't argue.

The com took an unusually long time to pick up.

"Rona. Dirk. What can I do for you this morning?" Adams looked distinctly disheveled, as if he had spent the morning running from place to place in an attempt to fulfill an unending list of to-dos, like some sort of housewife.

This thought made Dirk laugh. Housewife...that was funny.

Wait...stop laughing. You're angry.

"Where are the Magician and Xui Li?" asked Dirk. "You told me that they'd be escorting us all the way to the site."

"That was a lie," said Adams, cracking his neck in a nonchalant manner. "The truth is that Xui Li and the Magician have different mission priorities. It was important for you to travel as you did to this point, but that's no longer necessary. Hence, Xui Li and the Magician left."

"Dirk, relax," said Rona, touching his arm and running her thumb over the taut skin of his bicep. "We don't need the Magician or Xui Li. We are perfectly capable of taking care of ourselves from here on out."

"Listen, Dirk," said Adams in his infuriatingly calm manner. "I don't mean to be the bearer of bad news, but you should've heard the conversation I had with the Magician just to convince him to allow you and Rona to travel with him. I hate to break it to you, my friend, but the world's greatest assassin finds you obnoxious."

Dirk glowered. "Even if that were true—which is just ridiculous, because who on earth could ever find me obnoxious—that's not the point. The point is that you promised me he would escort us to the site, so you lied to me. I can forgive you for lying to me. I lie all the time. It's part of being a relic hunter, but I cannot forgive you for allowing Xui Li to go off with the Magician. Absolutely unacceptable."

Silence and surprise bordering on awkward coated them like mist. Rona was too shocked for words, and Adams' eyes mirrored his amusement.

"He's an assassin, is he not? How do I know he's not going to kill her and dump her body in the river?"

"Well, for one, there aren't any rivers on the way to... wherever it is they are going."

Dirk's eyes narrowed. *I saw that, Adams,* Dirk mused to himself. *Don't think good old Dirk didn't notice.* The Magician had some sort of mission in the Empire, and Xui Li was going to help him.

"Where are the Magician and Xui Li going, John?"

The smile faded from Adams' face. "Sorry, Dirk, top secret. On a need-to-know basis. Besides, you and Rona have other things to accomplish right now."

So basically, Dirk doesn't need to know, Dirk thought it but held his tongue. He changed tactics.

"The Magician and Xui Li go off on their own, and you want Rona and me to continue. I didn't ask this before, but while we're talking about 'need-to-know' items, what's the real reason you need this particular site surveyed by yours truly?"

Dirk carefully studied the reactions of Adams, and to a lesser extent, Rona. He continued, "This trip into the inner provinces of the Empire seems stupid and reckless. Don't get me wrong. I love reckless as much as the next nitwit. But I'd like to know why. There aren't any indications that D-list items are here. At one point, there were over a billion and a half people in this nation—"

"India," interrupted Adams matter-of-factly, "yes, I'm familiar with it."

"Then you know that any chance there was of finding D-list items here was lost centuries ago. Something that valuable remaining untouched for that long? Not possible."

"I'm not sure I agree with that assessment," Adams busied himself off-screen, presumably with an interface of some sort. "The last D-list item was found in Sanzarubi, which, as you know, is the home of one of the oldest recorded civilizations in history."

Dirk sneered. "Egypt never had the amount of people that India did. Nor did Egypt receive a barrage of disassembled warheads. The items we're looking for are already a long shot. The relics are literally not supposed to exist. Not a single one of the D-list stories starts here. We're talking about a place known for overcrowding, a landscape that received rounds of weapons designed to level mountains—literally, Adams: The entire country was bombed into nothingness— and items that are more myth than fact. I don't see how sending us here helps us. Even if we had an inkling of a D-list item here, odds are it has either been stolen or destroyed. I know you know this. So why are we really here?"

Adams studied Dirk's face momentarily. "You know, Mr. Garrett, ever since I met you, you have never ceased to amaze me. I assure you that the mission protocol here is of utmost importance for our overall goal. You have to get to that site, survey it, and bring back as much information as possible."

Dirk started to protest, but Adams held up his hand. "Remember, Mr. Garrett—you signed up for this. Do as I direct. Adams out."

The com link died.

Rona watched Dirk nervously. He sighed and stood. "You know I don't like that guy, right?"

"Not surprising; nobody likes him. But don't pretend that you aren't impressed by just how slippery he is."

Damn. Rona already knew him way better than she should. "Perhaps. We need to get moving."

Despite the fact that Dirk wanted to punch Adams in the face, as Rona so promptly pointed out, Dirk found it difficult not to be impressed by the man. His intellect, his tactical sense, and his ability to read people were second to none. But who was he? Who was this man who ran this shadowy anti-government establishment with near impunity? He was a hacker, one known all over the world. But there was not an inkling of who he really was. Not a one. And how could he run an organization like the Republicans and remain completely anonymous? Was he that careful? Or was it something else? If Rona was to be believed, and really, Dirk did not have any reason not to believe her, then Adams wasn't fighting for justice or equality, nor was he fighting for the ability to build an all-you-can-eat salad bar where he could get a good old-fashioned bacon salad. But if not for freedom or equality or bacon salads, or whatever catchphrase the Republicans were using, then for what? He was just bored? It couldn't be for nothing—he had to have a reason—but if it wasn't for the Republican mantra, what was it? Obviously, there was no way to find out with the information he had. All of it just stank like a sweaty Gangan. Dirk, since the very beginning of this strange venture, had been so preoccupied with the adventure that Adams offered that he hadn't taken the time to find out what his employer was truly after. He was starting to wonder if that had been a mistake.

So it begged the question: What if Adams was more dangerous than the Empire or the UWC? Dirk laughed inwardly. Ironically, Dirk already knew the answer to that question. Adams was more dangerous than the Empire or the UWC combined. He had tracked him down, caught him, and somehow convinced Dirk—not forced, blackmailed, or tortured, but convinced him—to work for a purpose that Dirk neither knew nor cared much about. Dirk had always thought, even before he had known for sure he was real, that the Magician was the most dangerous person on the planet. He now realized that that was not necessarily the case.

"Dirk, snap out of it," whispered Rona. Dirk roused himself from his brooding and turned to gaze at the Scottish beauty.

"What is it? I was in the middle of some me time."

Rona rolled her eyes. "You can have me time on your own time. You're on Rona's time right now. So snap out of it and look around you."

They were on the crest of what looked to be a three-sided valley. The sight was breathtaking but couldn't be right.

"I don't remember this topography." Rona's voice betrayed the slight panic she was feeling. "I think...I think we might be off course."

Dirk cocked his head in surprise. "You got us lost."

Rona scowled. "You didn't have to say it like that."

"But you did."

"Yes, I did."

"That's why you never let a woman drive."

"What are you talking about?"

"Never mind. It's not a big deal; we just need to—"

Boom.

Dirk and Rona both jumped as the reverberated noise

rained down upon them and the ground shook beneath them. Dirk's first thought was of an earthquake; they had become common in this part of the world after China, the mother country of the Jade Empire, attempted to use old strategic nuclear weapons to trigger volcanic eruptions against the United States and its allies in the last Great War. It was a desperate plan that didn't really work, but it did reposition the tectonic plates, hence all the earthquakes. But Dirk had a feeling that wasn't the case here. The shaking and noise lasted only a moment but were powerful enough that Rona fell on her butt.

"Oh no, how...what—" Rona's voice sounded fearful. "Dirk. I don't think that was an earthquake."

Dirk stepped forward and offered Rona a hand. "Only one way to find out."

Dirk and Rona crept forward. The jungle noise masked any footsteps, as did the continuing booms and shaking in the distance.

"I think you're right," Dirk said to Rona, pulling out a pair of finder specs.

Rona nodded like she knew she was right. "The patrols shouldn't be this far south, especially in the jungle. What are they doing here?"

"Well, we're not sure that they're Jadian," replied Dirk, removing something from his pack. "Rona, you stay here."

He continued up the ridge and peered down into the valley through the lush vegetation. Dirk cursed. Rona was right. The valley floor was crawling with Jadian soldiers. It was just then that he realized that he and Rona were on the side of a mountain and their destination was on the other side of the ridge. With the patrolling Jadians, he and Rona were going to be found if they didn't do something.

Dirk's skin stood, reaching so high that Dirk thought it might salute the oncoming danger. Dirk did not hesitate; he knew that when his skin responded this way, his life was in danger. He hit the ground. Thank Allah he was wearing his camos.

"Xing, what is it that we are looking for?"

Dirk froze. The voice was less than four meters away from him.

"Anything suspicious, Alexander. The captain said that we might be getting some unwanted visitors—"

Screams from a ways off made Dirk's blood run cold, but he was temporarily distracted by sounds coming from what sounded like an old shortwave radio.

"Lock and load, boys. We have an intruder—repeat—intruder found inside the perimeter. Fan out. Check if she's alone."

The soldiers heaved their concussion rifles to their shoulders. They took off, moving quickly towards the sound of the screaming—screaming that Dirk recognized as Rona's.

———

Dirk thought long and hard about his next step. He had two choices. One, he could leave and allow Rona to figure it out on her own. Two, he could rescue her, which sounded dangerous. Dirk was not a fan of dangerous.

Dirk watched the Jadian camp from one of the large redwoods that stretched high from the bottom of the valley. The redwood was not native to this part of the world. He had no idea where this tree came from. But he was thankful for it. It made a great hiding spot and would have made a wonderful treehouse. Too bad it was in the Jade Empire. He considered his problem.

He hated moral quandaries; it wasn't like Dirk was a very moral guy. So gods or fate or whoever was pulling the strings back there should just stop it. He was going to fail the character test every time. The fact was that the prospect of leaving Rona had its merits. The Jadian soldiers would be preoccupied with her and whatever project they had ventured out to the stinking jungle for. It would be easy to sneak past them and head to Adams' silly site. It was really the logical conclusion. Adams might be upset, but really, what could he do? He needed Dirk. He had already proven that. So what was the problem? Why did he find it difficult to simply walk away? Just walk, or in this case, crawl through the mud, away. And why did his stomach feel like it was trying to jump up his throat? Whenever he tried to leave, his stomach kept him there.

So Dirk took this time to think. And think he did. Dirk

thought long and hard about the two options, then he thought about the world. He thought about Rona. He thought about Adams...oh, how he wanted to punch Adams. To go, or not to go, that was the question.

After several futile attempts to move from the spot and move on without her, Dirk relented. He had his answer. He was going to save Rona. Stupid conscience.

————

Dirk could be very stealthy when he wanted. Not that it was difficult in the jungle. The sounds, the smells, the rain, the wildlife were all in such abundance that any noise he could make, short of throwing a fire bomb in the middle of the camp, was fairly minor. Plus, this group of soldiers wasn't particularly disciplined. Sure, they set up their perimeter and patrolled on occasion, but they seemed more interested in gossiping and sleeping. The whole thing bothered Dirk; it felt like the soldiers were trying to lull him into a false sense of security. It wasn't just luck, their lack of discipline, or the fact that they were this far south, either. Something was wrong with these soldiers. But Dirk couldn't seem to place his finger on it.

"I'm tired of waiting."

Dirk froze flat on the ground in one of the few spots shadowed from the spotlights that were cast methodically around the camp. Two soldiers were nearby, rifles swung haphazardly from their shoulders. One was smoking a cigar, pulling deeply from it.

"We've already commenced; now it's just a waiting game."

The first soldier, who incidentally almost stepped on Dirk, fidgeted with his rifle. "It's an obnoxious assignment. Why are we doing this again?"

"You know how the boss is," said the other soldier. "He wants to know the who's who before the shindig gets started."

"That stupid accent of yours is coming through again."

The soldier with the accent laughed, "My accent is sexy. Just ask your mom."

"A mom joke? What are you, ten?"

"That's exactly what your mama asked me. I told her, more like ten and a half."

"Nice."

The soldier with the accent twisted and cracked his back. "Come on, let's finish our rounds. I hate the jungle."

Dirk waited until they were out of earshot. He sat up, still trying his best to remain hidden in the shadows. From his hiding spot, he searched for additional soldiers, his skin going crazy. Something was wrong with this whole situation—he just needed to figure out what. Regardless, it was time for him to get Rona and bug out.

———

"Thank you, Dirk. I appreciate you coming back."

Rona and Dirk, their shoulders almost touching, hiked away from the soldiers. It had not been difficult to find Rona, as they simply kept her tied up in the tent of the group's commander. Given the situation, it had been surprisingly easy for Dirk to release Rona with a quick swipe of the knife. He smiled at her.

"What can I say? I couldn't just leave you. Bad karma. And Fate and I aren't really on the best of terms as it is."

Rona tried to conceal how pleased she was but gave him a burst of a smile that could have lit up a room. "Well, I for one am glad you came back. I wasn't sure that you would."

Dirk gave her a little shove as his face flushed slightly. Rona. She was too cute. Why hadn't he noticed before?

"Come on, we need to get to the site and complete this survey. I can assume those soldiers will notice you're missing after not too long. Let's get there and show Adams how stupid an idea this was."

Rona nodded her head. "Well then, Mr. High Adventure Man, let's get a move on."

It took Rona and Dirk another six hours to reach the site, and it was a delightful journey. The pace, while brisk, was hardly grueling. Dirk tried to move Rona along, but she didn't seem particularly anxious. He had been attempting to figure out why but was coming up blank. She had just been captured by Jadian soldiers. Shouldn't she be more concerned?

Dirk stopped just before they topped another hill. "We're close; the coordinates have the site in a valley just ahead."

Rona nodded. "Let's go and do what we came to do."

They crested the last hill and looked down into an expansive valley of...

"Goats?" Dirk looked at Rona. "Rona, there's nothing here but goats."

CHAPTER 17
TRUE LOVE

Time: Just before dusk

Scene: MagVac train en route to Chengdu in the Jade Empire

Xui Li stared out as the scenery whizzed by the windows of the mono-car train. At speeds approaching the speed of sound, the sections between the small window ports on the Vac-tube blurred together, giving the countryside a slightly shaded look. It was a definite improvement from the almost pitch-black section she endured while traveling under the Bay of Bengal, but still not as good as air transport. Xui Li preferred to travel by air, but the Magician had insisted on using the MagVac; something about fewer security checks. She had ridden it once before when she was younger, and back then, the information vid she watched had intrigued her. She was fascinated by how the MagVac used electromagnetic

propulsion within a vacuum tube and how the train's aerody-
namic design, combined with the reduced atmosphere inside
the tube, allowed it to race all over the Empire at incredible
speeds. Of course, the vid always touted the importance of
the Empire's biofuel generators, making the MagVac not only
an inexpensive public transportation system but energy effi-
cient as well. She remembered how the Empire's propaganda
used to bother her a lot as a child. It just rubbed her the
wrong way. It didn't anymore, not since she was now a part of
said propaganda. She had also stopped feeling intrigued by
science and how things worked. She was a Jadian princess,
after all. She had more important things to ponder.

Xui Li returned her thoughts to the terrain speeding past,
and inevitably they drifted to the mysteriously wonderful
man she was traveling with. She thought back to their trek
across the jungle and how incredibly sexy she found his
macho outdoorsman skills. His tight-fitting black clothes
accentuated his ripped physique, and while she had to admit
his insistence on the creepy faceless mask was a small setback,
what she saw when it came off on the outskirts of the city was
well worth the wait.

The man in black had led her to an outcropping of rocks
just beyond the city border. There, he *magically* produced a
new set of clothes for both of them, in addition to a standard
travel case. While she did not get to see the Adonis undress—
and not because she didn't try to peek—once out of his black
fatigues and clothed in a sleek business suit, he was a picture

of perfection. Sun-bleached blond hair hung just in front of his bold blue eyes, while strong cheekbones accentuated tanned skin and a firm jaw.

She assumed that he must be in some sort of disguise, but there was no way to hide those strong male features of his with makeup. Even with the suit on, she could see the athletic build of the man, and soon realized that every woman they passed on the way to the MagVac station did as well. Xui Li had tried to keep herself right at the side of the Magician as they walked through the crowds, if only to send a message to the sirens around her that he was off-limits. But just like in the jungle, he seemed to have an almost supernatural ability to flow through the crowds. She, on the other hand, being used to crowds moving out of her way, found herself trying to catch up to him most of the time.

Once onboard the train, the sly peeks from other women only seemed to increase. She returned her fair share of glares at them, but it did not seem to affect the Magician in any way. The man was stoic and rigid, yet after watching him for a while, she saw how his eyes were constantly taking in what was around them. Rather than it looking like he was intentionally on a recon mission, his sly vigilance blended in perfectly with his demeanor, never seeming obvious or purposeful. His whole super-spy coolness merely stoked the growing infatuation she was feeling towards him. It had only taken her that first hour of the trip to firmly commit to herself that one way or another, she was going to land that fish. After all, she was a princess. None of the other cows on the train had anything near her status.

Despite that status, however, the Magician booked them in the business-class section of the train instead of the more private first-class cars. He hadn't exactly *asked* her where she wanted to stay for the trip; it was more like he *told* her where they would be for the five-hour journey. Their early discussions had mainly consisted of normal small talk: which part of the Empire they were in, which other parts of the Empire each had visited, and the like. In spite of her comments about how striking his eyes were or how roguish his wind-swept hair looked, the conversation never moved past the mundane.

Currently, he was using the facilities; thus, she was left with the scenery and planning her next move. She glanced from the window only to see the handsome man sitting quietly across from her, reading something on his interface.

That was the one thing, besides his stubbornness about giving in to her charms, that she just could not get used to: the man moved like a ghost. First, he was there, then he was gone, then he was back again—all without making a single noise. No wonder they called him the Magician.

"We will reach Chengdu in just under two hours," he said softly. "I suggest we retire to the dining car and finalize our plans there."

A bolt of excitement ran through Xui Li. He was asking her to dinner. Perhaps all of her feminine wiles had worked on him.

"Oh, that would be lovely. You and I alone, sitting together for a delicious meal." Xui Li gave him her sexiest smile yet. "That will give us the privacy that we have been lacking." She looked around distastefully at the few passengers in the business cabin.

"Exactly," he replied quietly. "We need to discuss some things prior to our arrival, and the dining car is best suited for that conversation. Are you ready?"

Was she ready? This was what she had been hoping for: true private interaction with this smoldering man. Calming herself so as to not let her exuberance at her good fortune spill out, she politely bowed her head and stood to exit the cabin. He stood alongside her, and they made their way back to the dining car.

They were greeted by the hostess and shown to a booth at the very end of the dining section. Xui Li was about to say something as they were seated when the Magician caught the hostess' hand. With an impossibly debonair smile, and in perfect Mandarin, he asked the hostess to keep the tables next to them vacant as long as she could. That smile found its mark, and the youngish hostess giggled slightly and replied that of course she would do so, then promptly blushed and retreated to the hostess stand.

Xui Li was fuming. He totally flirted with that girl to get his way. How come she got to be the recipient of his attention, and all Xui Li got was unfulfilling small talk? The Magician called up the dining car's menu on his interface and looked through the selections. With more than a slight harrumph, Xui Li retrieved the menu from the table and tried to read it. After reading the wine list three different times, she set the menu down and took a deep breath. *You are the one eating dinner with him,* she reminded herself. *He only used his charm so that your conversation with him could be private. It was nothing. She is nothing.* Xui Li felt better. She again picked up her menu and looked through the dishes.

"The ginger crab is excellent here," remarked the Magician, not looking up from the interface.

Xui Li swelled inside a bit. She absolutely adored crab. It was by far her favorite dish, and somehow, he knew that. She let out a small contented sigh.

"That sounds lovely. What will you be having?" she asked softly, batting her eyes.

"The pork and vegetable stir fry looks appetizing," he replied.

No sooner had he said it than the waiter was at the table taking their orders. Xui Li impatiently gave her order, wanting the old man to leave their table quickly so they could get back to their alone time.

"So, do you travel this line of the MagVac often?" she asked coyly.

"Often enough to know what food is good but not so often that I need a frequent commuter pass," he replied, again without looking up from his interface. Xui Li was becoming increasingly jealous of that infernal device. *Better up the flirting*, she told herself.

"Well, I always find it comforting to be around a man who knows what he wants," she responded while delicately nibbling on her fingernail.

"Indeed. And what I want right now is to go over the future of our relationship."

Xui Li bit down hard on her nail as the shock of his statement hit her. She suddenly felt very hot and grabbed her ice water, downing a mouthful to cool herself off. Once she felt somewhat recovered, she asked, "Our *future* relationship? Oh my, I would love to discuss that topic with you." This was it, she knew it. He might keep his emotions to himself, but this was definitely it.

"Good," he replied matter-of-factly. "I believe the best place to start is upon our arrival at Chengdu in the outer city. Once there, we will have little time to review anything, so it is imperative that you leave here with everything you need to know to make this work."

She had to admit that this had gone very differently in her head, but as long as he was opening up to her, she didn't mind the stuffiness of his courting style. "Oh, I agree. *Our* arrival is most important."

"Once at Chengdu station, transportation to the Fifth Ring will need to be arranged. I think it is most prudent that your identity stay hidden until beyond the Fifth Ring. While I am sure there are those in the outer rings who would be helpful, there are also those who take advantage of their distance from the Capital."

Xui Li liked that; she liked that a lot. As soon as her identity was revealed, her private time with this man was over. More private time equaled a happier Xui Li.

"I have some contacts in the Fifth Ring who can escort you to a security center there. Once your identity is confirmed, the security center will notify the proper authorities and arrange transport."

That would be the difficult part. How would she explain who the Magician was? Based on her extensive interaction with him, the rumors she had heard about his ruthless nature certainly were blown out of proportion. Yet, how was she going to smuggle him back with her to the Capital without the security force arresting him on the spot?

The elderly waiter brought their food. Xui Li was too lost in her planning to be irritated by his return. The Magician paused as the various dishes were set in front of them. Upon thanking the man and watching him move away from their table, the Magician continued.

"Once within the Second Ring, I will contact you to begin the last part of the infiltration. We will use your clearance to enter the central city for retrieval of the asset."

Perhaps she could get ahold of the foreign relations minister. He had always been kind to her. Maybe he could pull some strings so that— Xui Li stopped. *Did he just say he would contact me?* she thought to herself. *Why would he have to contact me if we are together?*

"I will make sure that my presence is in no way traced back to you. Once the asset has been secured, I can arrange my own exfiltration through local contacts."

Exfil-what? What was he talking about?

"That is the big picture. Any concerns so far?"

"Concerns? No...not really...," she said with obvious concern in her voice. "Questions...yes. When you say 'contact me,' are you going somewhere without me?" Xui Li tried to keep the small bit of panic she felt in her gut out of her voice.

The Magician cocked his head slightly. It was a minute before he said anything. "What were you briefed on prior to leaving Sanzarubi?"

"*Briefed?* You mean, what did that old guy talk to me about?" she asked.

"Yes, Adams. What do you remember Adams telling you about this trip?"

"Something about going through the jungle, meeting up with you again, at my request, then coming back into the Empire. Why, what did he tell you?" That little bit of panic seemed to edge up her gut a bit.

"Xui Li...," the Magician started. He paused, almost looking like he was searching for words. "Xui Li, why do you think I'm here with you? What do you believe my motives are?"

Her panic was now in full bloom. "Well...you are taking

me back home. You and I are going home, and then I was returning to the Empire, and it was...my home...through the jungle and the city...I...is it hot in here? I'm really hot all of a sudden."

The Magician reached over and handed her the glass of ice water. "Here, take small sips."

She hurriedly accepted the glass and started to down the cool liquid.

"*Small* sips," he said insistently. She did so, slowing her breathing. The water felt good going down her throat.

Calm started to return to her. This obviously was just a miscommunication. After all, as a princess of the Empire, she would obviously have been given more details than anyone else. *That must be it*, she assured herself. *He just isn't as well-informed about this whole undertaking as I am.* Once firmly convinced of that explanation, her panic quickly abated.

"Sorry," she said politely. "This whole trip seems to be catching up to me." Of course, he would have to hide his true feelings for her. He was probably just unsure about his place by her side after her return. That would be totally understandable for someone not used to the privileges of court. Xui Li visibly relaxed as her thoughts became more and more rational.

"Are you sure you're OK?" he asked, a hint of concern in his voice.

"Yes, I am fine, thank you. Just not used to this much excitement. The kidnapping, my return—everything just seemed to hit me all at once." She smiled meekly at him to put his mind at ease. *He has enough to worry about,* she thought. *I can choose to keep this to myself for the time being.*

With a slight look of concern still on his face, the Magician continued the conversation. He detailed the specifics of each of the phases of her return and gave her a chance to ask questions. For the most part, Xui Li merely nodded and agreed with everything he said. Ultimately, it really did not matter what his plans were. As long as she was returned to the Empire with him by her side, everything else was inconsequential.

"Xui Li," said the Magician. "Are you paying attention?"

She refocused her attention from his incredible eyes to take in his whole face. "Yes, of course I am. I'm staring right into your bottomless eyes. How could I not pay attention?"

The Magician continued to stare deeply at her. She had the distinct feeling that he was trying very hard to keep his emotions in check. *Poor thing,* she thought. *Can't help but be torn between throwing himself at me and his sense of duty.*

"Xui Li, I think we should take a different approach to this whole thing," he said reservedly. "I think you are right; this is a lot for one person to take in all at once. Especially someone like yourself, who is so far removed from her accustomed environment."

He held her gaze for a few more moments, then took up his tablet and started working. After a few minutes, he addressed her again.

"I believe that this will be a better plan, much simpler." He finished tapping on the tablet and turned it over so she could see it. "Tell me what your thoughts are on this."

Xui Li reluctantly turned her gaze from his face to the tablet. She read through the notes and diagrams he had displayed on the page. There were a few times she had to re-read something, as her mind continually wanted to drift, but she took in the basics of it. Once finished, she looked at him again.

"I think that will work just fine," she responded. "Very...to the point, I suppose."

The plan *was* simple. She would contact the security office in the Fifth Ring and be escorted back to her home. He would contact her later, and they would meet up again. He would take care of the whole wanted-by-the-Empire business of his, and then everything would be fine. She felt relieved that he had set aside the whole "mission" mumbo jumbo. It seemed that his desire for her was edging out the more rigid side of his personality. This was indeed simpler.

The remainder of the meal was quiet and much less stressful. She, of course, flirted with him more, hoping to continue shifting him away from that unyielding duty-bound sense of his. Her efforts seemed to have worked, as at the conclusion of dinner, he asked to escort her back to the sleeping cabins. She gladly accepted the invitation and was sure she could expand its meaning. A night with him would be—well, incredible.

Once at her cabin door, she lingered there long enough to give him the opening she was sure he wanted. He looked like he was holding back as he stood by the window ports. Time for her to make her move. "Thank you so much for taking care of me. I don't think I have said that enough. Everything you have done for me—it's...well, it's unbelievable. I am truly...," she paused and stepped towards him, "truly in your debt."

"Those are kind words, Xui Li. Thank you."

"No, thank you. Thank the gods for you." She took another step closer. "Thank all heaven and earth for you and your strong muscles, rugged physique, and determined bravery." Another step. She was now just below his face. "I am not sure where I would be right now without...." Xui Li closed her eyes and leaned forward. "You," she whispered softly. She leaned farther forward, looking to find that strong, chiseled face of his.

Instead, all she found was cold glass as her nose was squished against the window port. Xui Li stumbled in surprise and threw her hands up in an attempt to catch herself. Too late. Her awkward forward-leaning center of gravity won out, and she half-tumbled, half-slid down to the floor. Looking quickly to her left and then to her right, all she saw was an empty hallway.

"Bloody ninja," she cursed quietly. Xui Li grabbed the handrail next to the window and stood. Taking a few cleansing breaths, she walked in her most regal and dignified manner across the hall, unlocked the door, and swung it shut.

CHAPTER 18
SANCTUARY

Time: Mid-afternoon
Scene: The Seven Cities

The trek through the fifth, sixth, and seventh rings of the Seven Cities was one word: breathtaking. Sam didn't know that such splendor could exist in this dystopian world. She had been impressed with the MagVac system and the journey through the first five rings of the Seven Cities. Those rings were greater—grander—than anything she could have ever hoped to see back in the UWC; even the Capital, where Chancellor Himms resided, fell short by comparison. But the seventh Ring, or Seventh City, was even more epic than all the other cities combined. It was much different from the rest of the sprawling metropolis.

A group of soldiers, arm cannons and light shivs at the

ready, surrounded them the moment they stepped off the monorail. Sam inched toward Misaka and Chen.

"No sudden movements," said Misaka, going as rigid as one of the many green rhodium columns that held up the train station. "The Red Guard—they're the keepers of the Seventh City, the personal guards for the Emperor and his household, and the last line of defense for the Seven Cities. They are the most decorated men in the Jadian Horde."

Sam watched the weapon-wielding men, careful not to move. "I could be wrong, but I don't think they want us here."

Misaka smiled at Sam's casual tone. "The only reason they haven't killed us is that they recognize me and Chen, plus the Mogui who are with us."

Chen shook her head disapprovingly and then shouted at the soldiers in rapid Mandarin. This seemed to anger the soldiers more than anything. One of them, who seemed to be the ranking officer among the soldiers, approached and spoke directly to their Mogui guards. The two elites argued rapidly and loudly in words that Sam did not understand. If she was going to be here, she should put some effort into learning Mandarin.

After a few more choice words, the leader of the Red Guard called to his men, who formed up around Sam, Chen, Misaka, and their Mogui escorts. He barked an order, and the group began moving.

"Misaka, Chen—what's happening?"

Misaka answered but kept looking straight ahead. "The young captain of the Red Guard is taking us to the Valley of the Mystics. If we don't get the acknowledgment from the Madam's office that we are allowed to be here, the Red Guards will kill Chen, you, and me, and the Mogui will be *Diūliǎn*."

"*Diūliǎn?* What's that? It doesn't sound good."

"It is not. *Diūliǎn* is Mandarin; it means *lose face.* It's the lowest dishonor a Jadian can be cursed with. Not only will the Mogui be killed, but all family members over ten years of age will face the Fields of Slaughter, and the younger ones will be banished to the Ice Beria in the north. You are correct, Gōng Zhǔ—*Diūliǎn* is not good."

Sam felt her stomach fall to her feet. "Let's hope that Adam called to confirm our appointment."

Sam would be lying if she said she wasn't scared out of her mind, but the backdrop of the Seventh City helped her to forget momentarily. A perfectly manicured forest with gorgeously exotic trees and other vegetation from every corner of the Empire greeted them as they trekked up the main bi-way. Intricately built shrines from obscure or dead religions crowded the moving sidewalk as priests conducted ceremonies among their followers, all while paying homage to a green and yellow flag and an oil painting of an opulently dressed man. The man was too far away to see, but it was not hard to guess to whom the priests were showing reverence.

Just past the priests and their shrines, the large bi-way opened up and broke off into different roads. Off in the distance, Sam saw a building of historical splendor that wasn't totally unlike the castles of her dreams.

"The Sanctuary of the Mystics," observed Misaka in awe. "It never ceases to impress."

Sam turned to look at Misaka. "Mystics?"

Misaka returned the look with a confused expression. "Do you not know of mystics, Gōng Zhǔ?"

Sam shook her head.

"What do they teach you at those academy cities, Gōng Zhǔ? How could you not know of mystics?"

Sam didn't have an answer. "Sorry, I've never heard of anything such as mystics. What are they?"

Misaka bowed her head. "I am not the one to explain this to you, Gōng Zhǔ. It should be a question that you ask the Madam."

They finished their journey in silence, leaving Sam to ponder. She suddenly felt apprehensive about everything—the Seven Cities, mystics, and even the nickname Gōng Zhǔ. She wished Richard were here. He would know what all this —Sam sniffed as images of both Richards, fat and super, entered her mind. Unexpectedly, a tear rolled down her face. Richard...he was gone. She tried to push him out of her head. The memory was too painful to think about.

"I am sorry, but getting in to see the Madam today is impossible. She is simply too busy."

Sam surveyed her surroundings. They were inside a building, she just now realized. Misaka was arguing rather boisterously with a man at a long black wood table. The guard, or more likely, some sort of receptionist with whom Misaka was arguing, was a handsome youth with deep blue eyes and striking blond hair. He was probably from the northern end of the European Archipelago.

"I don't care if she's the next Jadian Sun. The Madam does not take visitors unless they have an appointment."

"We do have an appointment," replied Misaka curtly. "Talk to the Madam's—"

"Do not speak her title with your unworthy tongue, hand-maiden. She is not to be defiled with thoughts from your lesser mind."

The statement made Chen ball her fists; Misaka showed no reaction. "Listen, curator, time is of the essence. This young lady is not only *Gōng Zhǔ*, but also the Delphic Candidate expected at the Emerald Palace before the ceremony can commence. If you make us late—"

Delphic Candidate? thought Sam. *Now that's a new one....*

"Hey, Chen, what's a—"

"I already know your question, Gōng Zhǔ, and we will discuss it later."

Misaka was starting to sound frustrated. "Please, curator, we need to see the Madam."

"You shall not leave until you have proven to *my* satisfaction that you are here by invitation."

"Well, if you would do as I—"

"Sebastian, what seems to be the problem?"

A woman with long raven-black hair and porcelain skin stepped from the recesses of a large set of double doors. She was young, no more than nineteen, and walked with a finished elegance that Sam knew she would never possess.

"Ms. Alena," stammered Sebastian, the receptionist, "I apologize for the commotion. These *handmaidens* and Mogui requested an audience with the Madam. I explained that she must not be disturbed because of the Ceremony of the Changing Seasons, but they insist that the Madam do a reading tonight and that this *girl*...."

Sebastian pointed at Sam.

"Is a guest of the Emperor."

The young lady didn't say anything but studied Sam with keen interest.

The voice of the young guard/receptionist became less sure. "I was about to have the Red Guard dismiss—"

Alena surprised them all as she stepped in front of Sam and took a knee.

She held her head to the floor and spoke. "Gōng Zhǔ—nay, your Grace the Delphic Candidate—it is a privilege, oh appointed one. I would have you forgive any trespass and unworthy—"

"Alena. Please, you're going to embarrass the girl."

Another woman stepped out from the double doors. She was a bit older than Alena, perhaps in her mid-twenties. She, too, was beautiful.

"Lady Sasha," breathed Alena, "I apologize if I stepped out of turn. I just thought that I would greet her and show—"

"Alena! Please."

Alena bowed her head, this time in a sort of shameful display, like a dog scolded by a master. Sam felt sorry for her. The pity came on suddenly, and before she knew it, she was down by the girl's side.

"I don't know why you would bow your head to me, as I am no one of consequence, but if it gives you pleasure, I would have you accompany me."

Sam stopped at the end of her statement. Now where did that come from? The words flowed so naturally, Sam was unsure that the statement came from her mouth.

She looked into Alena's face. Her eyes were wide, her lip quivering; the girl's expression was a mix of horror and wonder. Sam did not know why she did it. It was uncharacteristic of her. But she touched the girl's arm and guided her up. "I am Samantha Montgomery from Academy City 676. It is very nice to meet you."

The girl's wonder shined as her face broke into a smile. "Alena of the Black Northern. I am aide to her Premier Eminence Alexandra, personal assistant to the Madam, the Emperor's favorite wife and holy mystic. Gōng Zhǔ, thy holy

Delphic Candidate, welcome to Seven Cities...welcome home."

———

"You must not be worried," said Alexandra, better known as Sasha. "The Reading is merely a formality—something for your DragonNet File."

Sam walked beside Sasha, who guided her through the Sanctuary to where the Madam was waiting for her.

"Is it going to hurt?" Sam hated that she sounded so childish, but she had to be honest. She didn't want it to hurt.

"No, my dear, it will be like any other read you've ever had."

Sam remained silent, and Sasha perceived the reason for this. "Gōng Zhǔ, is it possible that you've never had a reading before?"

Again Sam remained silent. Sasha did not press.

Their journey was a long one, or perhaps it simply seemed so because of all of the wondrous structures and art throughout the building. Sam had to hand it to the Jadians. They knew how to decorate a space.

"We are entering the Inner Sanctuary. You are not allowed here without the specific invitation of the Madam herself. It's a safe space where the Madam and others like her can cultivate their talents. They have to exist on a different level, a different plane from the rest of us. The Mistress, the mother of our current Madam, established the Sanctuary and the guidelines for finding and training mystics, and ever since her impeccable wisdom helped to establish the Mystical Order, the Empire has prospered."

Sam listened with rapt attention. This schooling, history, and discussion were much different from what Sam had been forced to endure for the past weeks of travel with Adam and his gaggle of goons. Her questions, at least the superficial ones, were being answered before she even found the voice to ask them. This could be her chance—the opportunity she had been looking for to get all of her questions answered. She picked the most obvious one first. The question that had plagued her since she escaped the mountain facility and MESA, since she lost Richard and journeyed around the planet to the other center of the world: Why was she here?

Sam took a deep breath to ask the question she wasn't sure she was ready to learn the answer to when, to her surprise, she said instead, "Lady Sasha, you speak...you speak of Madam as if she is some other species."

Lady Sasha smiled at Sam. "Those who have the privilege of being called mystics are as different from us as we are from our evolutionary forefathers. But worry not about this divide, this obvious difference in status, as you, Gōng Zhǔ, you are special—special above all others."

"Special?" questioned Sam, coming to a stop in front of another pair of highly ornate double doors. "Special? I think you've got me mixed up with someone else, Sasha. How am I special?"

The doors to the left opened with the heavy creak of moving metal, followed by the scent of jasmine, juniper, and crushed pine needles. A green illumination, like what one would see in a cave of emeralds and green rhodium, spilled from the room and across Sasha's face. She looked down to the ground as if to compose herself.

"It's time, Gōng Zhǔ. The Madam...she waits for you in her tabernacle."

Sam looked into the darkness of the room before returning her gaze to Sasha. "You didn't answer my question. You can't do this to me, Sasha. You say that I am special. Please tell me why."

"I wish I could answer your questions, Gōng Zhǔ. I am sure you have many. However, I am not the one to give you those answers, and even if I could, I am unable to guarantee that my answers would not lead to a legion of other concerns. But I can tell you this: If there is anyone able to offer you answers, then it is the Madam. You must go, Samantha Montgomery—she awaits."

Sasha turned her back to Sam and proceeded to walk back up the hall. Sam watched her briefly, then squared up to the double doors, peering in through the shadows created by the unnatural green light.

"Samantha," Sasha called out.

"Yes, Sasha?"

"Can I give you a piece of advice?"

"Of course."

"The truth—don't fight it. The Madam might not reveal everything, but know she will never lie."

With this enigmatic statement, Sasha resumed her retreat up the hallway. She turned the corner and disappeared. Sam took a deep breath and entered the Madam's tabernacle.

———

"Hello?" Sam called out, stepping gingerly. "I'm looking for the Madam."

Nothing but silence and dull light greeted her. Sam wondered if, in all the commotion, someone forgot to inform the poor lady of Sam's arrival.

"Hello, Samantha."

Sam jumped, taking a quick step back as her flight-or-fight response kicked into overdrive. A woman materialized out of the darkness immediately in front of Sam. What a woman she was! Long golden hair flowed around her shoulders, and her eyes were glowing sapphires of blue. Rosy cheeks, high cheekbones, and a perfect smile—this was not merely a woman, but perfection personified. God's finest work—a woman so beautiful that one could not help but be impressed. Despite the woman's thoughtful expression, a burning within Sam's gut told her that she was not one to be trifled with. Sam took another step back, involuntarily putting up her fists in almost the same movement.

"Peace, child," said the woman in a whisper. "I assure you, I mean you no harm. You can put those away. I promise this room is about as safe a place as there is in all the Empire. No one will hurt you here."

Sam abruptly felt stupid. Had she really just put up her fists? What was she going to do, box her? Dumb. Sam let her hands fall to her sides. "Sorry. I didn't mean to threaten you. You just startled me."

"And your first instinct was to fight. Interesting."

"What's interesting?"

"I mean no disrespect, my dear." The Madam turned her back and not so much walked as floated between pillars set two meters apart up a path that carried them into the recesses of the building. Sam followed without realizing it and could not have stopped herself even if she wanted to.

"How do you like the Seven Cities, Sam Montgomery of Academy City 676?"

Sam chewed on her fingernail. "How did you know my name?"

"You'll find that I know a great deal, Sam. That is what you prefer to be called, correct?"

Sam nodded her head but saw the flaw. "You know a great deal about me, but you're asking me how I like the city? Is that just really terrible small talk?"

Sam cursed her tongue. This woman, whoever she was,

commanded respect and power like no one she had ever met; she was all she had heard about since arriving at the Capital. It probably wasn't wise for Sam to mouth off to her.

The Madam's smile was warm and inviting, genuinely flowing with real affection. Sam didn't know how to react to it. She smiled back, but the gesture didn't seem like enough. "I see your point, Sam. Yes, that was particularly egregious small talk."

"Umm...Madam—that's what they call you, right? Madam?"

"Yes, my child, that is both my name and title."

"OK," said Sam, "Aren't you supposed to be testing me or something?"

"Yes, my dear, that is right. Shall I?"

Sam nodded. "Might as well get it over with."

The Madam gestured to a sitting space where there was a kettle and two tea glasses waiting. Sam noticed the absence of any chairs, just giant cushy-looking bags. She stepped to one of the bags and sat, instantly aware of the material adjusting, seemingly of its own accord, around her body. It took a brief moment to find a comfortable spot. Once she was settled, Sam looked at the Madam, who sat directly across from her. She found herself staring at the woman as a wave of familiarity washed over her. The Madam matched Sam's gaze.

"I feel...I feel like I know you," Sam said without thinking.

The Madam pushed a golden lock of her hair out of her face. "I hear that often. Now, Samantha, shall I begin?"

"Is it going to hurt?"

"No, child."

"Then let's do it."

"Show me your neck, dear."

Sam stretched out her neck, for some reason not at all surprised by the odd request. The Madam reached out her hand and touched Sam. Her hand was warm. She remained still for a few moments. Sam closed her eyes until the Madam removed her hand.

"I am glad to say that you have passed. Congratulations."

"That's it?"

"That's it."

Sam scratched at her head. "That was rather anti-climactic."

"Yes, indeed. They make such a fuss about my readings. They are really to see if you bear the Emperor any ill will. It doesn't take long to ascertain the truth."

"And?"

"You're more confused than anything else. You don't know why you're here or why someone would take so much trouble to get you here. But be of good cheer, child. The answers you seek will soon be revealed. For now, there are many wondrous things I would like to show you, if you are so inclined."

"Are you allowed to do that?" Sam said, cocking her head

to the left in a gesture of confusion. "I'm sure you have more important things to do than show me around."

"Child, I have all the time in the world. Please allow me to show you the Emerald House. You'll have a room a stone's throw away from mine; it's absolutely beautiful."

"I'm sorry, Madam, but why would I, of all people, have a room next to you?"

The Madam's expression was sympathetic. "My dear, all the daughters and wives of the Emperor live in the Emerald House. You should be no exception. Now come. I have much to show you."

CHAPTER 19

BREACH

Time: End of the working day
Scene: MESA's Harmonics lab

Thurman sat and stared at the day's reports. He wasn't really reading them, more just using them as a place to focus his eyes. He had tried to go through the schedule, tried to process the day's events and how they fit into the overall progression of the Harmonicum research. But after reading the second cycle description six times, he realized that it was no use pretending. His mind was well occupied somewhere else— with something else. For what seemed like the sixty-fifth time that morning, Thurman looked up at the East wall. It wasn't a casual glance, that of someone just looking around the room. No, this was a complete and utter fixation on the white rectangle.

Next, his eyes roamed to where Warrick was standing in

the lab. If the East wall was occupying the majority of his thoughts, what little remained of Thurman's mental capacity was spent worrying about Warrick. The man was definitely up to something. Thurman had not trusted him when he first met the wiry man, and since then had been glad that he hadn't. Between his constant doubts of the cycle timelines and the incessant questioning about his well-being, cognitively, Thurman was tapped out.

Not to mention Kingston and his continual visits to the lab. For some reason, he seemed to be showing up at the lab almost every day now. In the preceding months, Kingston had visited sporadically. Now, he felt the need to poke around daily. Thurman knew he could only hold the man off for so much longer before Kingston would take action. What action that would be, he was not sure, but he was not looking forward to it.

Add all of this drama in his own lab to the fact that he spent way too much time scouting the hallways for those crazies working in that infernal Feedbacker lab, and it was no wonder that he had to re-read his schedule multiple times. Something had changed in the dynamics at MESA, and Thurman was pretty sure they knew about his side research. How they knew could only be explained by that vile lab.

Thurman caught a glimpse of his reflection in the glass of his interface. He felt even more tired than he looked.

There was an uncomfortable silence as the transport vehicle rumbled along. It was not like the team was typically chatty when they were coming up on a mission, but something about this op was different, and each of the team seemed to feel it. Palin and Teddy had their noses buried in their tablets, going over final checklists and reviewing last-minute updates to their recon and intel. Even those two seemed to be more on edge than usual when running an op.

Palin noticed the incoming update at the top of her screen. The SkyEagle was inbound to their location and was reporting zero tangos for the moment. Once it arrived in their area of operation, the cloaked recon ship would provide them with live feeds of the MESA campus and security force movements. From that data, she would render the insertion map one final time, running through the mission protocols to make sure they were all in the green. As soon as she processed the SkyEagle's update, her mind went right back to the schematics in front of her.

Teddy sat next to her, busy with his own last-minute work. The main part of his screen was dedicated to real-time updates of the cyberwarfare team's progress on the MESA security grid. They had put every available tech on this assignment, plus splinted-celled another hundred or so free-lancers for the diversion attack. Each of these fringe hackers had jumped at the chance to bombard MESA's grid—a holy grail of hacking if there ever was one. Teddy just hoped it worked. They were putting a lot of faith in people who consumed only candy bars and energy drinks—all day, every day.

A small vid popped up as Bravo team's leader checked in. He reported that all shape charges had been rapid-primed and all other ordnance had been locked and loaded. Teddy acknowledged the man and dropped the call. Seconds later, Alpha team's leader messaged in that their load-out was complete. Teddy sent a quick reply and returned to the security grid progress. He checked the digital timer at the top of his tablet. One of their insertion windows was approaching. If they missed this one, they would have to hold for another twenty minutes for the next one to open. That waiting made Teddy nervous. Twenty minutes was a lifetime during a—

Teddy's board lit up green as each of the cyberwarfare divisions reported their success. Diversion was green, counter-image was green, recon and real-time vids reported green as well. That was it. They had to go now or not at all. Teddy hit the group comm icon. "All teams: Christmas tree is lit. Start the clock."

———

Thurman sat at his desk sipping his tea. The warm liquid was incredibly soothing to his nerves, even if it did nothing to alleviate his problems. Warrick had, only minutes before, *finally* left for the day—but not before doling out his usual interrogatory end-of-the-day report. Warrick's departure relieved a significant amount of Thurman's stress. Thurman looked around at the remaining personnel mulling about the lab, wrapping up the day's work. Most were lower-level employees and techs merely catching up on messages, reports, and the like. At the pace they had been running the lab, Thurman was not at all surprised to see people still working. Despite the madness of the past months, they really had been making significant headway.

Thurman sat at his desk as one by one, they wished him a pleasant evening and chided him for staying so late. Thurman merely replied with half-hearted pleasantries. While the tea seemed to calm his nerves and the relatively empty lab put his mind somewhat at ease, each passing minute eroded that peace as his anxiety mounted over the unknown event Jameson had warned him about. Inevitably, he glanced at his timepiece. It was close. Whatever this thing was, he would find out very soon.

———

Teddy and Palin led their teams down the dark underground tunnel. The stench stung Teddy's eyes even through his combat eyewear. He motioned for the teams to split and take up breaching positions on either side of the storm drain access hatch. Once in position, Teddy looked at the heads-up display on his forearm. All teams were in position and awaiting the go/no-go. Teddy watched the digital clock tick down the seconds.

———

Thurman absentmindedly brought his cup up to his mouth. It was empty. He looked around the lab. It, too, had cleared of all the remaining staff. It seemed he was alone. He let out an audible sigh, the product of half-holding his breath for too long. It was one thing for him to get mixed up in whatever Jameson had cooked up, but after the explosion in the Interface lab, he was incredibly relieved that none of his staff would be present. He looked at his timepiece. Almost there.

———

Palin took a deep breath. This was it. Cyber-ops had breached the main security grid, and Alpha team had already started their insertion. Everything they had been planning rode on what transpired over the next twenty minutes. Palin closed her eyes and offered a short and simple prayer. Eyes open again, she patted the shoulder of the man in front of her and followed him into the proverbial lion's den.

———

A small flickering at the top of his vision caught Thurman's eye. He stared at the overhead light in the corner of his office. There was a very slight flutter, almost imperceptible, but the longer he stared, the more noticeable it became. The report currently displayed on his desk interface shifted slightly and then shifted back. Then again, ever so slightly. It was like there was a power surge and the interface was trying to compensate by re-rendering the image. Thurman stood from his desk and walked over to the large window in his office. The two terminals that he could see looked fine. Nothing seemed out of the ordin— There it was again. He looked more closely and could see that they both had a slight wobble to the images on their screens.

As he leaned forward, Thurman placed his hand on the glass but immediately withdrew it. The glass was vibrating. He again placed his hand cautiously against the smooth surface. It was slight, but definitely there. A small, subtle low-frequency vibration. He held his hand against the glass for a minute or so, trying to figure out what was causing it. As he stood there, Thurman felt the vibration grow. He could now feel it in his arm and upper chest. It was then that he noticed that the window was not the only thing vibrating. Thurman felt a low rumble through the soles of his shoes. He dropped his cup, and it smashed on his office floor.

———

"Scramble Four, Scramble Four, this is Alpha Two."

"Alpha Two, this is Scramble Four. Please code in."

"Whiskey, Zulu, nine, five, seven."

"Alpha Two, hold for comm relay."

The seconds that passed seemed to tick by very slowly for Coda. His arm twinged with pain, and he clamped the gauze tighter on the wound.

Scramble Four's voice sounded again. "Alpha Two, Fabius One has the relay."

Washington? Coda thought. *Why was Washington on comm?*

"Alpha Two, what is your status?"

"Sir, where is Adams? He was to be our comm point for this op."

"He was assigned to a higher priority meet-and-greet. Now report. Our recon feed went black shortly after insertion."

Coda felt another stinger up his arm and gritted his teeth. "Objective One fulfilled. Package and ribbon are safe. Objectives Two and Three were not met, repeat not met. The Interface and Harmonics labs were heavily damaged, and cyber-ops reports seventy percent server corruption. The Feedbacker lab was hit after the initial insertion, but we took heavy casualties. Full extent of damage to the lab is unknown. We have a small feed giving us intermittent updates, but I'm not sure how long before it's discovered and severed."

"Speculation on failure to complete secondary and tertiary objectives."

Coda paused as another wave of pain flowed up his arm. Where was that medic?

"Based on my limited data, I...honestly sir, it was like nothing I've ever seen. It was...." Coda let out a frustrated grunt. "It was like they knew we were coming. Almost like the demo team's diversion didn't have any effect on that section of the campus. We would clear a corner, and then out of nowhere, more patrols would show up."

"You reported heavy casualties. Give me the totals."

Coda pulled up the most updated report. "Alpha team, thirteen percent. Bravo team, seventeen percent. Cyber-ops, ninety-three percent. Recon—"

"Hold on, Alpha Two. Check those figures. Why did Cyber-ops sustain the heaviest casualties when they were not in the primary engagement zone?"

"Sir, those are survivor rates."

Coda only heard faint static for many moments as the information inevitably sunk in. Coda continued. "Recon, eighty-seven percent. Medics are attending to the wounded."

More silence.

"Alpha Two, confirm again the package and ribbon are secured."

Coda bristled with anger. Did the old man not hear what he had just reported? Who brickin' cared about the package or the ribbon?

"Alpha Two!?"

"Confirmed, the package *and* ribbon are secure. We are currently at waypoint Epsilon. When should we roll out to the primary extraction zone?"

"Negative on rollout just now, Alpha Two. JA is inbound to your twenty. He will be arriving at LZ Sigma Three. Continue periodic status updates on sched. Fabius One out."

Coda was just about to yell at Washington for dropping the call like that when the medic finally reached him to attend to his arm. He might have been royally pissed at Washington, but his arm was killing him. He nodded, and the medic peeked below the blood-soaked gauze. *Adams was inbound?* Coda asked himself. *Didn't Washington say he was engaged elsewhere?*

————

Thurman sat near the infrared heater, a thin thermal blanket wrapped around his shoulders. His thoughts were disjointed and random. Somewhere in his mind, he reasoned that he was in shock, and elsewhere in that same mind, he was ready to throw off the blanket and run. With the Shadow-glass erected, the area he sat in looked like an old greenhouse. Everything was dark, as the only illumination came from phosphorescent strips placed throughout the structure. Thurman's mind started to wander again, and he remembered one of his colleagues at the university working on the material for these shadow structures. From what he could recall, they were quite incredible. They combined heat and EMF suppression technology with active camouflage, thus creating a hidden dome wherever they were erected. The only risk of discovery was from someone accidentally bumping into the outside wall. It was a very effective portable hideout, especially at night.

Thurman clutched his leather notebook closer to his chest with one hand and pulled the blanket tightly around himself with the other. What had Jameson gotten him into? Everything had happened so fast. Explosions, screams, alarms, shooting. Then Thurman and his notebook were grabbed and roughly moved along smoky corridors. After that, his memory was a complete blur. The next thing he remembered was sitting in front of this heater holding his notebook.

A medic walked over to him. Thurman barely noticed the woman.

"How you holding up?" she asked softly.

"What? Oh, um...fine, fine...just fine." Thurman's brain seemed to be on autopilot. "How are you?"

The medic smiled. "Busy. Just came by to check on you. We have some hot soup. I think it may help you feel a little better. Here." The medic pulled out a small thin canister, twisted the bottom, and placed it in his free hand. Almost immediately, the canister grew warm.

"Now don't slurp it all down at once. Just sip it, OK?"

Thurman absentmindedly nodded, and the medic left to

check on the others lying around the camp. Thurman's gaze floated down and rested on the can of soup. Roasted red pepper. He wasn't sure if he had ever had that flavor before. Perhaps he had. It sounded somewhat familiar.

A flurry of activity brought him out of his stupor as several people started scurrying around the enclosed space. Thurman's heart started to race. It was only after he saw them in their state of excited activity that he noticed a sound coming from outside the structure. Thurman swore he heard a faint humming accompanied by the rustling of leaves and trees. The sound stayed consistent for a minute or two, then whined down. Except for the noises inside, it was silent.

Thurman saw the level of activity in the structure simmer down. Whatever was out there, these people had determined it was not a threat. Noticing the soup in his hand and feeling the pounding heart in his chest, Thurman decided to take the medic's advice. The steamy liquid gave off a delicious aroma. Thurman brought the can to his lips and took a few small sips of the hot soup. It was heavenly. Despite the heater and blanket, Thurman still felt a chill inside. The warm, flavor-packed meal-in-a-can seemed to chase that away quite effectively. He took another sip and let the liquid sit on his tongue for a moment. Thurman closed his eyes as the warmth spread from his mouth to his throat into his chest.

"How's the soup?"

His breath caught, and his eyes flew open. He remained

completely still. He knew that voice. Suddenly, the chill in his chest returned in full force.

"Professor?"

Thurman slowly turned to look up at the man standing next to him. He looked tired, and his clothes were disheveled and soot-stained, but CJ had a very kind expression on his face.

"Professor, I think it's time you and I had ourselves a nice heart-to-heart."

Thurman gulped down the soup.

CHAPTER 20

REALIZATION

Time: Afternoon

Scene: Goat farm in southeastern jungle, Jade Empire

"Did Adams get his coordinates wrong?" Dirk looked to Rona, who seemed neither upset nor surprised by the turn of events. "There's nothing here."

Dirk swore. He knew this was a fool's errand.

"I wouldn't describe it that way, Dirk."

The voice startled Dirk so much that he reached for the old six-shooting pistol on his belt. A weapon from the turn of the twentieth century, a Smith and Wesson .455—sure, it was old, but it had some special rounds that Dirk made himself. Some of which were pretty nasty. The gun was out of its holster before Dirk realized—

"Adams?"

The holographic image of a beaming Adams, standing

with hands folded in front of him, was just a meter or so from Dirk, precisely where Rona had been standing. Dirk searched for the elusive Rona, who was suddenly nowhere to be found. Dirk ignored the development and spoke to Adams as he re-holstered his weapon.

"There's nothing here but brickin' goats." Dirk pointed to the valley and the farm just below. "You'd better have a—"

"Llamas," interrupted Adams.

"Excuse me?" said Dirk, his temper starting to rise.

"This valley is known for raising llamas. Those are llamas, not goats."

Dirk stared at Adams incredulously. "You'd better be joking."

"No, I'm not—"

Dirk again pulled out his six-shooter, drawing like a western cowboy, pulling the hammer, and cracking off six rounds into where Adams' chest would have been, had he been real.

Adams' eyes widened in surprise; he had not been expecting that. "You shot me."

"No, actually I didn't," said Dirk. "I shot a picture of you. Which is lucky for you, because had you really been standing there, this would have been a huge mess. It might have killed you instantly, but even worse is the knowledge that wild animals were undoubtedly going to gnaw on your pitiful corpse."

"Dirk, I sense that you're angry."

"What was your first hint?"

The two men stared at each other, neither daring to break the silence. Dirk's anger finally boiled over as he reeled from this strange, crystallizing moment where everything became clear and he was finally able to put the pieces of this venture together. Dirk called to Rona, knowing she could hear him. "Rona, you can come out now. I promise I won't shoot, at least not right this second."

Rona stepped out from the bushes, followed by her Jadian captors, confirming Dirk's suspicions about the whole escapade. He returned his gaze to Adams. "There was never a site you wanted me to survey, was there?"

Adams didn't answer immediately, but after the moment stretched, he finally responded. "What would you like me to say, Dirk?"

"I want you to say that there was a very important historical site here that you want me to investigate and that we need to run like hell because the men standing behind Rona are actually regular Jadian military and not some cronies of yours just dressed up as Jadians."

Rona cautiously stepped forward. "Dirk, I'm really sorry that we had to do this. But we had to know—"

"Rona, love." Dirk shot her a scathing look. "It'd be better for you not to talk right now. All I need to do is reload the gun —and it's one of those cylinders that swings out, so you know I can load it really fast."

He turned back to Adams. "Well, John, what's the good word?"

"Sorry, Dirk, if I told you all those things, I would be lying to you."

"Since when is lying the problem?"

Adams answered calmly. "Dirk, I understand that you're angry with me. I get that. But you need to understand—we had to know what you were capable of and what you would make of the situation presented to you. The question: Can we count on you when the going gets tough? We had to ask it, and you had to answer. It was an important test. I am happy to say that you passed with flying colors."

Dirk shot at Rona, "You knew about this?"

Rona nodded. "We all go through something similar, Dirk. In our business, the single most dangerous thing isn't some new weapon; it's a traitor from within who knows our secrets. You had to be tested, and we had to do it in a way that would avoid raising your suspicions."

"You thought I would be suspicious?" In a strange turn, this knowledge pleased Dirk. As weird as that sounded.

Adams answered. "Of course. You evaded the Empire, the UWC, and us for the better part of two years. We are all very aware of your intellectual prowess. The test had to make you believe what was going on."

Dirk knew there had been something wrong with the situation—for one thing, the guards had spoken English. That alone should have given him pause.

Dirk looked at the "Jadian" soldiers. "Which one of you has the Colonies accent?"

For a brief span, there wasn't any movement. Then one of the soldiers raised his hand. "That would be me, sir."

"You sound ridiculous. Who seriously talks like that?" Dirk gestured to Adams and Rona. "So I passed your little test. Now what?"

"Don't worry, Dirk." Adams grinned widely. "We take care of our own. Rona, would you please handle the rest?"

"Sir." Rona dipped her head respectfully.

"I will see you two back at base. We've got some things to discuss."

Adams touched his brow and disappeared, leaving the sounds of the jungle and the smell of gunpowder.

Dirk and Rona ended up backtracking to the camp of the phony Jadian soldiers. Rona had left a few items that she wanted to retrieve before the long journey home. While Rona grabbed her things, Dirk ventured off on his own. He needed some time to think.

"Dirk," called Rona after him, "don't wander off too far; we're still deep in Jadian territory, so we don't want to miss—"

Dirk disappeared into the jungle, melding with the dark green background, allowing himself to be swallowed up by its depths.

Rona called after him, but her words fell upon deaf ears as Dirk retreated into the trees. The jungle was truly a different place. The noises, the sounds, the atmosphere; it was at the same time a place to be revered and feared. He'd been to the jungle during his adventures around the world, but it felt like he was truly seeing it for the first time. Why was that?

Dirk pushed up a worn game track and crested a moss-covered hill. He looked out over the treetops. Birds were flying, insects buzzing, and creepy crawlers scurrying across the ground. An invigorating sight, so full of life—it was amazing how quickly this part of the world had recovered after the last Great War while the Burning Plains and the European Archipelago had forever changed their landscape and people due to the weaponry used. But this part of the world, the southern reach of the Jade Empire, had been lucky. The disassembled warheads, while just as destructive as the nuclear weapons of the twenty-first century, were much more targeted and did not have the drawbacks of radiation and nuclear fallout.

Dirk almost walked headlong into a massive tree that reached high into the heavens.

"Sequoia?" wondered Dirk aloud. "You aren't indigenous to here...who would have put a sequoia tree here?"

The answer didn't matter. He scaled to the nearest branch. For some odd reason, he felt inclined to reach the top of the towering tree. Dirk continued to climb until he was about two-thirds up the tree. A sequoia on top of a hill...Dirk could see for kilometers in either direction. Including the fake Jadian camp, which was a ghost town; all it needed was a vengeful spirit or two to become truly haunted. The equipment and tents were packed up, and no one was around. Dirk settled himself on the branch and closed his eyes. Warm skin...the playful nip of scented breeze...they coalesced and...

"There is something amiss," spoke the voice, "so we should proceed with caution. There may be another mystic near... perhaps more than one."

"Cai, how about you reflect your namesake for once in your life and bring us some good news."

"My name means 'fortune,' Anton. Fortune is as pliable as the baker's dough, as the potter's clay, or the painter's canvas; fortune is what you make of it. Nothing more, nothing less."

"You mystics are all the same. We've been stomping around in this gods-forsaken jungle for hours because of the disturbance in your mojo, or whatever you call it."

"Meridians, Anton. They are called meridians."

"Like it matters."

"Cai adjusted and cracked his neck."

"Anton resumed his complaining. 'Now hurry up and start being the inhuman monster we know you are and that the Emperor loves so much, and do something useful for a change.'"

"You provincial military are all the same. We are people— the same as you."

"I've seen what that Madam of yours can do. Don't talk to me about being 'people.' There is nothing normal about you."

"Cai sighed. 'OK Anton, and what did you have in mind that would allow me to be helpful?'"

"Stop speaking in riddles for once, and give me something. What are we looking for?"

"Intruders—mystics specifically. They've been here in the last couple of hours. There is one...one in particular who is strong. The imprint is unbelievable. Her presence is almost as stifling as the Madam's."

"Great. More freaks. I'm calling in the cavalry. Last thing I want to do is run into someone like the Madam."

"Dirk?" Rona's voice pierced the space. "Dirk? Are you here? We need to leave."

Dirk awoke to the dusky whisper of twilight; his skin was prickling, and his throat felt on fire. Like he had been talking for hours. His head hurt, and he felt...distant. Through the groggy haze, Dirk heard his name again.

A figure stepped through the haze of humidity and tempered darkness. Rona walked and called for Dirk. He knew she would come eventually. How long had he been gone? Judging from the retreating sun, it had been a while.

Rona passed right under the tree Dirk had climbed. She wasn't speaking but searching through the branches of the jungle. The scattered rays of sunlight that pierced the darkness of the jungle floor lit her up in an alternating fashion of light and shadow, bright illumination and dark relief. The moment was striking, breathtaking...beautiful. She was beautiful. Was Rona always this beautiful?

Dirk was just about to call out to her when she found a rather large spider in her hair. Rona croaked out a yell, then launched into a sort of crazy, screaming dance that was funny enough to leave Dirk speechless. He laughed, and the magic was gone. Perhaps he should have helped, but he was feeling more inclined to just enjoy watching; besides, he was still mad at her. Rona composed herself and continued among the trees. Dirk watched her go. Yeah, he was definitely still upset with her.

The setting sun dipped below the horizon as the nightlife of the jungle came out of its hidden and secret places. The moon made its appearance in the east and reminded Dirk of Rona's perfectly porcelain skin. He sighed.

OK, that wasn't really true; he wasn't really upset with Rona over the whole lying thing. He had been honest before in his conversation with Adams. He lied all the time. He had to; it was part of the profession. No, if he was completely honest, he was more upset with himself than with Rona.

How could he have fallen for such a production? There had been signs—signs all over the place that something was wrong with this particular scenario: Adams' insistence that they travel to a place where none of the D-list items were located and that they take Xui Li, the ease with which Rona got caught, the lack of regular Jadian weaponry, the accents of some of the "soldiers," and the fact that they spoke English. There were so many signs, and he had noticed the inconsistencies. Yet, instead of questioning, he pressed on. He went after Rona regardless of the situation. Why?

Dirk didn't feel like answering the questions. He was charmed by Rona: her rough ways, her coarse accent, and her many other perks like her personality and idiosyncrasies. Despite the warnings of an unbelievable situation, Dirk had pressed forward after Rona *because* it was Rona—and to Dirk Garrett, that was the scariest thing imaginable.

"Dirk." The voice came from directly under him. "I know you're up there."

Dirk looked down, and sure enough, Rona was gazing up at him.

———

"I'm sorry, Dirk. How many times am I going to have to say it?"

Rona tried to keep up with Dirk as he almost flew down the crisscrossing path that led into the Llamas' Valley. Llamas' Valley—it wasn't the most original name, but in Dirk's current discombobulated state, a more clever description eluded him. He was still upset by the results of his soul-searching and was currently taking his frustrations out on Rona. He was finding it difficult. Her concern and sincerity really dug at him. He found it nearly impossible to stay upset with her.

Rona caught Dirk's arm, a look of concern splashed across her features. She paused as if she were at a loss for words. Dirk just stared at her.

"You're bleeding." Rona stared at Dirk's hand where, sure enough, bright red blood was flowing down his fingers. He had not noticed.

Rona took Dirk by the wrist, and before he realized what she was doing, she was examining the wound. It wasn't serious, just a couple of moderately long scrapes on the upper arm. Dirk tried to protest Rona's touch, but she shut him up with a single glance.

"You know that you can't stay mad at me forever." She dabbed antiseptic across the wound.

Dirk tried not to show any reaction. "No, I can't. Your impossibly cute ways will make sure of that."

"You think I'm cute? I thought you were into Jadian princesses."

"Har har har, I love how you think you're funny. I'm still pissed at you, remember?"

Rona smiled. "How can I forget? I've been apologizing to you for the last hour, ever since I found you all dazed in that tree."

"Speaking of which, you do realize that you passed under me once before? I saw your anti-spider dance...."

"You saw me run into that webbing?"

"Yes, it was quite humorous."

Rona glared.

Dirk held up his hands. "Don't get mad at me. Find the spider; I'm sure he'd go a round or two with you."

She glared harder. "So you *were* in the tree that whole time?"

"Yep, all you had to do was look up, and you would have seen me; you would have saved yourself quite a bit of time, too."

"It certainly took me longer to find you than I expected, that's for sure."

"You sound surprised."

"I am. It should not have taken me that long."

Dirk's eyebrow rose inquiringly. "You going to elaborate on that?"

"Nope."

"And why not?"

"Because you're mad at me, remember? Why would I share my secrets with you?"

"That's exactly what got you in trouble last time. Not sharing secrets."

Rona placed the bandage on Dirk's wounds, pushing down a bit harder than was absolutely necessary. "If there was anything that this little exercise should have taught you, Dirk, it's that trust is earned, not taken."

Rona let go of his arm and turned to leave. Before she got more than a few steps from him, Dirk caught her hand. She froze in place. Dirk didn't mean to grab her hand. That was not his style. He just wanted to ensure that she didn't leave. To make sure that she was listening when he spoke to her. He let go as soon as he knew she wouldn't walk away before he finished. "You should remember that statement, Rona, because it goes both ways. Trust is not taken; it's earned. So I want you to ask yourself: Should you ever again find yourself in a situation that would require my assistance, what have *you* done to earn *my* trust?"

The jungle was far from a silent place. But in that moment, Dirk and Rona could have been on the moon for all the sound that was between them. The silence that distance created was long and deafening. The pressure was heavy, the buildup of the unknown, intolerable. Rona turned her head as if to glance over her shoulder. Dirk's skin prickled like never before. She wanted to talk, to say...something. She wanted to spill...there was a moment of revelation just beyond out of reach...

She did not. Rona walked away so quickly anyone watching would swear she was running. Dirk knew better. He watched her leave. They had taken a step forward. Whether it was a step towards friendship and enlightenment or betrayal and continued ignorance, Dirk did not know, but he did know that if you weren't moving forward, even in the wrong direction, then you were moving back. And moving back was never an option. She disappeared from sight, moving out of the jungle into the clearing that was to be their exit point. The NightHawks should be there to pick them up anytime now.

Explosions ripped through the air as the sounds of gunfire, the smell of smoke, and the latent heat of artillery coalesced on Dirk in one single defining moment. It was coming from the clearing. Sounds of battle, of dying men and women, screams of agony stabbed Dirk's eardrums. He rushed forward without thinking.

Dirk had barely reached the tree line of the clearing when he took a smack to the side of the head. He looked up to see a soldier wearing a red and green uniform and holding a light shiv in his hand.

Dirk gulped. The Horde was here...for real this time.

CHAPTER 21
CONFESSION

Time: Early morning
Scene: Outer ring of the Jade Empire

Xui Li was torn. On one hand, what that infuriating man did to her was absolutely unforgivable. On the other, he was beyond gorgeous and her soul mate. Thus her dilemma. If she told him how rudely he acted, it could damage their relationship. If not, well, she *was* the princess here. She couldn't very well have people treating her that way. What would be next? Foreigners taking over the palace?

They had arrived in the outer ring of the Seven Cities the day before. Instead of her romp through peasanthood coming to a quick close once inside the Empire, the incorrigible man had insisted they lie low for at least a day. Why was beyond her, but in her current state of dress, it wasn't like she could go up to the nearest security officer and tell him to call for a coach to pick her up. In fact, she wasn't entirely sure how she was going to manage to convince anyone that she was who she said she was. Perhaps the Magician had already thought of that.

It was the early morning of their second day in the outer ring. Why she was up at this ungodly hour was also beyond her. Apparently, normal people didn't get up when they wanted to; rather, they awoke when incredibly sexy yet annoying men told them to. Still, even at this time of the morning, he looked incredible. And because it was the sole redeeming feature of this whole ordeal, she was not going to miss an opportunity to spend time with him.

Dressed in her commoner's rags, she was eating what was supposed to pass for breakfast. While her appetite for the bland food was almost nonexistent, her appetite for soaking in the beauty sitting across from her was a different story altogether.

"Once you're finished eating, we can head out. I have some business to attend to, and once that is finished, we can start working on getting you home." He spoke in a quiet yet confident voice, almost as if he never had a need to shout.

"Well, while I am not accustomed to traipsing around town on other people's business, I suppose since I'll be with you, I can make a small exception—this one time." She smiled coyly behind her spoonful of...whatever it was she was pretending to eat. "I do have to say, it will be interesting to see my country through different eyes. I don't believe I have ever had the pleasure of *walking* through one of our nation's fine streets."

A slight smile crept onto the handsome man's face. "I suppose that is very true. Nevertheless, you will need to set aside your wants for a little while. I cannot have you leaving my side for any reason."

Xui Li grinned devilishly before replying, "Oh, I don't think that staying close to you will be a problem at all."

————

Xui Li was determined to stay next to her prize catch as they navigated through the city, and for the most part, she was successful. While they both got the occasional stare from passersby, the Magician had insisted on a more muted wardrobe than Xui Li was used to, and in fact, they blended into the crowd quite nicely. The Magician seemed to know exactly where he was going. He made several stops at various markets and shops, picking up odds and ends. Before long, they had arrived at a very curious shop that seemed a little out of place in the bustling town. Upon entering, the Magician warmly greeted the old shop owner in perfect Hmong. Xui Li didn't have the slightest idea what they were talking about, how the old man knew the Magician, and how he recognized him in disguise. Yet the mere fact that this incredible man spoke the many dialects of her homeland just intensified her conviction that they were meant to be together.

The two men continued their conversation and eventually shook hands in what seemed like the close of a deal. Since neither exchanged any product or currency, Xui Li wondered about the exact nature of their transaction. She was determined to find out.

"What was that all about?" she asked.

"Just catching up with someone I know," he replied coolly.

"How in the world do you know that ancient old man?" she asked indignantly.

"He's an old friend. I was asking him about the local security activity in these parts and the next inner rings. From what he told me, we have our work cut out for us."

Us, she thought. *He said 'us.'*

The Magician led her over to a small café and ordered some afternoon tea.

"Let's go over today's events," he said calmly as he sat across from her. "I know this is all new to you, and I want you to feel as comfortable as possible."

He is always looking out for me, she thought. "Yes, I think that is a good idea. I'm not sure what I would ever do without you."

The Magician paused and then began to review the plan. "There is minimal security in the outer four cities, at least not enough that it will pose a problem for you to pass through unquestioned. When you arrive in the Fifth Ring, security is stepped up considerably. That is where you will need to

contact the security office and reveal yourself. Those posi-
tioned there are at a high-enough pay grade that they will
contact the Empire immediately and see to your swift return.
You should not have any problems. Do you have any
questions?"

Xui Li was only half-listening. "What? Questions? Um,
no. I don't have any questions."

"Good. Then if you are finished with your tea, you should
get going." The Magician stood up from the table and handed
a bag to Xui Li. "I've packed some things for you: water,
snacks, and some money in case you need anything else."

Xui Li took the bag and melted a little more inside.

"Thank you for doing this, Xui Li. It shouldn't be too long
after you are settled in that I contact you."

Xui Li's heart skipped a beat. She had almost forgotten
that he was not coming with her. She needed to act fast. Her
mind was racing.

"Oh, as I said before, I am the one who owes you thanks.
You have been just incredible." She was stalling. She needed
to figure something out quickly, or he would be gone forever.

"I do have one little favor to ask," she said sweetly. "I am
still a little nervous about traveling alone. Do you think you
could escort me to the gate just so I know you're there...
please?" She put on her best sad puppy-dog face.

The Magician simply stared at her, his expression never
wavering. Finally, after a long minute, his eyes softened...a
little.

"Of course. But as we've talked about, we cannot be seen together moving forward. I will take you to the gate, but you will need to be strong and go on through by yourself. Will that work for you?"

Oh sweet gods, this was really happening. She was really going to be alone without her true love.

"Yes, that would be very kind of you. Thank you again." What was she going to do when they reached the gate? Her mind continued to race.

———

The two walked up alleys and back roadways. Xui Li was too occupied with her planning to notice anything about where they were headed. During the short walk, she had come to only one conclusion. It was risky, but she knew it would work. It *had* to work.

Xui Li noticed that they had stopped at the edge of a darkened alley. She looked out into the street and saw the city gate not far off. Her heart was thumping in her chest. She could do this.

"Well, I guess this is it," she commented offhandedly, trying to keep the nervousness out of her voice.

"Right. All you need to do is blend in with a group of people that are heading through the gate. After that, take your time so that you do not appear to be rushing, but don't spend more time than you need to in any one city. Always move forward to the next gate. You'll be just fine. I know you can do it."

This was it. This was her last chance.

"I...I need to tell you something. Something very important." She wasn't sure where she was going with this. In fact, there was no way she could think straight while she was looking right at his incredible face. She turned from him, took one step, and drew in a deep breath.

"I have to tell you something very important, and if I don't say it now, I fear I may never have the chance. Ever since you rescued me, I have felt this electric connection with you. You are so amazing and wonderful and mysterious and... just everything. I know you feel it too. You are so kind to me and take care of me. That shows me that you share my deep feelings. It shows me that...that we belong to each other. I know I don't even know your real name, and of course, I know you are in disguise, and you have a shadowy history. I know the lies that have been told about you. There is no possible way that you are the man they call the Magician, for you are far too kind and loving. Your heart is too pure and gentle. And I know that we have only known each other for a short time, but you can trust me with your secrets. I know...." Xui Li took a deep breath and let it out. "I know that I am deeply, madly," she turned around to face her love, "in lo—"

She stopped mid-sentence. Her hands balled into fists as she stared at the completely deserted alley. "THAT'S TWICE!" she screamed.

———

Xui Li was furious. Like blood-boiling, raging bull furious. There was no taking her time. After she had stormed through the first gate without so much as a backward glance at the startled guards, she headed straight for the next, then the next. Several hours later, she had reached the security station in the Fifth City. She was sweaty and sticky, her hair was completely disheveled, the rags she was wearing were wet with perspiration and slightly mud-caked from all the walking, and her mood had not improved at all.

"Look, you little peons!" Xui Li yelled. "I will have all of your heads if you do not get me what I want!"

The negotiations to have the security station contact the royal palace had definitely moved into the hostile phase. It was her against two buffoons in the small interrogation room, and things were not going well.

"Like I told you, miss...what did you say your name was again?" asked the rotund guard with the bristly mustache.

"Xui Li Fen Fang Sun, as in *PRINCESS* Xui Li Fen Fang Sun, you dolt."

"Right, Xui Li. The same name as the young woman who was kidnapped a short time ago by slavers. I keep forgetting that. And Xui Li, you say that you escaped from Sanzarubi, carved your way through the jungle, and waltzed all the way to the Fifth City gate. Is that correct?"

Xui Li closed her eyes in disdain. "No, that is not correct.

I don't merely *say* that all that happened. It *did* happen. Now, contact the palace at once before I completely lose what infinitesimal patience I have left."

The portly guard nodded his head as he smoked a large, foul-smelling cigar. "Yes, of course. You *did* all that. My humble apologies, your highness," he replied with dripping sarcasm. "You see, Xui Li, or whatever your real name is, all of this is pointless. We have contacted the Empire and sent your bio-profile. As soon as it comes back and proves that you are not who you say you are, you will be charged with impersonating a royal figure, and we can be done with this little charade."

Xui Li smiled and cocked her head. "Oh, well, that is fabulous. Why didn't you just say so in the first place?" Her whole demeanor changed, and she settled, very relaxed, into her seat in the small room. She started inspecting her nails.

The two guards looked at each other, both concerned about the mental stability of their suspect. The far-fetched story, filthy clothes, and crazy mood swings all were indicative of a person who had been living on the street for some time.

A sharp knock on the door was followed immediately by the appearance of a well-dressed older man. Both the guards jumped up and saluted him. He sneered at them and nodded curtly, indicating they should leave. They did so without question.

Once gone, the well-dressed man placed a hand on his

chest and bowed as he knelt down. "My deepest apologies, your royal highness. I have no words to describe my absolute shame in the treatment you have received at the hands of my men. I can assure you they will be appropriately punished for their actions."

Xui Li did not look up from examining her fingernails and did not speak for some time.

"I assume you are the captain in charge of this unit," she asked without looking at the man.

"Yes, your highness, I am. And I can assure you, as soon as I was informed that you were here—"

"And as the captain, you are responsible for the operation of this unit, correct?"

The well-dressed man shifted uncomfortably. "Yes, your highness. But you see—"

"Then as the ranking officer, I see no reason that you should not suffer the same consequences as the idiots that you command here."

The captain looked incredibly nervous. A few times he started to say something, but then thought better of it. Xui Li merely continued to look over her nails.

"You are dismissed, captain. Please connect this comm directly to palace security on your way out." With that, the captain bowed again, awkwardly, and exited the room. Moments later, the comm connected, and a man's voice offered a reverent greeting. Oh, how she had missed that.

"I am sure you are aware that I am currently in this vile

gatehouse just outside the Fifth City. My patience has run thin. You will arrange immediate accommodations for me at the most lavish hotel in this disgusting hole. Make sure there are attendants to help me bathe and to scrub off this filth that I have been exposed to. Further, I wish to speak to my hand-maiden at once."

The man on the comm voiced his understanding of his instructions and transferred the call to Xui Li's handmaiden. After a minute, an older woman greeted her in a deferential tone.

"Mei, it is so good to hear a familiar voice. You would absolutely not believe what I have been through," pouted Xui Li.

"Yes, child, we were all overjoyed to hear that you were alive and will be returning to us," replied Mei.

"Oh, I will tell you all about it when I arrive. I will be staying here until the coach arrives to escort me into the palace grounds. I can't imagine that they will have all of the bath salts and perfumes I need to truly clean up, but I suppose it will have to do. I will not spend a minute longer here than absolutely necessary."

"Mistress...."

"I am not sure what to do about my hair, though. Do you think you could send my hairdressers with the coach that is picking me up? Yes, let's do that. I can't imagine being paraded through the palace grounds without looking absolutely stunning."

"Mistress...."

"And also send some dresses that I can choose from. There should be that gorgeous red one—oh, and the deep emerald, send that as well. Oh Mei, I can't tell you how excited I am to sleep in my own bed."

"Yes, about that, Mistress...."

"Don't interrupt me, Mei, these things are crucial to my return. The long-lost daughter of the Empire returned to her home. Oh, my entrance to the palace grounds will be exquisite. I have dreamed of something like this, but never did I believe it would have to happen this way."

"Xui Li!" Mei yelled.

Xui Li was taken aback. She and Mei had been close for a long time, but for her to be so informal and brusque with her...

"Mistress," continued Mei, "there have been some...developments in your absence."

"Developments? Mei, what are you babbling about?"

"I do not believe that there will be more than a standard welcome for you when you return. And as for your room, well, it is currently...occupied at the moment."

Xui Li felt a familiar feeling of frustration and helplessness creep into her gut. As she listened to Mei, it slowly morphed into anger and then into a budding rage.

"Occupied? Standard welcome? By the gods, Mei, you better start spilling." She found her hands once again clenched in fists.

"As I stated, mistress, your room is currently occupied... by another long-lost daughter of the Empire. *The* Gōng Zhǔ has been restored to the palace. There are already plans for her welcoming banquet and ceremonies. I fear that these will overshadow your return. I am also sure that once your return is relayed to the royal court, you will be expected to attend the gala."

Xui Li was woozy. Her head felt like it was spinning. "But what about me?" she asked feebly. "I returned, too. Where's my ceremony?" Xui Li started to cry. She rapidly flipped between sorrowful sobs and screams of anger. This was not happening. Not to her. Not to a princess of the Empire.

"Where's my gala? I want my gala, Mei!" she screamed as she slumped out of her chair and continued to bawl on the cold, hard floor.

CHAPTER 22
LORD OF THE RINGS

Time: Late morning

Scene: Outer rings of the Jade Empire

A man dressed in common, unremarkable attire approaches the city gate. With any luck, the vain girl he left in the alley would continue to blabber for some time before she realizes he is gone. He walks towards the city gates without a hint of reservation or apprehension. He had done this many times before, and this time would be no different. He approaches a group of people and slides himself into the middle of them as they approach the gate. No one seems to pay him any attention, as his mannerisms and behavior blend in perfectly with those around him. He passes through the checkpoint with ease, knowing that at this time of day, the guards want to maintain the flow of people rather than stopping them to check IDs.

In the Second Ring, the man stops at various shops and buys a few articles of clothing. Next, he makes his way to a more rundown part of the city and deftly donates some of the clothing he is wearing to the local population. Putting on his new purchases, the man continues to mill about the city. He travels in an eastward direction, following the curve of the city. He takes a transport to the southeast quarter and arrives there a few hours after the transport's departure. It is now midday, and he stops at a local café and orders tea and a bowl of seasoned rice. He sits quietly at the café, never engaging anyone in conversation, but never appearing to look out of place. Upon finishing the meal, he tips the waiter moderately and continues to make his way around to the easternmost gate.

He checks his timepiece and heads purposefully to a tavern close to the gate. There, he sits at a side table and orders a local spiced beer. Casually, he pretends to sip the drink as he moves his unobtrusive gaze across the bar. Memorizing the number and location of all men and women present, he focuses his attention on a guard sitting at a back booth. Without staring, he keeps track of the movements of the bar patrons, always keeping the guard at the back in his peripheral vision. He checks his timepiece and takes another false sip of the beer. A few minutes later, another guard enters the bar and begins to look around. Noticing the guard at the back, the man stops to ask the barman for a drink and then proceeds to join his comrade.

The first guard greets the second warmly and asks if he wants something to eat. The second guard declines, explaining that his drink is on the way. A steady influx of patrons enters the establishment and finds places to sit and order. The two guards continue to talk amicably until the second one looks for the barman and his drink. He sees the man busily attending to the new customers and shakes his head in frustration. The first guard checks his timepiece, swears, shovels another two bites of food into his mouth, and bids his friend farewell. The second guard nods and makes some sort of joke about his friend always being late. As the first guard hurriedly exits the tavern, the second guard sees the waitress coming over with his cold drink.

The commonly dressed man pretends to drink from his beer, watching the waitress make her way over to the back booth. Nonchalantly, he closes his eyes and taps his foot lightly against the floor. Just as the waitress approaches the booth, she stumbles, and the cold drink comes splashing down onto the guard's lap. Horrified, the young girl starts to apologize profusely. The second guard, while surprised by his now-wet pants, collects himself and tries to calm the girl down. He grabs the towel from her arm and starts to wipe the drink from his pants. Still apologizing, she points him to the facilities and says when he gets back, his new drink will be waiting for him—on the house, of course.

The guard nods and hands her the wet towel as he walks to the bathroom. He does not notice a plainly dressed man walking slightly to the side of him until they reach the restroom door at almost the same time. The man looks at the guard's wet pants and hastily swings the door open for him. Thanking him, the guard walks into the restroom and over to the sink. Grabbing towels, he tries to pat dry his soaking pants. He grabs another handful, and just as he looks down, he feels a sharp pain in his neck. His vision goes blurry and then black.

The man grabs the guard before he hits the floor and drags him to an open stall. Quickly, he strips the man of his uniform, then undresses himself. The man puts on the uniform and adjusts the clothing to fit around his tactical harness and weapon straps. Lastly, he dresses the guard in his ordinary clothes, sits him atop the toilet leaning to one side, and then pours the spiced beer down the man's front. He rolls underneath the stall door and walks over to the sink. Retrieving a small vial of white plastic crystals from his chest harness, the man holds the container in his hands and then shakes the contents onto the wet pants. Almost instantly, the plastic crystals begin to fluff up as they rapidly absorb the liquid. After a few moments, the pants are dry. The man sweeps the now-fluffy particles off his pants and onto the floor.

Donning the guard's cap, the man checks his appearance in the mirror, then exits the bathroom. He purposefully walks around the long way to avoid the waitress as she brings the new drink to the back booth. Now outside the tavern, he heads directly for the gate. His posture has changed. His shoulders are back, and there is a swagger to his step. His eyes and face look hard, and people instinctively move out of his way. He briefly flashes his ID to one of the guards, who motions him through without a second glance. As the man walks away from the gate, now in the Third City, a smug smile creeps across his face.

———

Moving swiftly but not arousing suspicion, the imposter guard makes his way towards the northern gate to the Fourth City. It is getting late in the day, and the man welcomes the coming darkness of night. Continuing towards the gate, the man locates a back alley. With the sun now set, he finds a secluded space and strips off the stolen uniform. In the last glimmers of ambient light, the man's skin color changes to a deep, pitch black. Anyone who witnessed this metamorphosis would swear they had seen a man being engulfed by surrounding shadows until, from head to toe, he was nothing but a walking shadow himself. Now clothed in darkness and keeping to the edges of alleys and buildings, the man weaves his way ever closer to the northern gate.

Just over an hour later, the man crouches near the formidable wall. Calling up his infrared HUD on his forearm, the man reviews the security intel he has gleaned. A guard passes twenty-five meters from the man. As his IR display cannot be seen without night vision goggles, and since he blends perfectly with the darkness at the foot of the wall, the man makes no attempt to further hide himself.

Once the guard has moved an adequate distance away, the man silently creeps to a spot along the wall a few hundred meters up from the last guard patrol. Here the wall is more run-down, as is the area around it.

Quietly, the man sits and observes the space around him for many minutes. Slowly, he continues to slip around the wall until he finds himself at an old sewer duct. He crouches as he walks to the sewer opening. Large rusted metal bars cover the opening in a crisscross pattern, and a vile stench wafts out of the sewer drain as a slight breeze picks up around him.

Carefully, the man stretches his arms towards the metal grate. Just as he is about to touch it, his arms freeze at a small noise. Instantly, he whips around to scan what is behind him. A slight movement at the corner of a building not too far off catches his eye. Sprinting towards the building, the man closes in on the small movement. As he approaches, he sees two small boys duck behind a crate. Slowing his pace, he rounds the crate and looks down at the two cowering boys. A few lights at the top of the building provide a tiny amount of illumination, just enough that he can make out their dirty clothes and ratty hair.

The man in black crouches down and puts a finger to his lips, indicating that the boys should be quiet. Still cowering close together, the boys reluctantly nod their heads. The man holds up both of his hands, showing them the front, then the back, and then the front again. At this gesture, the boys seem to calm down just a bit. Their heads cock to the side in curiosity as they stare at the man. Now that he has their attention focused on his hands, the man places his palms together and then slowly brings his fingers down until they all touch in a small clump. With careful movement, the man pulls apart his hands to reveal a tasty-looking meat stick. The boys both open their mouths in amazement but are stopped from making any sound as the man once again brings his finger up to his lips.

As the man holds the meat stick in the palm of one hand and holds up one finger on his other hand, the boys become excited to see what will happen next. The man covers the meat stick with his hands and brings them up again in front of him. Then, with a little flair, he fans his hands out to display four meat sticks. Again, the boys look amazed by this bit of magic. Once again holding his finger to his lips, the man offers the food to the boys. They look at each other in disbelief and then carefully reach out and take the gift. Both begin immediately to chow down on the treats. The man places a hand on the shoulder of one boy and motions for them to get home. They both stand and start to walk towards the building. The man turns and begins to walk back to the wall when he feels a small tap on his back. Turning around, he sees the two boys standing behind him.

They smile and motion for him to follow as they scamper towards the wall.

Looking around and seeing no one else in sight, the man follows the two boys. They pass the sewer drain and continue to curve around the wall. The boys move through the brush as if they had made this run many times before. About a hundred meters from the sewer, the boys slow down as they approach a spot on the wall overgrown with thick vines and dense bushes. They stop just in front of the tangle of vines and point towards the wall, motioning for the man in black to come closer.

Carefully, the man walks closer. They continue to motion for him to come even closer and keep pointing to a spot on the wall. The man approaches the spot and sees what they are showing him. Turning his back to them, he nods and then shoos them off back the way they came. Once they are out of sight, the man inches closer to the wall. Pulling back the thick vines, he uncovers a hole in the wall that would be completely unnoticeable if he weren't standing almost on top of it. Taking one last look around, the man slips behind the vines and disappears through the wall into the next city.

———

The man locates a high-end suit shop and lets himself in through the back. Making quick work of the rudimentary alarm system, he continues to the sales floor and peruses the clothing. He selects a dark-colored suit, a muted shirt, and a traditional tie, in addition to conservative shoes. Once dressed, the man looks at himself in the mirror to make sure the cut of the jacket and pants does not reveal the bulges of his harness. Satisfied with his appearance, he slips out the way he came and walks at a comfortable pace towards the business district. Once there, he locates a café that is just opening for its pre-dawn customers, sits at one of the outside tables, and orders a strong tea.

Once again, he observes all those around him as he waits patiently. As the usual crowd of businessmen rolls into the district, they are accompanied by grifters, panhandlers, and others with dubious intentions. Now, with both groups of businessmen present, the man searches for his mark. It takes only an hour to find him.

A rotund, affluent-looking Gangan man and his significantly skinnier and more attractive female companion sit at a table at the same café. Immediately, the well-dressed man notices the attention of more than one "entrepreneur" zero in on the foreign couple. Keeping the couple and the others in his sight, the man inconspicuously finishes his tea and begins reading a copy of the local news. It isn't long before the couple finishes their breakfast and stands to leave. Almost immediately, a small man walks straight towards them, a determined look in his eyes. The rotund man pulls out an expensive-looking personal interface and starts to check his schedule. Upon his lovely companion's complaint that he is attached to that "thing," the large man offers a less-than-sincere apology and places the small interface in his jacket pocket. He looks around the café and spots an empty table with an empty teacup and a copy of the local news. After grabbing the news, he and the woman walk towards the center of the business district.

By now, the small man is merely a few paces away from the couple. Walking casually, he brushes past the two, slightly bumping into the man. Without losing a step, the small man turns to apologize profusely and begs the man's pardon, then swiftly turns back around and continues on his way. The rotund Gangan smiles the polite smile of a foreigner, realizes the small man is no longer looking, and changes his smile to a look of annoyance.

The small man heads straight for the corner of the closest building, rounding it as he picks up speed. He darts down the first side street he sees and finally comes to a stop behind a large trash receptacle. The small man looks around and then squats down to inspect his acquisition. The interface is very expensive and a foreign model not available for purchase within the Empire. A scratching noise at the corner causes the man to pop up and peer around the receptacle. Seeing nothing there, but not wanting to stick around, he pockets the interface and heads for the other end of the street.

As he walks, the small man constantly checks over his shoulder. His pace is brisk and at times speeds up to a half-run. Another sound echoes off the wall at the other end of the street, causing the man to look behind him as he rounds the corner of a building. Before he can turn back around, he runs into a well-dressed man in a dark suit. The well-dressed man stumbles back from the smaller man, yells at him to watch where he is going, and then begins to dust off his clothes. The other man, startled, apologizes and turns to jog away from the corner. The well-dressed man yells after him, which only causes the small man to break out into a full run.

Out of breath, he rounds a corner three streets down and hides in a doorway. Leaning over to catch his breath, it takes him a few minutes to calm down. Wiping the sweat from his brow, he reaches inside his coat to look at the interface again. Pulling the object out of his pocket, the small man stares confusedly at the thin rectangular piece of dirty scrap metal that he holds in his hands.

———

Somewhere near the business gate to the Fifth City, a well-dressed man in a dark suit, muted color shirt, traditional tie, and conservative shoes passes a Gangan man and his lovely female companion. He overhears the rotund foreigner arguing with a local security officer about a stolen personal interface.

As he approaches the business gate, the well-dressed man shows the gate officer his ID displayed on his expensive-looking foreign interface. The guard looks at the picture on the interface and motions for the man to register it. Holding the device close to the scanner, the security matrix searches for the man's clearance. The gate officer checks the ID clearance on his display and sees the Gangan businessman listed with full access to the Fifth City in addition to a schedule showing meetings with a number of local commercial venture partners later that day. The gate officer nods to the well-dressed man and waves the next person forward.

With a knowing smile on his face, the well-dressed man walks into the fifth of the Seven Cities. A short distance from the gate, he checks his timepiece and calls up a map of the city on his new interface. Locating a spot on the map, he heads towards the western gate. With any luck, the annoying princess he is to meet there will not be late.

CHAPTER 23

THE JADIAN SUN

Time: Mid-morning, one day after Sam's arrival in the Seven Cities

Scene: The Emerald House

"Why didn't you tell me?" Sam glared at Misaka and Chen, who had prostrated themselves on the floor in front of her. Sam initially thought this behavior was strange, but considering her newfound knowledge that she was some sort of Jadian princess—or at least that everyone here thought she was—the action became less weird. In fact, it actually explained quite a lot of the behavior from everyone over the past weeks. "Misaka. Chen. Get up off the ground immediately."

The two handmaidens did as they were commanded. Their expressions were a delicate mix of horror and awe as they watched Sam's personal makeup and body assistants make her over.

Chen was the one to answer the question. "We are sorry, Gōng Zhǔ! We were ordered not to reveal any details to you in case we came in contact with enemy mystics. For you to have the information before we were on Jadian soil was too dangerous for you and Da Xiao. I assure you, Gōng Zhǔ, we meant no offense."

The two women again prostrated themselves on the floor.

"Chen. Misaka. Get up off the floor. Geez, it's hard to have a conversation with you when you keep doing that."

The two women reluctantly did as they were told. Misaka stepped forward. "We are ready to accept any punishment you bestow upon us, but we promise that we had only your best interest at heart."

Sam rolled her eyes. "I'm not going to punish you, Misaka. You were doing your job. I get that. I just thought...I just thought that we had become friends during our time together, and friends wouldn't keep that kind of information from each other."

Chen and Misaka exchanged looks of genuine surprise, and Sam realized the gravity of her words to the two young ladies. If she was royalty, as stupid as that sounded, then these two women were her servants in every sense of the word. It was hard to cultivate a friendship under those circumstances.

"Sam, child, are you ready?" The Madam entered with Lady Sasha and Alena in tow, the two assistants holding tablets and trailing at the ready behind the Madam. "Oh, my dear child—you look marvelous."

"Madam," Sam bowed her head respectfully. "Thank you for your compliment, but I feel foolish. Who actually wears this stuff?"

Sam pointed at the amalgamation of strange clothing she was wearing. "I feel like we are mixing styles here, and that's saying something, because I have the fashion sense of a beetle; you should ask my friend Cammie."

Sam stopped herself. Like the times when Richard came up in conversation, thinking about Cammie was too painful.

The Madam stepped to Sam and touched her face affectionately, a gesture that did not surprise or faze the onlooking crowd. "Child, you have to be aware of what this dress represents. The different pieces represent the heritage of the Empire: a Chinese qipao, a Japanese veil, a Russian shawl, and an Indian headdress. The Empire was designed to be a melting pot of different cultures all under the guidance of the Holy Emperor. The princesses of the Empire all wear such garb at their launch. You are the princess who was lost and now is found. You will be received like no other princess in history. You have to look the part."

Sam averted her eyes. "I still think it looks stupid. I cannot believe you all want me to go outside like this."

The Madam smiled. "I know, child, but endure. Your dress tonight will be of the finest Jadian silk, and you shall be the sparkling emerald of the ball at the Ceremony of the Changing Seasons. All will look on in envy."

Sam smiled as Adam popped into her mind. "OK. I suppose I could do it just this once."

The Madam offered Sam a hand. "Then let us go, child. The Seven Cities await your return."

———

Sam had never been part of a parade before, let alone had one thrown in her honor. The sights and sounds of the Jadian honor parade were like nothing she had ever seen. Sam tried to take it all in as she was chauffeured around in a car that looked to be hundreds of years old. Sam sat with the Madam as it rolled through the narrow streets of the Seven Cities. Sam had to admit, she did like the rumble and vibration of the vehicle. The hum of the fossil fuel engine was alluring.

After the parade, Sam was whisked back to the Emerald House and forced to endure more primping, but this time it was a lot more fun. Expensive gowns from every designer in the world were marched before Sam and her stylist as Sam pointed and made a list. Sam was not usually a girly girl and had always been rather low-key about her appearance. She didn't feel that she was particularly pretty, and she didn't have the know-how or desire to learn how to fake it like so many of the High Tracks girls back in Academy City 676, with their surgical alterations and armies of stylists. Now, she didn't have to worry about dressing and looking pretty because it was going to be done for her. Unexpectedly, a memory of shopping with Cammie for dresses popped into her mind. Sam quickly brushed it aside, not wanting to deal with the emotions accompanying it.

Alena materialized next to her. "Gōng Zhǔ, you look fantastic."

"Thank you, Alena. I must admit it feels a bit on the revealing side."

Alena came and inserted herself behind Sam, taking a hairbrush from one of the stylists. She started to brush Sam's hair. "True, it is a bit revealing for my tastes, too, but it's the style for the celebrations here in the Seven Cities—rest assured that it won't be the most revealing. The royals often try to outdo each other in their manner of dress. It's become very much a spectator event."

"How so?"

"Lady Sasha went to great lengths to turn this year's Celebration of the Changing Seasons into a celebration for you. The Emperor's only other daughter, Xui Li, also just returned recently, and now that you've come back to us, it's an opportunity for the Emperor to poke back at some of the other noble houses of the Empire."

"Sounds complicated."

"Court politics always is. The Emperor is absolute in his authority, but he couldn't run the Empire without the help of his nobles. It's simply too big. The balance becomes precarious at times."

"I bet."

Alena stepped out from behind Sam. "But tonight you don't need to worry about any of this. You simply need to hold your head up high and smile. You are the daughter of the Emperor, and tonight, Samantha Montgomery, is your night."

Sam found herself in a full-length mirror and admired the handiwork of Alena and the others. "Now if only I could be excited for it."

Sam examined herself in the mirror. At least she looked good.

———

"Where are we going again?" asked Sam as their hover transport cleared a security post. Sam rode with the Madam in the royal compartment of the vehicle. Sam knew that Chen, Misaka, Alena, and Sasha were somewhere behind them, but she could not see them at the moment.

The Madam touched a delicate finger to her lips, something that Sam knew to be a nervous habit. It was amazing how quickly these things became noticeable. "The Fourth Ring, child. There isn't a reception space in the Seventh City big enough for all the provincial nobles, businessmen, and other guests, not to mention that security procedures there are too stringent. There is a castle in the Fourth City specially constructed for just such a purpose. There you'll meet the Emperor and be launched into Jadian society."

"Can't wait," muttered Sam under her breath.

"What was that, child?"

"Nothing."

Picking out their destination was easy. Bright spotlights and music could be seen and heard for minutes before Sam's procession got even close to the venue. Located exactly in the center of the Fourth City, the Madam had not been joking when she said "castle." The local venue for the Ceremony of the Changing Seasons was a castle in every sense of the word, a place that Sam had only seen in history books and really old 2-D movies. Huge towers, medieval battlements, and buttresses aplenty. Sam knew that Richard would have gone crazy for a place like this. Well, the *old* Richard would have. He would have spent a bunch of time pointing out historical inaccuracies in structure and material, of which Sam knew there had to be some. He would have done so until he frustrated her and everyone else around them...gods, she missed him.

The hover transport pulled into what Sam could only assume was the gateway through the flashing lights; the crowds of people made it difficult to be sure. The Madam touched Sam on the shoulder.

"Before you enter, my dear, let me give you a piece of advice."

Sam leaned towards her.

The Madam smiled gently. "For now, let me do the talking. Follow my movements, bow when I bow, but only at three-quarters length. You are a princess of the Empire; the other nobles will look for any reason to discount or mock you. I will give you more instruction when you go inside. And Sasha will be there should you require any advice."

"You're leaving me?" Sam didn't like the sound of that. She was completely out of her element. There were enough people here to make Cammie's famous ragers look like a small gathering of friends.

The Madam again touched Sam, this time on the cheek. "Peace, child. I shall be but in shouting distance. No one will dare hurt or even openly mock you for fear of my wrath. All you must do is avoid embarrassing the Emperor and your mother."

And my mother? thought Sam. *Yeah, if only she could see me now. What an odd thing to say.*

The hover transport came to a halt, landing in front of a sea of people, just behind a couple of other transports. A green carpet stretched from the road in front of their craft up and into the recesses of the castle that towered above. Just outside her door, Sam could hear one voice in particular.

"This is Ling Lang, reporting to you from outside the Pendragon for the Sixty-Seventh Annual Ceremony of the Changing Seasons. The nobles are dazzling the green carpet this year with their display of opulence and finery. And look who we have here—it's Xui Li, the Second Daughter of the

Emperor. Gōng Zhǔ, do you have a moment to speak with us?"

"Yes, of course, Ms. Lang. I am always happy to speak to the people of the Empire."

The hover transport moved out of earshot, and Sam couldn't hear the rest of the interview. Finally, it was their turn. Sam, in a red qipao with an emerald design, and the Madam, in her black and diamonds, glanced at one another. Sam admired how the Madam's dress and eyes sparkled in the reflected lights of cameras and show illumination. The Madam peered at Sam. "Are you ready, my child?"

Sam felt like she was going to throw up, but she nodded. A half-second later, the door swung open.

———

"Over there is Zou Qin of the Han Province, his two daughters Mei and Jiao, and his son, Michael." Sam watched as Lady Sasha pointed to various persons around them. "Just behind the Qins, you have Dmitry Rurik of the Russian Expanse, and his sons Ivan, Igor, and Iosif. It looks like he left his wife home again, the pig. You'll want to watch out for Ivan and Igor; they have been trying to catch an inner province noble for years...."

Sam stopped listening. Lady Sasha was a wonderful personal assistant, but she took her job way too seriously for Sam's taste. The woman had spent the last hour reciting every noble, major or minor, as well as every official from across the Empire. Not even the historical beauty of the Pendragon Castle could enable Sam to recover from Sasha's endless drone. Basically, she was boring Sam to death.

"Samantha, dear, don't slouch, child." The Madam stepped beside Sam and touched her on the shoulder. "People are watching, remember."

Sam scowled. "This is supposed to be a party, right? Are all royal gatherings like this? If that's the case, then I don't think I want to be a noble anymore."

Not that she really believed she was one to begin with.

The Madam laughed, a beautiful sound, vibrant and full of life. Apparently, this was a phenomenon because people standing close to Sam, Sasha, and the Madam looked at the Madam with something akin to disbelieving wonder—Sasha included, though her smile was more knowing. "Yes, Samantha, this is supposed to be a party, but the appearance of the Emperor always puts people on edge. He makes quite the impression, you see."

Not knowing how to reply to this statement, Sam scanned the massive ballroom, searching for a familiar face— a specific familiar face, actually. Adam...Adam...where was he?

Sam's breath caught in her throat. There he was, standing among a gaggle of noble girls. She couldn't hear what they were saying, but she could imagine what the conversation was like.

"Oh Adam, look how handsome you look. So manly. Would you like to take me away with you?"

"I am sorry, random girl, but my heart belongs to another. She is my world, my sun, my moon. I traveled across this gods-forsaken world in search of her. In fact, I must go to her, find her, and tell her such things that are in my heart, the heart that she has stolen and is hers and hers alone."

"Gōng Zhǔ, do you realize that your mouth is hanging open?" Sasha tapped Sam on the shoulder. Sam closed her mouth; her face went crimson. How embarrassing.

At that moment, trumpets flared, accompanied by the pounding of bass drums. Guards wearing green and red—the Mogui and the Red Guard—walked through the hall, clearing their path by their mere footsteps. The nobles, staff, and performers stepped out of the way for the soldiers, who moved in perfect synchronicity. The red- and green-clad men stopped when they were spaced evenly across the room. The second they were in place, the pounding on the drums subsided to that of a heartbeat, the trumpets quieted, and the subtle lull of a flute wafted through the air. There was a creaking as a massive stone double door inched open, filling the room with a nerve-grinding grating sound. Finally, the doors came to a rest.

A voice loomed out from all around, a voice that didn't appear to be coming from any one place, that instead seemed to meld with the air itself. It said:

"Noble men and noble ladies, honored guests, I am the sol

who peaks in the east, the moon that hides in the west, I am the sea, the wind, the life, the breath, the blood of the Empire, I am he who welcomes you to my cities, my Seven Cities, I *am* the Jadian Sun."

Four men carrying a palanquin walked slowly across the room. As the procession passed, servant, performer, and noble alike bowed, kneeling much like Alena did the first day Sam came to the Seven Cities. There were some noted exceptions —about twenty people bowed but did not get down on the ground. The Madam was included in this group, as were a couple of other women and boys Sam had seen in the Emerald House; a gorgeous teenage girl standing not far from Sam, staring at her as if she wished nothing more than for Sam to die; and then Adam, which was strange. The men holding the litter stopped as a section of the floor on the far side of the room began to rise, revealing a great throne made out of green rhodium. The four men set down the palanquin. Two of them knelt, mimicking most of those in attendance. The other two removed the top covering of the silk and offered their hands to the occupant. They helped out a man clad in riches of all kinds, so much finery that it was hard to make out the individual within. The Emperor, the Jadian Sun, stood and walked to his green rhodium throne. He turned and sat upon it.

"All rise," he commanded, this time with a voice that carried from his position. "I am overjoyed that all of you could come, and it seems that we've an even larger group in attendance than usual. Could it be that all of you have come to see the first, the first who we thought was lost?"

No one answered, but Sam could feel the tension...no, not tension...excitement. She could feel the excitement of the people rise.

"I understand your feelings, my people. I too am over-joyed that the First Daughter of my Favorite Wife, Irina Fen Fang Sun, has returned to us. My little Irina, I would have you come to me."

Sam craned her neck, as unladylike as that was, just like everyone else in the room. She looked, but she couldn't find this Irina anywhere...

The spotlight landed on Sam, and it took her no more than a second to realize. He was talking about *her*.

"Child," whispered the Madam, "go, your father awaits you."

Sam walked towards the Jadian Sun. Every step was excruciating as all eyes fell upon her. Some looked with inten-sity and desire, others with hatred and disgust, others still with simple curiosity. By the time she reached the top of the raised podium, she thought her legs might give out. The Jadian Sun smiled as she neared him. He dropped the pretense and threw his arms around her.

"Irina, welcome home."

The crowd cheered.

CHAPTER 24
THE NEXT JADIAN SUN

Time: Late evening

Scene: Gala reception at the Pendragon Castle, in the fourth ring of the Jade Empire

"Hello, Father?" Sam managed to squeeze out. The Emperor had a death grip on her that was making it hard to breathe.

"My dear Irina," said the Emperor. His voice was higher than she would have expected but held a strange weight to it. "You were lost. Now you are found. I will never let you out of my sight again."

The Emperor let her go and studied her face, looking directly into her eyes. He looked young; his face was smooth, devoid of wrinkles, and his hair was black as night—the spitting image of one in his late twenties, though Sam knew that he was much older. His eyes gave him away; they were old beyond their years, shrewd and calculating. No wonder he was in charge.

"I am sorry, child. I must go. The Empire never sleeps, even if my harpy nobles are here. I cannot be away from the affairs of the Empire too long."

The Emperor turned abruptly and walked back to his throne. He waved to her as the throne sank back into the ground, leaving Sam standing alone on the platform. All eyes were upon her. She was saved by the soldiers' retreat. They left the same way they entered, in perfect uniformity, step for step. They were mesmerizing; everyone watched them as they left the room. Once the soldiers were gone, the eyes turned back to Sam. She wasn't sure what to do. It was quiet, like those few seconds before a firing squad takes aim. Unfortunately, this group wasn't going to put her out of her misery.

"Gentle ladies and lords," rang out a voice, clear and feminine. It was close to her, but Sam did not recognize it. A girl stepped forward next to Sam, the same one who had been glaring at her so fervently during the Emperor's entrance.

"As my father said with such simple words, we are very glad that our long-lost sister has returned to us. I, Xui Li Fen Fang Sun, Second Daughter of our Jadian Sun, present to you the First Daughter of our Jadian Sun, Irina Fen Fang Sun."

Everyone clapped, some more enthusiastically than others, and then people started lining up at the bottom of the stairs.

"You'll be expected to talk to them, UWC pigdog." Xui Li

turned to Sam and smiled in a very fake manner. "I do not know why you think you can come back and claim the position of First Daughter so readily, but you have not heard the last of me."

"I don't know what you're talking about. I'm not even sure who you are. So why don't we start there?"

Sam put out her hand in a friendly gesture. Xui Li stared at her hand and then smiled darkly at Sam. "I am the owner of the bedroom in the Emerald House that you are currently occupying. I leave for a few weeks only to come back and find that some *commoner* pretending to be a princess has stolen what is rightfully mine."

Sam took a deep, controlling breath. The gravity of the situation was starting to get to her. She had been kidnapped from the UWC and forced halfway across the world, only to have the Emperor of the Jade Empire claim her as his daughter. She was confused, irritated, and now: angry. Sam stared at the gathering crowd, trying to will herself to calm down. People were watching—including the Madam. Sam purposefully put on a fake smile for the crowd and spoke very softly. "I'm not sure why you're so upset with me, but I'm sure we can work it out if you just calm down and explain—"

Xui Li assumed the same position and mirrored her smile. "Can you not hear, UWC pigdog? Has your lack of education, your lowly existence, destroyed your ability to understand simple words? You are an eyesore. I do not care if you are the Delphic Candidate. You make me sick. You are lucky my beloved is not here. He would end your sorry existence—"

Sam interrupted. "I don't mean to cut in on this one-woman freak show delusion you are so deeply swimming in, and I really hate to burst your over-inflated bubble, Ling Zoo—"

"Xui Li."

"Whatever." Sam continued to smile for the crowd. "But if you think I give a damn about whatever slight, real or imaginary, you've concocted in that too-small brain of yours, you've got another thing coming."

Sam was surprised at the venom in her voice. It was not like her.

Xui Li's face morphed at the statement. Sam didn't know if it was shock or what, but Xui Li looked like she had just been slapped across the face. A sudden moment of clarity, like when fog suddenly lifts from a hillside and the expanse of the valley below becomes visible, made Sam know before it happened; she could clearly see Xui Li's intentions. She put up her hand to defend herself.

"Xui Li! Stop this shameful behavior immediately." Adam was rushing over to them. He wasn't watching where he was going, though it didn't seem to matter as people were sliding out of his way.

"But Gēge, she started it—"

"Enough, Xui Li. You are acting like a child. If you desire

to be the First Daughter of the Empire, then start acting like it."

Xui Li swallowed hard, turned on her heel, and stalked away, snapping at servants and guests alike.

Adam was still watching her. "I am sorry, Samantha. Xui Li is temperamental at the best of times. Her recent endeavor has not made her any more endearing." Adam glanced around the room at the hungry eyes of the spectators.

"Come." He took her by the arm and began marching her out of the room. "You could use some fresh air, I think."

Adam led her, without speaking, up a stairway and through a series of halls to a balcony that overlooked much of the Fourth City. The air was crisp and a bit cold. "This is one of my favorite places in the Seven Cities," said Adam, walking to a stone bench on the far end of the balcony. "So how do you like it here so far?"

Sam didn't know how to answer the question. She didn't know where to begin.

Adam smiled at her in an affectionate way...but not *that* way; affectionate, but not romantic. Sam tried to return the smile.

Adam gestured in the direction of the reception. "So your Jadian society debut was a hit."

Sam rolled her eyes. "I wouldn't say that. I didn't really say much, and I got in a fight, against the Madam's orders, in front of the 'Highness' people."

"Nobles."

"Like it matters."

Sam cursed herself. She was being rude, but it was diffi-cult to care at this point. He could take offense if he liked. She had other queries. "So the Emperor...."

"Yes."

Sam straightened up and looked at Adam. She found his eyes. "Is he always like that?"

"Yes, to an extent—" Adam cut himself off. "What do you mean, Sam?"

"It's just...," Sam struggled to find the word, "that he's a bit on the weird side."

Adam laughed. "Yes, I've heard the Emperor described as that—a bit weird."

Adam and Sam broke into laughter, though Sam wasn't really amused. That wasn't what she had intended to say, but she scared herself into not speaking. Because the truth was, the Emperor was cold. They may say he was her father, and she might have been missing or kidnapped or presumed dead, but any remorse he may have shown at her absence or joy at her return was a lie; this man known as the Jadian Sun didn't care the slightest for her. He probably never had.

She didn't know how she knew. She just did, but she couldn't tell Adam that.

He was scrutinizing her. She had remained silent too long. She tried to force out a smile, but none would come.

Adam placed his hands on the balcony and scanned the horizon of the city. "It's nice to be able to just relax here with you. I don't get to do it very often. Maybe I'll venture out after the ball and hit some of the spots."

Sam raised an eyebrow. "The spots?"

Adam nodded. "Yes, the Fourth City is where the scholars and non-noble-born merchants reside. Really, it's every bit as amenable and luxurious as the fifth or some parts of the sixth, but it's less restricted, so there's more to do here."

Adam pointed to another large building in the distance. "The Yellow Theater, for example. I used to try to get there as much as possible before my duties took me away from home too often. You'd love it, Sam. They perform many of the legendary stage plays from before the war, most from the original music scores: Les Misérables, Madame Butterfly, Il Trovatore—all beautifully tragic. It's one of my favorite things, going to the theater—Sam, what's wrong?"

Sam couldn't help it. She had tried. But she couldn't do it anymore. Tears ran fast and free. Her mom...her mom loved the theater. It was one of the few luxuries they had ever engaged in. Cammie's big parties with everyone dressed in beautiful gowns. Richard's genius wit, and Coda's unadorned perversion...the way the T. Tracks came to life after a rainstorm.

"Adam...why am I here? Why would you come halfway across the world to find me?"

"Sam—haven't you been listening? You're the daughter of—"

"Of the Jadian Sun, I know. But how is that possible?

Adam, I grew up in a nondescript place, doing nondescript things, living a boring, nondescript life. Sure, I moved around more than was probably normal, but how does my life translate into all this? This isn't how it's supposed to be. How does my mother, a normal middle province woman from the UWC, end up getting busy with the Emperor of Jade?"

"Getting busy?"

"Yes—well, you know what I mean."

Adam had the decency not to laugh.

"I don't get how I ended up here. I don't know why you would come to get me. As a matter of fact, I don't even understand how all of this started. What happened at the school? What about MESA? Is all of this why Richard died? Because of who I am? I don't understand, and no one seems to care."

Adam watched her as she talked. By the time she finished, his eyes lit up with some sort of revelation. He came and sat next to her. "So...you're wondering how your mother...how *your* mother ended up here?"

"Yes. How can I possibly be a daughter of the Emperor? And if that is the case, why did it take so long for you to find me? Why doesn't my father seem to care? Why didn't you retrieve my mom with me? And what—WHAT is a Delphic Candidate?"

Sam lost it. She broke down in sobs. All the fear, pain, anger, and grief came crashing into her like a raging river. She thought she might be swept away by it.

Adam didn't say anything, but Sam could see the recognition in his eyes. He understood her. She didn't know what it meant, and at that point, she didn't really care. She wanted him to go away.

"You haven't been told, have you?"

"Told what?"

"About your mother."

Sam sniffed.

"Oh Sam, you poor girl. I am so sorry. I truly am. For your kidnapping, your imprisonment, and my inability to answer your questions. You are here now, and you are a princess of Jade. You are a Gōng Zhǔ of the Jadian Sun, the First Daughter of the Empire, and the Delphic Candidate. I will answer as many questions as I can, starting with the most basic. Believe me, I would answer all of them myself if I could, but I cannot. Some answers I do not have. Others are not mine to share. But rest assured, Gōng Zhǔ, you are home, and you will be treated with the respect that you deserve."

Sam took several deep breaths in an attempt to get ahold of herself. A torrent of emotion had been unleashed, and reigning it back in took her some time. Eventually, her sobs quieted down.

"OK, let's start with an easy one. I am a princess of the Jadian Empire?"

Adam nodded. "Yes."

"You're sure?"

"Yes."

"How?"

"Your biometrics are a perfect match for Irina Fen Fang Sun, the First Daughter of the Jadian Sun, and the Delphic Candidate. The biometric tests are one hundred percent accurate. You are Irina, even if you go by another name now."

Sam took another deep breath. "OK, so I am a Daughter of the Jadian Sun?"

"Correct."

"I still don't fully believe you. I'm eighteen years old and have been living in the UWC for as long as I can remember—why did it take so long for you to find me?"

"That one is a bit trickier. Honestly, we thought you were dead. During the week of your birth, you disappeared; it was suggested that slavers were the cause. We never did find out who took you or how they got in and out of the mountains without a guide."

Sam listened, taking in every word. "So you're trying to tell me I was born in the Empire?"

"Yes, you were born at the maternal palace in the Tibetan Mountains to the southwest of here, which is why you should have been safe."

"Why would that be important?"

"The Palace of Jagged Peak in the Tibetan Mountains is one of the residences that the Emperor sets aside exclusively for his wives, of which he has many. There isn't any settlement within two hundred kilometers of the entrance. It should have been impossible to find the palace and get in and out without anyone noticing and without hurting a single person. It's one of the great mysteries of the Empire: how you disappeared that night and who took you. Whoever they were, they were like ghosts. It was proposed that it was an inside job, but there was never any proof."

"So we disappeared from the mountain?"

Adam sighed at this. "No, *you* disappeared from the mountain."

"But not my mother?"

"No. Not your mother."

"What happened to her?"

Adam shook his head. "Not something I can answer. I am sorry."

Sam raised her eyebrow. That seemed like an easy one. Why refuse to answer that of all questions?

Sam considered the information for a moment. She had been kidnapped and taken to the UWC, and during her travels, or maybe after her arrival, she escaped from her kidnappers. She didn't know exactly how, but she met up with her mom later. They had been living in the UWC ever since. Perhaps that was the reason she and her mom were always moving. But if that was true, then why not come back to the Empire? If that was where they truly belonged, then why stay in the UWC? There was no obvious reason to stay.

Sam cracked her knuckles. "OK, how about this. How did you find me? And when did you come to realize that I wasn't dead?"

Adam rubbed at his chin. "Another tricky one. The short answer is MESA."

"MESA?" Sam started to get excited. She was finally going to get some answers. "How does MESA play into all this?"

"After you were kidnapped, we waited for a ransom demand. When none came, the powers that be came to the conclusion that you were kidnapped by slavers or, at the very least, that the slaver routes were used to get into the mountains and get you out."

"What does that have to do with MESA?"

"I'm getting there. What you have to understand is the slaver trade is a booming business. After we lost hope of ever finding you, the Mogui made it their specific mission to stomp out the practice. A couple of years ago, one of our head intelligence officers, a defector from UWC, started noticing similar patterns of slaver movements both here and in the UWC."

"How did you get data on slaver movements in the UWC?"

Adam winked at her. "We have our ways. Once we started noticing that the slavers were still slaving but not taking their captives, their *payloads* out of the primary provinces of the UWC, we knew something was up. We followed a couple of the less careful slavers. They led us to MESA and their kidnapping operation."

Sam hung on Adam's every word.

"The rest was easy. I activated a couple of sleeper Mogui

cells in the UWC and had them raid some of MESA's less-secure facilities. It took longer than expected, but eventually, we were able to get our hands on a portion of their feedbacker research."

"What's a feedbacker?"

"You know what a mystic is, right?"

"I haven't been given an exact lesson, but I've surmised as much."

"Good. Feedbacker is the UWC's title for a mystic. They don't like the supernatural-sounding quality of mystic, so they renamed them."

"Why was MESA researching feedbackers?"

"We have no idea, but I'm glad they did. You were one of the samples they took from, I'm assuming, one of their trips to Academy City 676. We compared each of the samples to the bio-data, and you were a match. That's when I was sent in to observe and collect additional data."

"That doesn't make any sense," said Sam, pushing a lock of hair out of her eyes. "At this point, you thought I was dead for what, seventeen-plus years? How did you know I was one of the samples?"

"Honestly, it was purely by chance. All interfaces and interweb activities run by any op of my Mogui are handled by the DragonNet—the sentient intelligence system that helps the Emperor manage the Empire. The DragonNet literally runs just about everything in the Seven Cities and beyond. It's connected to every system, every transportation grid, everything. When you were born, your biometrics were fed into that system and flagged. Minus cloning, no two people on the planet have the same biometrics. The Emperor flagged your biometrics in the system, hoping to get a lucky break and find you. After time, it was assumed you were dead, but you were never removed from the system."

"So when your guys ran MESA's data through the DragonNet, I came up in the results?"

"In a routine data dump, you got it."

"So why not come and get me straightaway?"

"Because your sample was filed by general location only —no other identifying information was in the database we found. That stuff was corrupted somehow, by someone who knows a lot more about computers than I do. We knew you were around Academy City 676. So we came to find you."

"Is that why you attacked MESA at the school? You figured it out?"

Adam shook his head. "That was a mistake. I figured out who you were. We were trying to get you out before MESA really understood what was going on. We are far more advanced than they are in the mystic fields, but their blood products identified a DNA marker and enzyme that only mystics carry—they could find out if any specific person had mystic potential just by taking a little blood, even the ones that don't register with our current detection methods. It was only a matter of time until they figured out what was going on. That's why we had to get you. The timing was simply bad, and things got out of hand."

Sam laughed. A genuine, though somewhat ironic laugh. "Yeah, that is the understatement of the year. You're lucky Richard was there to protect me."

Adam exhibited a bit of relief. "I guess you're right—but why do you say that about Richard?"

Sam related her side of the story, explaining what happened to her in general terms on the day MESA showed up at Academy City 676 and finished by briefly describing Richard's relationship with the Republicans. Adam rubbed at his face.

"Richard was a Republican."

"Yes."

"I knew there was something strange about him."

Sam laughed. "Richard said the same thing about you. Apparently, you two had a good read on each other."

Adam again rubbed his face. "But what did you mean, I was lucky that Richard protected you? Were you in any real danger that day?"

Sam bit her tongue. She had been trying to avoid that part. Reluctantly, she detailed their flight through the school, the Mogui attack, Richard's transformation, and their escape on Dyson's bike.

"Those Mogui tried to do *what* to you?"

"Well—you know, they tried to—take advantage of me."

Adam started to stand up.

"Adam, sit down." Sam pointed to the seat. "I'm fine."

Adam seemed unconvinced. "Samantha, these actions taken against you must be punished—I will find their families and exact—"

"Don't you dare!" Sam yelled. Her voice seemed to carry a heavy weight with it.

Adam stopped talking and looked at her.

Sam looked back. "Their relatives are not to blame, especially not for something that happened thousands of kilometers away. Besides, all those men died in horrible, horrible ways. There is nothing to do now. Leave it alone. I won't have anyone banished or killed on my behalf."

She touched Adam's arm, and they watched each other. He hesitated but sat back down.

They remained in silence for a long while until Adam finally said, "Are you all questioned out for the moment?"

Sam was about to say no, but she found that these answers were easing her fears a bit. They were still there, but they were much less intense. She did have one more question. "Adam, why were you sent to get me?"

Adam looked surprised by this question. "Actually, I wasn't. I volunteered. I wanted to come and get you."

Sam thought back, remembering vaguely. "That's not what you told me back on the ship. You said you were commanded to come and get me."

"Ahh...yes, that was a lie. I apologize."

"How do I know you're not lying now?"

"You know."

And the truth was, she did. He wasn't lying. Odd.

Sam cocked her head. "So why *did* you come and get me?"

Adam smiled. "I had the best chance of identifying you without tipping anyone off. We still don't know who kidnapped you, and we certainly didn't want to lose you again."

Sam scrunched her eyebrows in thought. "Why would you have the best chance of identifying me? What's so special about you? Well, besides the obvious."

Again, Adam looked confused. He stared at her for a brief moment until a look of belated comprehension smacked him in the face. "Samantha, I must apologize most profusely. I cannot believe that I have not introduced myself to you properly."

Adam stood up and half-bowed, then stated, "I am Michael Hunang Sun. I am the First Son of the Emperor, the Royal Commander of the Mogui forces, and the Governor of the Islands of the East. I am the next Jadian Sun...and your eldest brother."

Sam's jaw dropped.

"Nice to formally meet you, my sister."

CHAPTER 25

A MOTHER'S LOVE

Time: Predawn
Scene: The Emerald House

Sasha picked up her teacup and took a long sip. "I believe things went well, do you not agree, Madam?"

The Madam, Sasha, and Alena sat in the Madam's room in the Emerald House. The Madam had let her hair down, so to speak, and changed out of her mystic robes into her nightgown. She looked tired, and simultaneously happy and sad—if that was at all possible—and most of all, the Madam appeared preoccupied. Sasha and Alena gazed at her, waiting for her to answer the question. The Madam didn't know what to say.

"Madam...," said Alena in a concerned voice, "are you... are you alright?"

The Madam started as if she had just realized that both of

them were there. "Oh, Sasha, Alena—I do apologize. My mind was somewhere else."

"I can imagine, my lady." Sasha bowed her head thoughtfully. "After this week, the return of Irina...after all this time...and Xui Li for that matter—walking up to the Fifth Ring guard house like it was nothing, demanding to be taken home. It's a wonder. The two eldest daughters of the Empire. Home at last."

"Yes," said the Madam simply. "It has been quite the week."

She reached for her cup of tea, brought it to her lips, and took a sip. "Ahh...Alena, child, could I trouble you for a warm cup?"

Alena almost jumped out of her chair and busied herself refreshing her cup. Fresh leaves with essential oils of peppermint and rosemary were dropped into the Madam's cup. The Madam smiled gratefully. "Alena, would you do me the honor of a favor?"

Alena blanched a bit. To her credit, it was far less dramatic than the Madam would have expected from her. *There may be hope yet for the assistant of the assistant,* she thought. Alena knelt in front of the Madam. "Anything, my lady."

"Irina—would you keep an eye on her?"

Alena lifted her chin to look the Madam in the eye. "Of course, my lady. What would you have me tell the Gōng Zhǔ of my purpose in being around her?"

"Whatever you want, my dear...but for the next couple of weeks, I want you to stick with her, and specifically, don't let her near the Mystic's Abode. They will all want to meet her. But she is not ready for that."

"I wouldn't dream of it, my lady."

The Madam smiled. "Then you are dismissed, Alena. Go to bed; you look like you are about to pass out where you stand."

Alena bowed to the Madam and Sasha. She left without another word.

Sasha watched her go, then turned to the Madam. "My lady."

"Yes, Sasha."

"If I may be so bold, how did Irina take the news? Has she reconciled herself yet?"

"I am afraid not."

Sasha attempted to hide her sadness. "I am sorry, my lady, but do not worry; I am sure that she will come around—"

"You misunderstand, Sasha. It is not that Irina was unable to accept the truth. I have not told her yet. She does not know."

Sasha bowed her head. "Ahh, I see."

They sat in silence briefly until Sasha stood up. She bowed deeply, much like Alena had. "Do you realize how special you are, my lady?"

The Madam smiled. "I love you too, Sasha. Now go to bed."

Sasha shot the Madam a warm smile. "Goodnight, Madam."

Sasha walked from her room, closing the door behind her. The Madam lingered, her fingers enjoying the warmth of her teacup, the smell of peppermint and rosemary soothing her nerves. She was anxious. When was the last time she was this nervous? It was probably then...eighteen years ago...when she said goodbye...the memory cut into her. She closed her eyes.

The Madam stood, walking to the large double doors that led to her balcony. She loved the balcony and the views it provided of the Seven Cities. The Emerald House had been her mother's brainchild; the Favorite Wife's room was the crowning jewel of the glorious structure that was the Emerald House. The upper balcony enabled views as far as the eye could see; the lights and wonders of the Seven Cities pushed back the blackness of the night in a brilliant cacophony of metallic sheens of gold, green, and blue. It was her place, one she used to get away from the world and the responsibility of being "The Madam." There was something else...something special that only she knew about—but she had to be sure.

The Madam walked up the spiral stairway to the roof of the Emerald House. Grow boxes containing all sorts of vegetables sat in neat rows stretching the length of the roof. It was about time to start harvesting...maybe she and Irina— Samantha—could do it together. That might be fun. The Madam enjoyed making things grow, but this space was much more to her than just a place to satisfy her green thumb... much more.

She moved up the rows and through the hanging non-native plants to the inner provinces of the Empire. She loved the different and exotic flowers and shrubbery. It made this sanctuary a place away from the world. She counted on that.

She neared the wall and touched a pendant around her neck, a piece of Jadian gold. The jewel warmed slightly as a tiny scanner inside inspected the area for listening devices or other types of electronic surveillance. The slight vibration her necklace gave indicated it was clear. The Madam then did something curious. She sang a single line of verse that meant something only to her. Another vibration from her necklace told her that the password had been accepted. The Madam waited briefly until...movement...just in front of her and to her right. Gears shifted, metal moved seamlessly, and a seemingly solid section of the wall opened to reveal a Madam-sized passage. The Madam slipped inside, touching her pendant once she cleared the threshold. The slab of rock closed behind her.

The lights flipped on the moment she entered the room. The Madam smiled. This was her true sanctuary. No one, not even Sasha and Alena, knew of this place. This was her room away from it all. The Emperor, the Empire, her role as the Madam...the Madam...when was the last time someone spoke her real name? She was not even sure she would recognize it if someone did.

She took a deep breath. The smell of roses permeated the air. Roses. They reminded her of times gone by, of simpler, happier times. Memories came that she pushed away because she must not linger. She had specific business to attend to before she was missed or before the Emperor came on one of his rare visits. The Madam stepped to a crystal orb resting on a pedestal in the middle of the room. She took a deep breath. She was nervous, nervous for what she was about to see. The Madam touched it.

The belly of the orb flared to life, colors dancing briefly. A hologram projected itself from the orb. A man looked at the Madam and smiled. She returned the smile instantly with genuine affection. She tried to stop herself, but tears began to form at the corners of her eyes.

The man's smile wavered ever so slightly. "My lady."

He dipped his head respectfully. "Are those for me or for your newly arrived guest?"

The Madam dabbed at her tears. "Both, I guess. It's been too long."

"Yes, it has."

"I miss you."

"And I you."

The man paced. He looked so real she almost called out to him to keep him from walking into some of the few furnishings in her sanctuary.

"I have to ask...how...how did this happen...I thought— well, I thought—"

"I thought as well." He interrupted in a gentle voice. "I will get to that. How are you doing?"

The Madam attempted to articulate. "I am feeling confused but elated. This should not have happened; it should have been impossible, but for the first time in eighteen years...my daughter...my daughter...has come home."

ABOUT THE AUTHOR

Collin Earl is a trial lawyer, entrepreneur, and lifelong storyteller. Known for blending sharp dialogue, layered world-building, and emotional depth, he's the mind behind The House of Grey and co-creator of the Harmonics series. When he's not in court or at the keyboard, Collin is running his firm, raising kids, or losing sleep to whatever creative rabbit hole he's fallen into.

Chris Snelgrove is a writer, producer, and corporate strategist with a background in psychology. He's best known for his collaborative work with Collin Earl on The House of Grey and Harmonics, where his character-driven storytelling adds a distinct voice to the narrative. He lives outside Denver with his wife and four boys, finding time to write between bedtime stories and business meetings.

Thank you for reading.

To explore more of their work, get exclusive content, and stay updated on upcoming releases, visit SilverstoneBooks.com. Whether you are looking for fantasy, sci-fi, or something in between—your next favorite story is waiting.